Also by Olivia McMahon:

Love as a Foreign Language

Poetry: *Domestic Verses* (Koo Press)

ROSE-TINTED SCISSORS

Olivia McMahon

For Brian, Tadg and Roisin.

Copyright © 2009 by Olivia McMahon

First Edition

The author asserts the moral right under the Copyright, Designs and Patents Act 1988 to be identified as the author of this work.

All Rights reserved. No part of this publication may be reproduced, stored in a retrieval system, or transmitted, in any form or by any means without the prior written consent of the author, nor be otherwise circulated in any form of binding or cover other than that in which it is published and without a similar condition being imposed on the subsequent purchaser.

Published by YouWriteOn.com

British Library C.I.P

The names, characters and incidents portrayed in this work are fictional. Any resemblance to actual persons, living or dead, events, or localities is entirely coincidental.

My thanks

to Jeannette King, Bill Kirton, Lindsey Fraser, Esther Woolfson, George and Jo Watson for their support and encouragement, and to Jo also for the title

to, among other sources, *Good Hair Days, A History of British Hairstyling* by Caroline Cox (Quartet Books, 1999) and *The Hairdressers' Journal* for 1960-1961

to Haworth Hodgkinson and Laurie Robertson for help with the cover

to Brian Farrington for almost everything, including reading through the final manuscript.

Chapter 1

I was really determined I was going to concentrate on hairdressing when I left Manchester and came to work in Paris. It had been a big decision. I knew they were all thinking that I shouldn't be gallivanting off like that, that I should be getting married and settling down. Twenty three and still not married. Most of the girls I grew up with have been married for years, they've all got two or three children by now.

'You don't want to leave it till it's too late,' my Mum kept warning me. 'You don't want to end up like Doreen Bright.' She was always reminding me of what happened to Doreen Bright - a nice-looking girl like me once, with lovely fair hair and big blue eyes who could have had her pick of the men. 'But she was too choosy and look at her now, she's on the shelf.'

Anyway, I really wasn't wanting to be distracted here in Paris by getting involved with any man. I love my work, especially creating new styles. Changing the way a woman does her hair's a big challenge. I love judging what would suit a woman from her height, her way of walking and holding her head, the sort of clothes she's wearing, how much make up she's got on.

A lot of hairdressers aren't like that. If a client arrives saying she wants a change but she's not sure what, they just give her one of the latest styles, regardless of whether it will suit her or not. So they give this dumpy woman with a large nose a chignon and she walks away thinking she now looks like Audrey Hepburn. Or someone who obviously spends her time in brogues and an anorak walking the dogs in

Boulogne goes off with bouffant hair like ate for lunch at *Maxim's*.

Actually, though, I've been a bit disappointed working at *Bertrand*, though it's a really posh salon just off the Champs-Elysées. It's not as challenging as I'd expected. In some ways Manchester was more exciting. I was winning practically every competition I went in for there, and my clients in the salon where I worked would never have anyone else do their hair. But since I've been here, I haven't had any chance of trying out any new styles. I'd imagined Parisians would be adventurous, wanting me to create daring hairdos especially for them, but most of the women coming into the salon are really conservative, just wanting a shampoo and set. This is 1961, not 1951 I keep wanting to tell them. It's very frustrating. And a bit boring.

That's maybe why I ended up getting so mixed up with Michel. Michel's one of the other stylists. He's very attractive. He's not very tall but he's got a really graceful figure and he has these steady intimate eyes. He's about the same age as me and almost from the first week we clicked. We were like kindred spirits because we were both passionate about hair, but we also had lots of laughs together. The other stylist, Jean François, who'd been in Manchester, is a real moan-a-lot and Bertrand always manages to look mournful even when he's feeling cheerful. He has these poached egg eyes quite a lot of French men have - something to do with their livers, I think.

But Michel was fun. He started helping me with my French from the first week, taught me the French for rollers - *bigoudis*. The way he pronounced the word made it sound much saucier than *rollers* which always remind me of something called a *roll-on* I bought once - a tight rubber tube, a sort of corset without the whalebones, that was actually more of a tug-on than a roll-on.

'Bigoudis,' he'd say.

'Bigoudis.' I'd try to imitate his way of saying the word.

'No, you have to push your lips out more for the *ou*.' He'd demonstrate and I'd feel self-conscious, knowing that Bertrand and Jean François and Marie Claire and the others were probably watching and wondering. Marie Claire's the receptionist and she told me, my first day there practically, that Michel was working class Parisian. She told me to be careful not to imitate his way of talking.

'Ee eez not a good exhampell. ee 'as a verree strong Parees accent,' she said.

'Listen who's talking,' I thought. But he's able to put on a posh accent when he's talking to the clients apparently. Otherwise he couldn't work at *Bertrand*, Marie Claire said.

By the end of my second week working in the salon I was becoming really attracted to him, I felt so happy always when he was around. And I sensed it was the same for him. I even started to imagine us having a future together. We'd get married and have a salon with *Lucy et Michel* over the glass door. I was sure that he must be on the point of asking me out.

But the days went by and nothing happened. Every morning, getting ready for work, I'd think Maybe today's the day he'll say 'Are you doing anything this evening?' So I'd look at my clothes and wonder if they'd be smart enough for sitting drinking Martinis in some fashionable café. I even went out one lunchtime and bought myself an expensive anthracite grey jumper that the saleswoman said was very very elegant. But no invitation came.

And then I found out why. It was a Friday morning. The salon was full of the scent of the yellow mimosa that Marie Claire had arrived in with. I was thinking that if Michel was going to invite me out for the Saturday evening he was leaving it a bit late. Then, just as I was about to snip round the ears of this stout woman, Madame Sentier, I heard the woman Michel was bending over asking him

'And how is your little daughter?'

I looked across at the face reflected in the mirror - a middle-aged woman with small eyes and a pointed nose.

'She must be *ad-or-ab- le*!' She strung the word out like they do in French as if she was unrolling a velvet ribbon. 'And what is her name again? Charlotte? Charmant!'

I stood there watching a small spot of blood appearing on Madame Sentier's skin where I'd nicked it with the scissors. I pressed my thumb down on it and managed to smile at her in the mirror but she hadn't noticed anything. It hadn't occurred to me that he was married. I thought he was completely free like me. He had all this life going on and I'd known nothing about it.

I couldn't bring myself to joke with him after that, I started trying to concentrate on work and improving my French, looking through the French hair magazines, trying to memorize the words for colours of dyes like *plum* and *ash*. I kept telling myself that it was better like that, anyway, as I'd said I didn't want anything to distract me from my ambition to become a top hairstylist. You've really got to be dedicated and single-minded, I know. But it was hard, being all by myself in Paris, not knowing anybody. It was fine during the day with lots of people around and two evenings there were training sessions in the salon but the other evenings and then the week ends...

I really appreciated that I was living in the Marcels' flat and not all alone in a poky room. It was through the hairdressing salon that I got the room in their flat. Madame Marcel's one of Bertrand's oldest clients. She's there every week having her hair washed and set. This amazed me at first. I'd never known anyone with money like that to spend on hair, even in the place I trained in in Manchester, though *Alexander* was pretty posh. I can still see my Mum and me right up to the time I started as an apprentice, bent over the sink every Friday evening. It isn't as if Madame Marcel - or Monique as she told me to call her - is particularly fashion conscious or anything, but I suppose she has to keep up appearances, being the wife of a businessman. Her husband's called Claude and he's director of a company that sells soap and things. They have two children, Daniel, who's seven, and a little girl, Catherine, who's four and a half.

Anyway when Bertrand told her he was taking on this English stylist, she immediately said there was a spare room in their flat I could have. She said it would give her a chance to practise her English - she's very pro-English because of how they were liberated by British and American soldiers during the war. I'm not sure but I think she had some sort of a romance with an American soldier at the time, something she said once about a guy called Bill. But also I think she's glad of the company. Claude's away a lot on business and even when he's not away he's not there in the evenings much, he's out - till very late, usually - entertaining business clients, or so he says.

Monique's thirty five and petite and very neat like the French are, with mousy hair that she just has off the face. I'm surprised Bertrand doesn't suggest she has it dyed, but then she's quite conservative, what my mother would call lady-like and refined. She likes things to be tidy and organized too, not like me. She was actually Claude's secretary before they got married. I'm sure she's horrified at the way my room's always in a mess but she's very nice, she doesn't say anything.

It's quite a big room with a window looking out on the courtyard. All the other windows in the flat have these voile curtains across them but I've pushed the one on my window right to the side so I can look out. I usually have the window open a bit too, so Monique hates it when I open my door because she says it creates a draught. They're terrified of draughts, the French, it's the same in the salon. 'Watch out, you're in a draught!' they're always telling you, like you were standing in the middle of a street with a whacking big lorry careering down on you.

Monique fixed the room up like a bedsit for me with a little electric stove and a couple of saucepans so I could boil up water to make myself a cup of coffee, or heat up a tin of soup and live sort of independently. But from the beginning I've usually ended up eating with her in the kitchen. I really appreciated her company in those first weeks and then after I found out Michel was married.

But then came the day of the downpour. I was standing at the exit to the salon, watching it hopping off the pavement. Michel happened to be there too - we were the last to leave that evening. I'd really been avoiding him, avoiding meeting his eye but there we were just the two of us.

'Where do you live?' he asked me. I told him and he made a face the way the French do and said

'Eh ben. Very bourgeois.' It's true. Monsieur Marcel earns a lot of money and they live in quite a smart district.

'How are you getting back there?' he asked me.

Usually I walked back to the *rue Galilée* up the *rue François I* and across a*venue George V* but today I could easily get the Métro, I told him. It was just down the road.

'I can drive you, if you like,' he said. 'Even walking as far as the Métro you'll get soaked. It's raining cats and dogs, you say in English, no?'

He had his 2CV parked just round the corner. As we ran to it, our bodies kept colliding as we dodged the puddles. I felt I could go on running like that with him beside me for ever and ever. When we got to outside the flat he switched off the ignition and turned to me.

'I'm married, you know,' he said, giving me such a serious look, quite different from his usual way of looking at me.

'I know,' I said, and then I found myself whispering, and this is what started it all, I think, 'I wish you weren't.' And then I tried to say 'It's a pity' in French. 'C'est dommage.'

'Do you really mean that?' he said, looking even more serious. And then he leant towards me and the next moment we were kissing and all the time I was thinking I was falling in love with someone who could never ever be mine.

Chapter 2

It wouldn't have been possible to bring Michel back to my room in the flat. In any case, there was no question of that at the beginning because it took me a while to decide whether I should 'give' myself completely to him or not - 'go the whole hog' as a woman I met on the ferry coming over called it. I hate that expression. She practically told me her life story between Newhaven and Dieppe.

I wasn't a virgin. I'd already 'given myself' to Andrew, the boy I left behind in Manchester – though only after we'd been going out together for nearly four years. Before that, it was just lots of what they call 'heavy petting' on the sofa late on Saturday night after my parents had gone to bed. And before that just necking in the back row of the cinema or in the back lane before I went home. Andrew wasn't like a lot of the others, forcing you to do things. That's probably because he was a good Catholic and going to bed together if you're not married is a mortal sin, which means you can't go to Holy Communion on Sunday unless you go to Confession first. And you wouldn't want to be confessing that sort of thing to Father Dwyer.

But, to be honest, with me it wasn't just because it was a mortal sin, it was because I was too scared or something. Once, at a party, this man had started kissing me and then he'd suddenly got hold of my hand and brought it down below so that it was on his thing. And then he'd started moving my hand up and down it in this frantic way and I didn't know what to do. There was never anything like that with Andrew - until last

October when his parents went away on holiday and his house was empty apart from his brother, Peter.

That's when it happened for the first time, when Peter was out for the evening. We managed to be there alone just twice after that, once for a whole Saturday afternoon when Peter was at a football match. I should have been at work but, at the end of the morning, I told them I wasn't feeling well and went back to his house. Andrew got worried because he thought I really was sick and maybe that meant I was pregnant. Which got me worried too because that was the last thing I wanted, though lots of girls I knew had got themselves in the family way so that the bloke would marry them. But we were being very careful - Andrew had managed to get a packet of French letters off a friend.

But I was never in love with Andrew. Life would have been so much simpler if I had been. There'd been a girl at school who was always saying about any feller anybody was keen on - 'Would you die for him?' I can still see her face wobbling like a jelly, quivering with excitement, waiting for you to say Yes. I could never have said Yes if she'd asked me about Andrew but it was sad because I was sure Andrew would have died for me. He'd die for me even now. At least I think he would.

The nearest I got to wanting to be with Andrew for the rest of my life - with me having my own hair salon in Manchester or somewhere - was one Sunday at the end of November. We took a bus out to Glossop and went for a walk up on the moors. It was cold but bright and sunny and the sky was light blue with only a few wispy clouds and you could see the horizon far away, not like in Manchester where there are always buildings blocking your view. Walking along this track together I felt so close to him.

Afterwards we came back down and had a big pot of tea and toasted tea cakes in a little café with red check tablecloths on the table and a black cat snoozing in the windowsill and I felt really happy. But there was this couple at the next table with a child in a push chair and suddenly Andrew smiled across at me and took hold of my hand. And I knew that what he was thinking was that one day that would be us. And I'd felt so close to him up on the moors but now I just couldn't smile back. Instead I asked him if he wanted the last tea cake. I'd been thinking we should cut it in two but now I didn't want any of it. I was suddenly sure that I had to get away. I didn't want to settle down with someone whose dream of happiness was sitting sharing tea cakes in a sleepy little café.

But with Michel it was different. I wasn't sure I could die for him – I don't know if I could die for any man – but I *was* sure that I wanted to be with him completely and all the time. I'd never felt like this for anyone else before. I felt I was on the brink of something calamitous and I was frightened. Sitting in the back of his 2CV parked at the bottom of the alleyway round the corner from the flat, every time his hand started moving up under my skirt I'd push it down. It was too big a step to take. But I knew it couldn't go on like that.

I started wondering about the maid's room - the *chambre de bonne* - that the Marcels had on the sixth floor and that I knew was empty. The top floor of all these old blocks of flats have little attic rooms for the servants and the Marcels' maid, Renée, lived in one. But then Renée left soon after I arrived. She was suffering from *aérophagie*. She kept going on about this *aérophagie* and I thought it must be something really serious, so I asked Monique what it was in English. She went into this room they call the library and looked it up in a huge dictionary and it turned out to be 'wind', only in English you'd probably just say you had tummy ache. But, in any case, she was lonely in Paris so she'd gone back to her parents' home in the country.

One evening as we were sitting in the kitchen eating the leftovers from the midday meal I asked Monique about the room.

'Will Renée be coming back, do you think?' I asked as I watched her turning leaves of lettuce round and round in a bowl.

'No, she's found a job in the local café, and I'm not looking for anyone else. I'm just going to manage with Nounou from now on.' Nounou's the cook and cleaner who comes in every day.

'So Renée's room upstairs is free?' I asked.

'Why, do you know someone who'd like to live in it?' Monique asked me. This possibility hadn't occurred to me.

'Yes, me,' I said quickly. 'I mean ...' What was I saying? I certainly didn't want to move out of my room in the flat completely. I didn't even know for sure that I was going to say Yes to Michel, that I would want the room on the sixth floor. 'I mean, sometimes I like to have a place to myself where I feel I can go and ...' I said, thinking this can't be me talking.

'Get away from it all,' said Monique sympathetically. I hadn't told her anything much about my life before coming to Paris but maybe she sensed a sad love affair, a tragedy even. Though, being French, it was more likely she imagined I wanted the room so I could take someone back there. The French are supposed to be famous for being romantic but I've been finding them much more down to earth and practical than me and not romantic at all.

'Yes, that's it,' I said 'but maybe you'd prefer to let someone else have it?'

'No, no, I'll give you the key. It's very cold up there though. You'll have to take up the paraffin stove that's in the cupboard in the hall.'

The little rooms on the sixth floor are off a long corridor. Not many of them still have maids in them, they're mostly occupied by poor people and students, who can't afford anything else. I thought the room looked a really cheerless place when I saw it first, like a monk's cell - with a sloping roof, and greenish lino on the floor, a table and chair in the window and a narrow bed in the corner. But Monique gave me a cover to put on the bed and I bought a yellow cellulose blanket and pinned up a bit of blue cretonne over the window. And I lugged the stove up the stairs and bought paraffin for it - called *pétrole* in French, just to confuse me - from a café advertising the sale of coal. And all the time I wasn't sure about whether I was ever going to be there with Michel.

We never ever lit the stove. Michel didn't like the smell of the paraffin. It reminded him of cold winters when he was a child, so we just huddled together under the new cellulose blanket. It was freezing cold, those first times we were there, with snow outside. But inside the cold brought us even closer together and I felt so happy, lying there with him. This is where we belonged, together in the little room on the sixth floor. This is where we should remain, for ever and ever.

But the trouble was when we weren't together in the little room on the sixth floor I was alone in the room downstairs in the flat with nothing to do but brood. Being with Michel was a mortal sin, which meant I'd a stain on my soul like it was a white teacloth with tea spilt on it. At Mass I'd sit and watch people queuing up to receive Communion, and then coming back down the aisle slowly, their heads bowed, their hands clasped in front of them. I couldn't go to Communion because I couldn't go to Confession because I was sleeping with Michel. I couldn't go into the dark box and kneel down as I'd done ever since I was a child and whisper 'Bless me, Father, for I have sinned. It is a week/two weeks since my last Confession.'

Would I ever be able to go to Confession again? I knew there were people who said it was all right for Catholics, they could commit as many sins as they liked as long as they went to Confession. But you're not supposed to get forgiveness unless you make a firm resolution not to commit the same sin again and the way I felt about Michel it was completely impossible to even think about never making bve with him again. Besides, as I say, I couldn't think of it as a sin.

To be honest what bothered me much more was that he had all this other life going on while I had nothing else apart from work. But what was wrong with that? I kept asking myself. After all this is what I'd come to Paris for, wasn't it? I did throw myself into it and that helped a lot. What I love most is thinking up new styles. Sometimes when you're doing a client's hair you sense there's another woman inside – a *femme fatale* or a hippie or a warrior queen - struggling to get out. I have this client, a Madame Chenier, a woman of about fifty. Her hair's mid length and permed and going grey and she just looks like any other boring respectable middle-class woman coming into the salon. But she's got a really strong face and a beautifully shaped head. She'd look great with a short jagged hair cut. I was aching to get to work on her so one morning I said to her - 'You'd look really good with an urchin cut.' But she said something about her husband having a fit if I gave her a style like that. He'd say she looked like a *voyou*. She kept repeating the word so I looked it up later in the little dictionary I carry around and found that it meant 'gutter-snipe.' So I had to just put her in rollers as per usual but I haven't given up on her. I'm still thinking I might persuade her one day.

However passionate I was about the work, though, it didn't help when I had to go back alone to the flat. Michel could only manage to be free once or twice a week when we worked late at the salon. He'd come back afterwards with me to the room on the sixth floor and I'd feel again this immense happiness: this is where we belong, this is our home, this makes up for all the unhappiness the rest of the time.

But it didn't really. Once or twice I went back up to the room by myself and lay on the bed and tried to remember being there with him but all I could think of was him with his wife and child and with friends dropping in and me all alone here.

'It's your own fault,' I kept telling myself. 'You've only yourself to blame for getting mixed up with a married man.

Going back to the flat on Saturday evening was the worst as I had the whole of Sunday and Monday to get through – the salon's closed on a Monday. I felt like something tossed onto the shore from the high seas, waiting for the tide to come back to sweep me out to sea again.

'How was your weekend?' Marie Claire would coo at Michel when he arrived back on Tuesday morning and I'd have to shut my ears.

So I suppose it wasn't surprising that I reacted as I did when Juan appeared that Sunday afternoon.

Chapter 3

I was all alone in the flat, sitting there looking through *The Hairdressers' Journal* that had come in the post the day before. Monique had taken the two children to the zoo so the rest of the flat was deathly quiet. I was just about to play *The Great Pretender* again for about the seventh time when the doorbell rang. I quickly took the pins out of my hair - I'd been messing around earlier, trying out a new style - put a bit of lipstick on and rushed to open the door.

    I recognized the man standing there because I'd passed him on the stairs one other Sunday afternoon when I was going out for a walk, a figure in a long flowing black robe that they call a *soutane*. Monique had told me afterwards that he was a Mexican called Juan who was studying to be a priest. I told him there was nobody there but me but he still wanted to come in. Maybe I could make him a cup of tea, he said. I don't actually drink tea here, the tea Monique has is nothing like what you get at home. It's called *le thé Lipton*, which I'd never heard of before, and it comes in little sachets with a string attached. It's very weak, it tastes of nothing at all so I always have instant coffee.

    I brought him into the library and then I went into the kitchen to put some water on to boil. All I could find were little china cups and the only tea pot was a pink one at the back of a cupboard with a lid made out of the top half of a woman in a crinoline that some visitor over from England must have brought Monique once. And the only biscuits were these things that taste of butter and vanilla and have a sickly smell. The French are not very good at biscuits.

When I came back he'd got one of Claude's enormous books down and had it spread out on the desk. It was full of pictures of French cathedrals.

'Look at this,' he said, showing me a picture of the face of an angel smiling. Apparently it's a very famous angel because of its smile. It reminded me of the way Marie Claire smiles when she's taking the coat off someone she doesn't like and she's trying to be charming.

There are two large brown leather armchairs in the library. He sank into one of them and I sat opposite him in the other one. As we drank the tea he looked at me and smiled and I felt like Alice in Wonderland must have felt when she fell through that hole. I was in another world to the one I'd been in only half an hour ago. He was so handsome, particularly in the black robe - lean and with high cheekbones and very straight black hair in a crew cut. I didn't know where to look or what to say. To my relief he put down the little china cup and got up and went over to put a record on the turntable.

'Do you know this?' he asked me as it began to play. I didn't know any classical music except for that piano concerto by Tchaikovsky.

'It's Mozart's clarinet concerto, the most beautiful music ever written. He wrote it the year before he died.'

We sat listening to it and I began to feel I was being transported to a place where everything was simple and good.

'How old are you, Lucy?' he asked me as it came to the end and he got up to put it on again. I was a bit surprised at the question.

'I'm twenty three,' I said. 'How about you?' I asked him. I didn't see why I needed to tell him my age if he wasn't going to tell me his. He was twenty three too. We smiled at each other then, as if this made our sitting together drinking tea in someone else's flat like some sort of conspiracy, especially when I began to notice the way he was looking at me.

'Lucy, in two years you will be twenty five,' he said then. I supposed that what he meant was that, at twenty five, it was high time a girl was married.

Nounou had said the same sort of thing to me the week before. I think she must have had a particularly bad night and was wanting to take it out on someone. Her skin looked sallower than usual and her eyes were like two newly opened oysters. I didn't actually understand what it was she was saying but Monique explained, making a joke out of it, but I didn't think it was very funny.

'She says that if you don't hurry up you'll end up wearing the special hat girls used to wear in the old days once they were twenty five. It's called a St Catherine's bonnet.'

'What business is it of hers?' I shouted as I went out the door, slamming it behind me. I was furious.

I should have been furious with Juan too now as he sat there because he was obviously thinking along the same lines. But instead I was feeling all disturbed. It was the way he was looking at me, as if he was in love with me.

'Yes, I hope, by the time I'm twenty five, I'll be a successful hairdresser,' I said, just to see how he'd react to this. I guessed that for him my job didn't count. Why should a girl be bothered about a career?

'Lucy,' he said gently, 'for a woman, what is beautiful is being with the man she loves and planning a future together, with the grace of God shining upon them. And in time, if God wills it, their union will be blessed with children.'

As far as I was concerned children didn't enter into it, but being with the man I loved, that would be a wonderful thing. Only I was beginning to feel a bit confused. Up to an hour ago, the man I loved with all my heart was Michel, but now funny things were happening inside me as I sat with the afternoon sun coming in, listening to the music and looking across at this stranger whose dark eyes seemed to be brimming over with emotion.

'I would like to see you again like today, Lucy,' he said as he left. He didn't use the lift, he ran down the stairs swiftly, gracefully. I watched his black soutane trailing behind him as he went.

He appeared again the following Sunday. At Mass that morning, as I stared at the priest in his green vestments, I'd thought of Juan and how attractive he'd look in front of the altar with his back to the congregation, and then swinging round to face us, moving his hands apart and bowing slightly and intoning *Dominus vobiscum*. I told him that the Marcels were away – they'd left for a ski-ing holiday in Switzerland. It occurred to me as I said this that he must have known they were away. Was that why he'd come, to see me alone?

He had a book in his hand. It was a children's story - *The Little Prince* - about an airman whose plane came down in the desert and this little boy appeared to him. I didn't really understand how the little boy with the golden hair had got there in his sky blue shirt and short trousers but Juan seemed to think the story was saying something very beautiful. There was a picture of the little boy holding a flower - a rose. And the most important thing in the world for the little boy was to look after this rose. The rose really represented a little girl, Juan explained.

What I was thinking was that the picture would make a nice birthday card for a little boy to give his Mum, and this reminded me I still hadn't bought a birthday card for my sister in law, Helen.

Juan sat cross-legged on the ground, next to the armchair where I was sitting with the book in my lap so we could look at it together, and I was thinking about that too, that our knees were practically touching. I wondered about offering him a cup of tea but it seemed easier just to open the cocktail cabinet and see what there was inside. The cocktail cabinet's a blaze of lights and mirrors when you open it, you're completely dazzled by the reflection of all the bottles and glasses. We ended up helping ourselves to little glasses of Chartreuse from the two tall bottles standing side by side at the back. Juan had a glass from the yellow bottle and I had a glass from the green one.

It was then that I found myself telling him about Michel. It was a bit like being at Confession but I could never have talked through the grill to a complete stranger, or worse, to someone I knew, like the priest at home. But sitting there with Juan in the library I just blurted it out, that I was involved with this married man. It sounded all wrong when I heard myself saying that – 'involved with a married man'. It made it seem sordid. It wasn't a bit like what I felt that me and Michel had between us.

Juan didn't say anything for a long time. We just went on listening to the music together and when it got to the really sad slow bit he put his hand over mine and whispered 'Lucy.' I didn't dare look at him, I just wanted the moment to go on with his hand covering mine and the music playing and the sun coming in.

I didn't say about taking Michel up to the *chambre de bonne* and he didn't ask. He didn't ask anything at all, which surprised me. At home the priest in the confessional would have asked lots of questions. He'd have given me a lecture about avoiding 'the occasions of sin' and I'd have felt his disapproval coming at me through the scrap of purple curtain, like the flames of hell fire.

But Juan just sat there quietly and then, when the music came to an end, he closed the book and went back to his armchair facing me and said again about me being twenty five in two years' time. It was a bit like he was practising for a sermon where the priest keeps repeating the same sentence over and over. 'Lucy, in two years' time you will be twenty five.'

Like as if I didn't know. Did he share my mother's anxiety about me still being single then - risking being on the shelf, a spinster, an old maid? Was he telling me I shouldn't be wasting my precious years, I should be looking for a nice Catholic boy I could settle down with? Like Andrew. Only he didn't know about Andrew.

In any case, Andrew was the last person on my mind at that moment. Sitting there looking at Juan, feeling his warm gaze upon me, and listening to that music together, an idea was growing inside me. What if I were to spend the rest of my life with Juan? He was going to be a priest so we would never be able to marry, but that was, in a way, what would be so good about it. Our love would be a strong secret thing, nobody but us would ever know about it. My parents would be worried because I wasn't getting married but that would be better than being with a man who was married already. There'd be no wife, no other woman at all, apart, of course, from the Virgin Mary and I could live with that. It would be a spiritual love.

I wouldn't ever have wanted the sort of marriage my mother had in mind anyway. When I was about thirteen, one morning she'd launched into telling me about what the magazines called 'the facts of life'. She was standing at the sink with a pile of washing on the floor beside her and I was standing in the doorway. And it was like the moment had come for her to give me the present she'd been saving up for me for years and I was at last able to unwrap it.

'You know that the reason people get married is in order to have children,' she started off.

It was like finding inside the parcel some serviceable garment like a home knit Fair Isle twin set. I'd always thought getting married was about being in love and not being able to live without each other, like in the fairy stories where there's a beautiful princess and a handsome prince and they want to be together but there are lots of problems to be overcome, like having to empty all the water from a lake and all you've got is a spoon with holes in it, but it all turns out right in the end.

'What's wrong with being twenty five?' I said now and he gave me the same look as he gave me last time, like I wasn't living in the real world. And then he went back to talking about *The Little Prince*.

As we said goodbye we stood at the door and I was all tense. Would he put his arms around me? But he just smiled and touched my cheek.

'I'll try to come and see you on Wednesday evening,' he said. The Marcels weren't due back till the Thursday.

After he'd gone I put the record on again and sat there listening to the sad slow tune and dreaming about opening a salon in Mexico City. I'd be this top hairdresser with the secret lover that nobody would ever know about.

He was actually waiting outside in the street when I got back from work on the Wednesday. He could only stay for a short while, he said, he had to be back in the seminary not long after eight and it took a whole hour in the Métro, changing at *Montparnasse*.

'Lucy,' he murmured when we were inside the door. He put his arms around me and we stayed like that for nearly a minute. It was the first time I'd been so close to him. We're about the same height so I could smell the soap he used on his face, it smelt like what they call *Savon de Marseille*, the soap I use to do my washing with. But then he moved away. He put the record on again and we sat in the armchairs facing each other, listening to it. It was as if there was a beautiful lake between us with treasure at the bottom of it that belonged to us, only we didn't want to disturb it. We sat there and it was so peaceful.

And then he started telling me about St Teresa. The St Teresa I knew about was French from Normandy and she'd become a Carmelite nun and died at around the age I am now. She wrote a book called *The Little Way* and after her death her body had smelt of roses, she had led such a pure life, utterly devoted to

God, so she became known as The Little Flower. There's a statue of her in the church at home, she's holding a wooden cross in her arms, covered in roses, and she's got this sweet serene expression on her face. Looking at her I always used to think how I could never be like that, and I couldn't think of anyone in my class at school who could ever be like that either.

But the St Teresa he was telling me about was Spanish. She came from the same part of Spain as Juan's father, only she lived in the sixteenth century. The main thing Juan said about her was that she was a mystic. I'd no idea what a mystic was and Juan wasn't very good at explaining. All he kept saying was that she had this passionate relationship with God. And in a way I could understand what he was meaning because of what I was beginning to feel about him and how wonderful it would be if I could live close to him for the rest of my life. I certainly liked the idea of St Teresa better than the little prince in the pale blue shorts.

When we came to say goodbye, though, he told me that he was leaving for Rome very soon. He was going to study there for a few months. I was five years old again, alone in the playground. Everyone else had gone home and it was getting dark. Was this the last time I'd ever see him? I was about to ask when he gave me a piece of paper with his address in Rome written out on it and underneath the word *love*.

'When you write to me will you put that at the end of your letter?' he asked. 'And when I write to you I will put the same - *love*.'

As I went back to my room I felt like I used to feel when we had retreats at school and had to fast and not have any breakfast till after we'd been to

Communion, sitting down in the canteen then and having the nuns smiling down at us for once and not minding too much about the nasty taste of the tea which came from it being made in a big metal kettle.

I decided I'd stop seeing Michel. It would be difficult because I was seeing him in the salon every day but I'd started going to daily Mass before I came in to work, so that sort of made me feel strong and aloof. I decided I'd tell him when he came back - he was on holiday from the salon at the time, down in the Marne visiting his wife's parents. I started putting everything into the hairdressing, staying on in the salon at the end of the day, practising on Agnès and Patricia, two of the apprentices.

Not seeing Michel lasted a whole two weeks after he came back from his holiday. Then one evening he caught up with me in his 2CV as I was walking home. He opened the car door and persuaded me to get in. He was very unhappy, missing me all the time. Life without me was unbearable. He was like a magician with his words. Juan vanished on the spot. I fell into his arms. I stopped going to daily Mass and the notion of opening a hair salon in Mexico City and having Juan as a secret lover began to seem more and more absurd.

All the same, my heart jumped a little when I got this long letter from him in his tiny handwriting, all about how he spent his days at the seminary in Rome. He ended up saying how he often thought of our times together in the library, listening to the music. 'I like to see you in Rome. It is possible?' he wrote in English at the end. He knew some people who could put me up – the relations of a fellow seminarian he'd got friendly with. At the bottom of the letter he wrote *love.*

The idea of exploring a strange new city gave me a thrill. It would be an adventure. Rome had been the setting of a film just out that I'd gone to with Andrew last year in Manchester - *La Dolce Vita*. It would be wonderful to be actually there. But no, I couldn't go - my life was complicated enough. I'd better write to say it wasn't possible. I was in love with Michel. There was no room for Juan in my life.

Then one morning the woman who'd asked Michel about his little girl was in the salon and I could tell Michel was talking to her about Charlotte from the look on his face. Michel's a Communist so he's quite critical of all these *bourgoises* as he calls them who spend their time having their hair done. He laughs and jokes with them but inside himself I know he despises them. Sometimes, when I see him standing over them with his scissors, I think he's going to jab the point in their necks.

This morning, though, talking about his little girl there was no faking. There was a real smile on his face. All of a sudden I realised how stupid I was to imagine that I was at the centre of his existence, how stupid I was to be making him the centre of mine. Why shouldn't I go to Rome? And why shouldn't I meet up with Juan again?

My parents wouldn't understand, of course. They'd be shocked if they knew. Leading a young priest into temptation, they'd say. They'd think it scandalous, like Father O'Brian going off with that girl he was supposed to be giving instruction to. I know my Mum was pleased when I said in a letter that I was going to Mass every morning - and I did mention Juan once but they probably imagined him like Vincent Sweeney who's studying for the priesthood and hasn't looked at a girl in his life. The only women that priests are supposed to have any contact with are their mothers and sisters. And nuns, of course, except with nuns they have to be careful. The only other women they meet are The Legion of Mary - women who are always around the church like flies, doing the flowers, polishing the candlesticks, leading the rosary, getting really excited about talking with the priest even when it's just about the weather or what flowers to put on the altar.

That evening I wrote and told Juan that I was coming. I've fixed it all up and tomorrow I'm leaving. It's too late now to do anything about it but go.

Chapter 4

Sometimes you've a feeling you don't know what you're about, like you've got on a bus and you're not sure where it's taking you, or why you got on it in the first place. That's the feeling I've got right now, standing beside this bloke at the military airport just outside Paris, waiting for a plane to take me to Rome. The sun's not yet properly up and I'm feeling a bit chilly. What am I doing here?

I've bought a French magazine because it has Jackie Kennedy, the wife of the new President of the USA, on the cover. *She* looks as if she knows what she's doing and where she's going. Straight black hair flicked round at the ends and a pillbox hat perched on top of it. I'm a hairdresser so I notice hair. I look at a woman and think - she's got a neat head, not a hair out of place, I bet she's the sort that vacuums under the bed and has the house nice for her husband when he comes home. Or the hair's swept off the face with loads of lacquer - someone's secretary. Or she's in her forties with the same style she's had since she was fourteen - hair neatly parted down the side and held in place with an Alice band, an old maid, still hoping. Or it's scrunched up into a cockeyed topknot and she's a goodtime girl. Anyway, if I was looking at myself at the moment I'd say 'It's nice and thick and curly so it suits her to have it chopped off just at the jaw line. And it's a good colour – the chestnut brings out the green of her eyes. But gee is it wild, going in all directions! That girl's a mess.'

The bloke beside me's called Alberto and he's a colonel in the Italian air force. He picked me up this morning in his red Alfa Romeo outside the Marcels' flat. I felt really conspicuous stepping out of his car when we arrived here because anyone watching would probably think we'd spent the night together. Actually, it was my first time meeting him. He's a friend of Bertrand. When I told Bertrand I was going to Rome he said this Italian colonel friend of his could probably get me a seat on a military plane. That sounded really exciting - I've never been on any sort of plane in my life - so I jumped at the offer. But now standing here I'm feeling nervous and a bit sick.

I very nearly didn't tell Bertrand I was going to Rome. I intended telling everybody I was going home to Manchester for a few days, but in the end it seemed easier to tell the truth – well, part of the truth, I couldn't possibly have told them the whole truth. I said it was my friend, Carmel, from Manchester that I was going to meet up with. Two nice Catholic girls in Rome together, that sounded okay - we could almost be part of a pilgrimage, an audience with the Pope thrown in.

Besides me and Alberto there are two other men waiting to get on the plane. One of them's very short and round with a bright red face and popping eyes, and a lock of straight greyish hair drawn across to hide his bald patch. The other's tall and elegant, with neatly cut dark hair, he looks a bit like Gregory Peck. Then there's a woman in her thirties with very straight silky shoulder-length dark brown hair with a parting down the middle. There's a glint coming off it – a Mahogany rinse. Plum would have suited her better. And she reeks of Jacque Fath's *Femme* – I can smell it from here. She's wearing a black duster coat with three quarter sleeves and stiletto heels and dazzling white kid gloves that look like white pigeons when she waves her hands around - which she does all the time when she opens her mouth to talk.

I hadn't expected there to be a woman like that on the plane. I'm in my flat black pumps and dirndl skirt and black sweater. I didn't even bother with any earrings. She's with a young boy who's probably her son - he's got the same straight dark brown hair. He's in a white shirt and shorts - he looks like an ad for *Omo* - and he's got these solemn brown eyes that keep staring at me. He seems to be looking at me accusingly, as if he's telling me I shouldn't be going to Rome, and his mother's looking at me too now as if she's thinking the same. Who is this English girl? How does she know Alberto? Why is she here? Where does she think she's going?

I'm wondering if I've time to escape from them and go off and spend a penny and do something about my hair but now we're moving towards the plane. Not far away there's another plane taking off, the engine's making an incredible noise and the smell coming from it's beginning to make me feel even more sick. But a bit of me's still thinking this is a thrilling experience, being so close to this great big roaring grey monster. The nearest I ever got to a plane up to now was making one out of balsa wood when I was a kid.

Then just as we're getting on this other bloke arrives. 'Luigi!' Alberto shouts and they greet each other like long lost brothers, hugging and clapping each other on the back and jabbering in Italian. My heart sinks - it's bad enough struggling with French like I've been doing for the last three months without having to cope with Italian. But once we're in the plane Luigi goes off to talk to Gregory Peck, thank goodness.

'How old are you?' Alberto asks me as we settle in our seats and he offers me a cigarette. He seems to be scrutinising me as I lean forward to light it from his posh silver lighter, as if he's checking me out for wrinkles. I'm a bit taken aback. I thought you weren't supposed to ask a woman her age but maybe it's all right in Italy. But why does he want to know? Also, I feel embarrassed, though he must be at least twenty years older than me. Should I lie?

'I'm twenty three,' I say as I take a deep puff from my cigarette. It makes it sound worse, saying it aloud. I'm about to tell him about my ambition to become a top hair stylist when he gets up and goes to sit beside Luigi. Just as well. My stomach's started to rumble and he'd be able to hear it in spite of the noise the engine's making. The woman's taken off her white gloves. She's got incredibly long fingernails painted pillar box red and she keeps running her hands over her son's head, smoothing down his hair. It's giving me the willies, looking at her. She reminds me of a witch in a fairy story I got out of the library once.

I look at the magazine, which is full of stuff about the Kennedys because they're coming to Paris at the beginning of June. There are more photos of Jackie Kennedy – 'the woman behind the President' - showing *le look Jackie* as they call it. There's a photo of her with a lacy wrap around her and her hair's coming forward in big curves round her cheeks and swooping onto her forehead. They'll all be arriving in the salon wanting a hairstyle like that - *le look Jackie*. Actually they annoy me, these fussy hair styles. When I've a salon of my own, I'll have nothing but sleek, simple styles. It'll all be in the cut. If you know how to cut you can get the hair to go any way you want.

'Where are you staying in Rome?' Alberto has come back to sit beside me. He must be about the same age as Bertrand but he's better preserved, not so podgy. He's going back home to his wife and teenage kids for a short break, but an idea is maybe running through his head, not to mention his trousers I'm beginning to think, which makes me feel uncomfortable. Is he expecting something in return for arranging this free trip on the aeroplane? I start imagining Bertrand telling him about *la petite anglaise* who's so *mignonne*. *Mignonne*'s a word I'm always hearing about me wherever I go - I looked it up once and it means *sweet.* I hate being called *sweet*. I try to avoid looking at him as we talk.

'I'm going to be staying with these people who live in ...' I produce the bit of paper with the address written on it and regret it immediately. He's going to ask me who the people are and how I know them and I'm not much good at lying. But he doesn't ask me any questions. All the same, this feeling of being on the wrong bus comes back to me.

'Rome is a very beautiful city,' he says, and he starts talking about all there is to see and I begin to feel more cheerful. I get out my packet of cigarettes, which are just about the cheapest blonde tobacco cigarettes you can buy, and offer him one, but he says *grazie* and gets out his *Benson and Hedges* and then goes off again to join Luigi. I don't think men like women offering them cigarettes, particularly when they're cheap ones like these.

'Look!' Alberto has come back and is leaning across me. I can feel the softness of his woollen jacket against my arm, and his skin smells of perfumed soap -

sandalwood. Out of the window down below there are all these snowy peaks.

'There's Mont Blanc,' he says, pointing. I look out and I see something that looks like a little white cap, sticking up just a tiny bit higher than anything else around it. Then clouds start whirling past the window and Alberto goes back to sitting beside Luigi.

To take my mind off how things are going to turn out when I get to Rome I'm trying to make sense of the article about the Kennedys but it's hard going because I only did a bit of French at school and I haven't made that much progress in the time I've been in Paris. When they know I'm English the clients often want to practise their English on me so I don't get to speak much French. Or else they're dying to talk but they know I'm not going to understand much so most of the time all they do is pull faces into the mirror and sigh and shake their heads and say things like I've no idea how awful their husband is and then more sighing and I have to nod my head and look sympathetic but it doesn't do much for my French.

Anyway, the article's about how elegant Jackie Kennedy is and how she detests hats and how the Americans don't like it because she chooses French designers like Givenchy and Balenciaga, instead of American ones. But I can't concentrate. This going to Rome is just about the most daring thing I've ever done in my life – after going to Paris – and maybe the most senseless.

The plane's lurching around like a drunken elephant. I can hardly see Alberto and Luigi through the fug of cigarette smoke but I can still hear them talking away in Italian and waving their hands about so I suppose everything's all right. But I'm beginning to feel queasy again. Popeye was offering me and the woman and the boy boiled sweets when we took off so we wouldn't feel sick but I didn't take one. Alberto's coming back to sit beside me again so I'll ask him to get one for me.

'Let me have your phone number,' he says. 'I would like to show you something of my city. One evening, perhaps we can arrange something.'

I'm not sure whether I should give him my number, but there's no reason really not to think that he's not just being nice, and also I'll be on my own in the evenings anyway. So I write it down for him and I ask him if I can have a sweet or something because I'm not feeling too good. He gets one off Popeye for me and then he pats me on the shoulder and goes back to Luigi and Gregory Peck. Maybe the thought of me throwing up's putting him off sitting beside me. Mind you, they're none of them taking much notice of Mrs Glamour Puss either. She's sitting there now with her eyes closed and the boy's got his head in a comic.

I've just got a pencil out and I'm giving Jackie K a funny hairstyle in the margin of the magazine when suddenly it's as if the engines have got fed up with making all that noise. I look up and there's Popeye standing there offering me another sweet and telling me we're coming in to land. And then *whack* and we're on the ground and everything's gone completely quiet like it's the end of the world. Except that none of them have stopped talking and the mother and son sound as if they're having some sort of row.

Outside there's a warm breeze blowing and I've pushed my sleeves up and Alberto's getting a taxi for me and telling the taxi driver to drive the *signorita* to the *Via Munia*. He makes it sound as if it's somewhere like Moss Side in Manchester. The woman and her son are being met by a distinguished-looking elderly man who's probably her father. She's got her gloves on again and she's waving her hands around and they're all kissing each other and stepping into a big white car. And I'm wishing with all my heart that I was her, knowing where I was going.

Chapter 5

Signor and Signora Bellini look like Tweedledum and Tweedledee, both short and dumpy. The flat's over heated and it's got quite a stuffy continental smell about it of garlic and olive oil and eau de cologne and drains.

They don't speak any English. We're waiting for their daughter, Angelica, to get back from work. She does speak English, they manage to tell me. Meanwhile I'm sitting there with a thimbleful of black coffee, smiling and puffing on my cigarette and nodding as they demonstrate the pull-out settee I'm going to be sleeping on. Then they go off into the kitchen or somewhere, leaving me with a book of pictures of churches in Rome. It's quite a small flat with lots of bits of lace covering things and there are statues of St Anthony and St Joseph on the mantlepiece and a big framed photo of the Pope sitting on top of the wireless.

Angelica arrives at last in a beige suit and white blouse with a crucifix on a chain prominent on it. She's got carefully combed longish dark brown hair that curls up at the ends. She's a bit older than me with brown eyes and a sallow complexion. She could do with putting some rouge on. I'm beginning to feel self-conscious about my dyed chestnut hair and my green eye-shadow and cyclamen lipstick.

'My parents want to know how long you've known Father Juan,' she asks me. I thought I'd noticed something a little hostile about them, a way of looking at me a bit suspiciously. I'm not what they'd expected - they'd assumed I'd be someone middle-aged and matronly, or young, like Angelica, but with the same

'Child of Mary' look about me. Definitely no dyed hair. I'm beginning to worry about what it will be like when he arrives, standing there with all their eyes upon us, watching us for signs – of what I'm not sure. He said he'd come round as soon as he could, just to welcome me.

A ring on the doorbell. That will be him. My insides are going all funny. Angelica goes to open the door and shows him in. I'm trying my best to keep calm but he appears in the doorway looking completely at ease. He's gracious to Tweedledum and Tweedledee, shakes their hands, bows slightly, the young priest in his long black soutane bringing his blessing into the house. He manages a little conversation in Italian with them. Or maybe he's speaking to them in Spanish because he's Mexican.

And then he turns to me. He doesn't hold out his hand. I can feel myself going beetroot red.

'Bonjour, Lucy,' he says, gazing at me. I say 'Bonjour' and look away quickly. Signor and Signora's eyes are upon us. He produces a sheet of paper from his pocket with a list of places to visit on it, like as if he was a tour guide. This makes me feel better. I'm here to visit Rome, not to see him. He's free tomorrow afternoon so we can meet at the foot of the Spanish Steps at 2 o'clock. He's drawn a map of how to get there. He makes it all seem so business-like, I'm hoping that the watching Signor and Signora will be reassured.

And then he's gone, leaving a strange emptiness behind him, as if we'd been visited by the Divine Presence and then abandoned. The table's laid and we eat some sort of meat paste like you get at home, only it smells like it's got a lot of garlic in it, as well as chunks of fat. Then we have something a bit like a lamb stew that's quite good. I'm starving, I've hardly had anything to eat all day apart from those sweets on the plane. There's a jug of water on the table and over by Signor B. a bottle of wine. He's poured himself a large glass. Would I like some wine? Would I not!

'Yes, a little, poco, poco', I say, hoping to charm them with my attempt at Italian. I regret it immediately as Angelica goes to the cupboard and comes back with a tiny glass and Signor B. pours me a lady's measure of the blood red liquid. Not much more than the priest gets to drink when he's saying Mass.

The next day at the Spanish Steps the sun is shining and he's there waiting for me. And for the first time I'm feeling glad I came. We walk towards a church that he wants to show me. He walks briskly and I'm trying my best to match his step but it's difficult because I'm in my high heels. He says the church was erected on what was thought to be Nero's grave. A walnut tree had been growing there, emitting evil spirits in the guise of crows. So they pulled up the tree and built the church in its place. We're standing there looking up at it and the people passing keep staring at us, a young priest with a young woman. I'm in my linen suit - yellow ochre - and I've got my hair swept up into a bunch at the back with a flowery chiffon scarf around it. I can see he's bothered by the attention we're getting. Maybe tomorrow I should wear my black woollen dress and a sober head scarf.

But I could be his sister, no? Except that we don't look a bit alike. I'm fair with pink cheeks and he's dark skinned with very short straight jet black hair in a crew cut. And then the looks he keeps giving me with his intense brown eyes. Between us it's as if there are little sparks darting around, like the ones you get as you comb out a client's hair after she's been under the dryer. He catches hold of my hand as we go through the door of the church and gives it a squeeze.

Inside the church, we stare up at a painting of St Paul falling from his horse, painted by someone with a name like *caravan*. Juan explains that what I think is a piece of drapery is a shaft of light. And the horse's hoof is in the wrong place as far as I can see but he says it's to do with perspective.

'Je t'embrasse,' he whispers as we stand there. 'I kiss you,' he ventures in English. He doesn't, of course. What he means is he's kissing me in spirit. And that's why I came, that's why I'm here - to be with him, safe and happy and whole and good and not in a state of sin. But then outside, back in the square, he gets all brisk again.

'Tomorrow, St. Peter's and the Sistine Chapel,' he says. It sounds a bit like a trip to heaven, which is what it is, I suppose, in a way, but I'm beginning to feel I've had enough of churches and statues and looking up at angels flying around on ceilings. I want to be back with him in the flat in Paris, listening to that music and being transported into a world where everything's simple and beautiful, not trudging around, having people staring at us. I try to look bright and smile as we say goodbye and I walk off in the direction of the Spanish Steps where I've arranged to meet Angelica.

What are we going to do this evening? Yesterday evening I'd suggested that maybe the two of us could go for a walk so I could see a bit of Rome but she seemed taken aback by the suggestion. Two women walking around on their own at night in Rome?

We'd be taken for tarts, she seemed to imply. Not much fear of Angelica being taken for a tart, I thought.

I've fixed up to meet her at some Tea Rooms. She's there when I arrive - looking worried. She explains as best she can in English. Apparently relations have arrived unexpectedly and I can't stay with them in the flat any more. But she's found a place for me in a *pensione* not far from the Coliseum. We go back to the *Via Munia* and I pack. Signor and Signora appear as I'm leaving, to wish me a formal goodbye. No sign of the relations but Angelica says they're expected *subito*. We take a taxi to the *pensione*. Angelica looks a bit embarrassed and I'm feeling quite upset because I think this is just an excuse to get rid of me. There aren't any relations. Her parents just don't want to have anything to do with me because of Juan, which makes me feel dirty. It's hard enough for a priest having to be celibate, they're thinking, without having young girls circling around them, leading them into temptation. They don't understand.

I ask Angelica to give my new phone number to anyone who might ring asking for me. I'm thinking of Juan, in case something comes up and he can't make it tomorrow, but I try to make it seem as if I'm concerned my parents might want to get in touch with me.

The evening meal in the *pensione* is a big plate of spaghetti and two tiny lamb chops and something like blancmange. There are just two other people at the table, two men who look like commercial travellers who sit reading their newspapers, taking hardly any notice of me. And now I'm sitting in this square room with a high ceiling and a heavy brocade thing on the double bed and the Sacred Heart looking down and the whole evening in front of me, and tomorrow evening too, and the evening after. I should never have come here. I try to think of Juan and the moments in the church but all I'm seeing is him walking away from me across the square.

But then I hear the Signora calling my name. I go to the door and she's there in her purple shawl gesticulating, pointing down the stone staircase to the phone on the wall. I run down. He's missing me, he wants to talk. Or maybe he's going to suggest meeting. I'll set out over the dark city to find him and we'll sit on a bench somewhere and I'll feel him close beside me.

It's Alberto. I try my best to sound friendly. Actually, once I've got over my disappointment, it's comforting to hear his familiar voice from the plane. He's concerned. Why aren't I still with the friends in the *Via Munia*? I say how they had relations arriving unexpectedly and how the *pensione* they've put me in is very nice. Anyway, he's inviting me to have dinner with him. We fix up to meet tomorrow evening in a little restaurant close to the *Fontana di Trevi* - the fountain Anita Ekberg threw herself into in *La Dolce Vita*. I begin to feel a little excited. At last I'm going to see something of Rome other than churches.

I go back up to the square room with the picture of the Sacred Heart above the bed and spend the evening thinking up a new hairstyle - *Style for the Sixties*. I hate the way women all go around looking so pleased with themselves with this hair style that's like a cage round their heads. I draw something sleek and geometric, hanging loose, with definitely no backcombing. I become totally absorbed and it's one o'clock before I climb into bed, pushing the heavy brocade thing onto the floor.

The next day I'm standing in St Peter's with Juan at my side. We're looking at a statue by Michelangelo of the Virgin Mary with Christ in her arms just after he's been taken down from the cross. It's the first thing I've seen in Rome that has really moved me and Juan is looking pleased, as if it was he the sculptor. But how come the mother of Christ looks so young, I ask him. If Christ, now dead, was thirty three, she must be in her late forties at least, but in the statue she looks like a young girl still. Juan explains that it's because the Madonna is a symbol of eternal beauty. 'Like you,' he whispers in my ear and I smile. But I'm beginning to be a bit tired of being treated like a Madonna, like as if I'm not a real person for him. This is not what I came to Rome for. He hasn't asked me anything about myself, about what I told him in Paris.

I'm certainly no Madonna to Alberto standing outside the *pensione* at midnight. I'd been worried this might happen, though I'd been careful all evening not to give him any encouragement. Dinner in a fashionable little restaurant with about four wine glasses in front of me, the women all around dressed in black with gold bracelets, pearls, shiny handbags, bouffant hair and Alberto talking about how he started out as one of the pilots that bombed Republican Spain during the Spanish Civil War. I felt a bit funny when he said that because Juan's father was a Republican. That's how Juan ended up being Mexican. His father had to leave Spain for Mexico when the Republicans lost to Franco so Juan was born in Mexico.

'You were on the wrong side, weren't you?' I said, as if I knew all about it, which I didn't but I didn't like the way he was sitting there all pleased with himself. He just laughed and called for the bill. *Three Coins in a Fountain,* he started humming as we stood in front of the *Fontana di Trevi* afterwards and I threw in all the coins I'd got. And now he's starting to kiss me as I'm searching for the key they gave me in the *pensione*, first my ear and then my neck and my forehead and cheeks and now my lips, trying to prize them open.

'Chérie,' he's murmuring.

'No, no. I'm sorry,' I breathe, pulling myself away from him and putting the key, which I've now found, in the lock. I gaze up at him with an *It's hard for me to resist you but I must, I really must* look in my eyes. I feel awkward because, after all, he's taken me out, paid for an expensive meal. But does that really give him the right to spend the night with me? Maybe it does, I don't know.

'Thank you for a wonderful evening,' I whisper and slip into the darkness of the pensione, pulling the heavy door closed behind me.

Friday. My last day. I'm meeting Juan early to take the Métro out to *San Paolo's* - he wants to show me the cloisters - and I'm sitting in the sunshine on the Spanish Steps writing a letter home to my parents. I write home every week. This week there's plenty to tell them, except that the one thing my mother's interested in is whether I've met someone yet, someone I could settle down with, if I really don't want to marry Andrew.

Dear Mum and Dad, I hope you are well …' I stare at the page for a moment and then put the writing pad back in my handbag and light a cigarette. It'll be my last for several hours as Juan doesn't like me smoking. I start daydreaming. What if I were to spend the rest of my life close to Juan? When he went back to Mexico City I'd go too. With my qualifications and experience I'd easily find work and one day I'd be famous and people would always be wondering about my private life. 'Lucy is such a devout Catholic, she's at Mass every morning. A pity she has never married. It must be because she's always put her career first. But maybe she has a secret lover.' A nun at school once held out her hand and pointed to the ring nuns wear. She said what it signified was that they were married to Christ. It would be a bit like that. I wouldn't be married to Juan but we'd have this deep spiritual bond that nobody else would know about. I see him coming towards me, walking quickly, lightly.

We're sitting in the cloisters. It's beautiful and peaceful gazing at the forest of thin columns and arches, and there's hardly anybody else about. The sun's quite hot and there's a lovely smell coming from the blossom on a nearby tree and somewhere there's a blackbird singing. Juan's hand is very close to mine. The thought suddenly occurs to me that I'm sitting beside a stranger. I know nothing about him, about his family, where he comes from in Mexico, why he wants to be a priest. I find this exciting, like a land waiting to be discovered. A bell starts to strike the hour.

'Lucy, in two years, you will be twenty five.'

Hearing him come out with that refrain again, I feel really irritated.

I don't see what that's got to do with this moment, sitting here together. 'Are you hoping I'll say that I don't want to get married, I want to be close to you all my life?' I'm tempted to burst out, just to see how he reacts. But instead I tell him that, by the time

I'm twenty five, I hope to be a successful hairdresser. I know this will annoy him. I start talking about the revolutionary hairstyle I'm designing that I can't stop thinking of, but he interrupts me.

'Lucy,' he says, 'this may be the last time we're together like this.'

'But you're coming back to Paris in June, aren't you?' I say.

'Only for a very short while, just for my ordination and then I go back to Mexico. But remember the story I told you about the little prince and the rose.'

'You never know,' I say, ignoring this, 'I may turn up in Mexico one day.' I try to sound as if I'm only joking.

'We will write to each other, Lucy,' he says. He puts his hand in mine, our fingers intertwine and he looks at me tenderly. And then he takes from his pocket a little gold medal with a picture of the Sacred Heart engraved on it.

'This is for you, Lucy.' He gives it to me. 'Look on the other side,' he says. I turn it over. On it he's scratched just the one word: *love*

'We will write to each other, Lucy,' he says again as we say goodbye at the foot of the Spanish Steps.

'Yes,' I say. We almost put our arms around each other but there are lots of people about, staring at us, so we just stand there for a moment and then he turns and walks away. I watch him until he disappears. I saw a film once when I was eight about a little girl who was a cripple. She was in a wheel chair and the thing I can't forget about the film is when her Dad took her to this orphanage and left her there. As her father walked away she started moving the wheel chair faster and faster to try to catch up with him. 'Daddy, don't leave me. Daddy, don't leave me.' As I stand there I feel a bit like the cripple girl in the wheel chair.

And then I move away. The facades of the buildings seem as if they're about to burst into flames in the evening sunlight. Tomorrow I'll back in Paris. With Michel. At least Michel understands that I care about my job.

Chapter 6

We're walking up the stairs to the *chambre de bonne*. Michel's close on my heels, studying my behind no doubt. I should have let him go first, I've put on weight, too much pasta and ice cream in Rome. Michel is lean, skinny almost, and muscular. The body of a dancer. He'd have made a good dancer. You can see that from the way he dances round the clients and from the way he raises his arms. Not that it isn't an advantage in the salon either. That was the thing I noticed about him, that first day, the graceful way he had of moving, of holding up the mirror so that his client could see the back of her head.

'Is Madame pleased with the way I have cut her hair? Would Madame like a little more off the top? I think maybe … .'

We're standing at my door and I'm searching for my key and he's looking at me with that steady gaze, the way he looked at me the end of my first week, as I was putting on my coat to go home.

I've found my key and now we're walking into the room with the faded bedspread of yellow and pink roses on a cream background covering the bed and the pale pink mat on the floor beside it and the bit of dark blue cretonne across the window that I don't ever bother taking down. We're only ever here for a few hours in the evening and the view from the window is of a dingy brick wall.

Michel helps me off with my jacket with a slight flourish like when he's helping an important client off with her coat. He's being a little bit distant. I've told him something about Juan but he doesn't realise that Juan's now in Rome and that's why I went there. But maybe he senses something.

'You make me feel like the Comtesse de Cluny,' I say. Marie Claire had whispered her name to me one morning as I stood watching Michel holding out a mink coat for a handsome woman with lightly permed grey hair.

We joke a lot about the clients and Michel imitates them - he's a good mimic. He's running his hands up the inside of my jumper now, caressing my breasts and then sliding his hands round to the back to undo my bra. And now we're moving towards the bed and I'm undoing my hair band.

We're lying there later between the cotton sheets and he's gone back to looking like there's something on his mind and I'm thinking that he doesn't need to worry. He's the man I'm in love with, not Juan. He's here beside me and he's real. I turn towards him to put my arm around him. I'm even wondering if I won't tell him more about Juan and ask him what he thinks of *Le Petit Prince* but Michel doesn't believe in God. He's a Communist. I couldn't bear it if he started saying anything against Juan, making fun of him or something. But I can talk about Alberto, tell him about us throwing coins in the fountain. I'm just launching into a description of this when he interrupts me.

'Bertrand has asked me if I'd like to go down to Nice to be in charge of the new salon.' He's looking straight ahead of him as he announces this. I lie there staring at the walls, suddenly noticing they need washing.

'So what did you say?' I manage to ask him at last.

'I said Yes. It's a great opportunity. I'd have all the setting up to do on my own, and then I'd have two apprentices and there's a stylist in London Bertrand thinks would be interested in coming over.'

The room's changing into the dingiest place I've ever been in and I'm noticing how chilly it is, even though it's well into April. I've taken my arm away and I'm lying there all rigid, like I'm on an operating table. He puts his arm around my shoulders but I don't respond. I'm feeling really upset. I thought he loved me, I thought he could never bear the idea of us being separated, that leaving Paris, leaving me would be impossible.

'You could transfer too,' he says, as if this is a thought that's only just struck him.

'If you think I'm going to give up my position in Paris and follow you like a little dog,' I almost burst out. At the same time, I'm struggling to reason with myself. I know I'm not being fair. After all I was thinking of leaving him for Juan, wasn't I? But somehow that seemed different.

He's turned and he's kissing me and guiding my hand downwards. I try to resist, I'm feeling so hostile towards him. I bite him hard on the ear but this suddenly makes me want him, makes me want him to want me even more so that he'll realise he can't go away like this.

But he is going. He's leaving tomorrow. I'm still struggling with the idea that he can bear to end what we have together here.

We're in the *Belle Ferronnière,* the café just up the road from the salon. It isn't a café that anybody else from the salon goes to, so we often have a drink there after work before he sets off - back to his wife and child.

'I always think there's something *louche* about that place,' Marie Claire said today as I walked past it with her at lunch time. We'd been to the big shop in the *Rue Marboeuf* that sells about a hundred different sorts of cheeses. As we sit there now, I ask Michel what *louche* means and he says it means something not very ... . He swivels his hand from side to side the way the French do. I think he means it's *shady* There are two men standing at the bar in camel coats and plastered down hair, smoking cigars and looking as if they might be arranging some deal. And there's a peroxide blonde in the corner all by herself, with a mass of gold bracelets on her wrist, smoking a cigarette on the end of a long holder. Otherwise me and Michel are the only people there.

That's all there's time for, this drink after work. I can understand - his little girl's upset that he's going and he has to get back before she goes to bed - but it doesn't make me feel any better. He's bought me a Dubonnet. It's my first time drinking Dubonnet, though I've been seeing the ads for it everywhere since I arrived. *Dubo ...Dubon ....Dubonnet*.

'Do you remember that large copper-haired woman who was in the salon yesterday morning?' Michel asks me. 'Bertrand was giving her a perm. Well, she's Madame Verrier, but she used to be Mademoiselle Dubonnet. Monsieur Verrier was just a clerk in the Dubonnet business and then he married Mademoiselle Dubonnet.' We start laughing at the idea of Monsieur Verrier's good fortune, bent over a ledger book one moment and sitting behind a mahogany desk the next and driving a Rolls Royce.

'Maybe one day a Mademoiselle *Cordon Rouge* will come into the salon and you'll seduce her.' I start to laugh and then realise that, from my point of view, that wouldn't be funny at all.

I've finished my glass of *Dubonnet* - what there was of it - within minutes so Michel has ordered me another one. He's drinking beer.

'Be careful,' he says as he sees me drinking this one too as if it was ordinary wine, 'it's quite strong.'

It's maybe the two glasses of *Dubonnet* that have given me the courage to ask him if Jeanne's going to be joining him in Nice. I don't like calling her Jeanne, it gives me a funny feeling as if I knew her, which I've no wish to do.

He's fishing for his packet of *Gitanes*. I'm still on blonde tobacco, though Michel keeps trying to persuade me to change to French cigarettes because he thinks they're better for you. He says French tobacco doesn't give you lung cancer like blond tobacco, but I can't get used to smoking *Gauloises*. I've discovered a brand of blond tobacco called *Raleigh* that's much cheaper than things like *Benson and Hedges,* only I've trouble pronouncing the *r* in a French way. I have to keep pointing. I've started buying them at the same kiosk every day, where the man knows what I'm wanting.

He isn't sure if they'll be coming down to Nice. Maybe. It depends how it all works out. He looks at me as he says this, as if he's meaning not just the hairdressing, and I have a feeling like you get when the bus goes round the corner too fast. There's no way we can get married because he's married already.

'But I'll be by myself until September at least. It will be too hot for them to be in Nice in the summer, so they'll be with Jeanne's parents in the Marne. You *could* transfer for the summer, you know, I'm sure Bertrand wouldn't mind. It's very quiet in Paris during the summer.'

He's said this before to me and the thought of two months all alone with Michel in Nice - even the possibility of spending one whole night with him makes me tremble. I can't imagine anything more wonderful than having him beside me till morning. Not having to listen to him fumbling round for his clothes in the dark, and then creeping down those six flights of stairs, lying there waiting for the sound of the 2CV to start up and then listening to it getting fainter and fainter as he goes on his way back to the second floor flat somewhere on the south side of Paris. Why am I hesitating?

But a bit of me's resentful still, I can't help it. How can he be going away like this if he's really in love with me? If it were me and I were offered a job, no matter how tempting, anywhere other than Paris, I'd say No if it meant not seeing him. But he said Yes without knowing if I was going to follow him or not.

The bracelets on the wrist of the peroxide blonde jangle as she lights up another cigarette and gazes out of the window. Is she waiting for some one? Probably resting between clients, Michel says. This hasn't occurred to me, that she might be a prostitute. She must be a very high class one.

'Come down to Nice, Lucy. Talk to Bertrand about it. It would be wonderful. Wouldn't it?' He's looking at me, waiting for my response. 'You said you'd come down but you haven't even mentioned it to Bertrand yet.' He's looking at me so intensely.

'Yes, I will, I will talk to him,' I say. But I don't like the way he seems to be almost bullying me.

Funny because I spent the weekend in the dumps, certain that he didn't really care if I came down to Nice or not. But also I want to know what my position would be if I went to Nice. Here we're sort of on an equal footing. I don't want to arrive down there and find I don't have the same status.

'I think it's better if I wait till you've gone before talking to Bertrand,' I say. Not that they wouldn't still put two and two together, all of them - Bertrand, Marie Claire, Jean François, Agnès, Patricia ..... .

'I'll talk to him next week after you've gone,' I say, catching hold of his hands.

Chapter 7

Bertrand's watching me, I can tell, as I do the Countess's hair. She's not at all pleased that Michel has gone off to the south of France.

'I am sure you will be delighted with Lucy,' he tells her. He would have taken her on himself but she was a last minute appointment this morning and he was busy with this French film star I'd never heard of.

'I think if I curve the hair round more over your cheek it will emphasise your lovely high cheek bones,' I say, patting them in case she doesn't understand. I'm talking in English as she's told me she'd like to practise her English.

'My Eengleesh is terreebel zee same like my 'airs.'

'Oh no,' I say. 'Your English and your hair are both ... .' I look for a word and end up with 'very nice.' Big laughs. I am too kind, she says. The English are always finding everything very nice. But we're getting on okay and I'm thinking the way I'm doing her hair is a big improvement on Michel's. Her face is too square and the style he chose used to emphasise this.

I help her on with her beautifully cut jacket in a dark blue face cloth. It's the beginning of May and it's warm and sunny outside and the salon is full of the smell of lily of the valley. It's the custom here to give people bunches of lily of the valley on the first of May - there were women on street corners yesterday selling it.

'Congratulations,' says Bertrand to me after she's gone through the glass door, looking at me with his large sad brown eyes and giving me a nice fatherly smile.

'I'll be sorry if you go down to Nice.' he says. 'I'll be sorry to lose you.' He knows about me and Michel, I'm sure, though neither of us has said anything to him. He's probably thinking I'd be better staying in Paris and not just for my career. He's thinking of Michel's wife.

'Yes, I'm not sure I want to leave Paris,' I say. 'Only ….' I can't finish the sentence - only I'm missing Michel and he's missing me. 'Only it might be good experience for me working in Nice during the summer with plenty of famous people about,' I say instead. Bertrand shrugs his shoulders but doesn't contradict. 'But I'm wondering what my position would be down there.'

He raises his hands and has another shrug of the shoulders. He knows nothing about that, he says. It's Michel who's in charge down there. He tells me to get in touch with Michel and discuss it with him. On the phone last week he was talking about the new stylist from London who's called George.

The new stylist from London? Michel hadn't said anything about him. Was he avoiding the subject? Would he be senior to me? Surely it went without saying that it mattered to me, the position I held in the salon. But maybe it didn't go without saying. Maybe I'd need to say something next time I was on the phone to Michel.

Marie Claire has asked me if I want to go for a drink with her after work today, which was nice of her. She probably guesses I'm missing Michel, though I'm sure she can't imagine how much - having him around all day, smiling across at me, feeling his lips touching mine as we find ourselves alone for a moment in the little staff cloakroom, his hand resting on the nape of my neck.

I still haven't said anything definite to Bertrand about leaving though I spoke to Michel yesterday evening and he says George won't be senior to me. So that's okay, though I'm glad I brought it up as I don't think he'd thought about it much. He says the salon in Nice is great, I'll love it. It's in one of the smartest hotels on the *Côte d'Azur*, on what they call the *Promenade des Anglais* because lots of rich English used to come here at the turn of the century. Lots of rich English still there, he says, so it will be great having me and George to speak to them in English.

I asked him where I'd live if I came down and he said it would be easy to get a little flat in an old block of flats nearby. 'But not too little,' he added, making me leap for joy inside myself. What that means is he'll be sharing the flat with me a lot of the time. His flat is some distance away from the hotel, he says. It's quite a big flat in a modern building. That's so his wife and little girl can visit him there, I suppose, though he doesn't actually say this. What would I be letting myself in for if I went down?

This is what's preoccupying me as I'm sitting now with Marie Claire in a little café in the Champs Elysées called *le PamPam*. Marie Claire's tall and skinny and she has her hair up in a Brigitte Bardot style and always wears spiky heels, which makes her look even taller. The café's crowded with men having aperitifs before going home. There aren't many women around so we're attracting quite a lot of attention but Marie Claire's doesn't seem to notice.

'I am verree taierrd. Or can I say 'I am verree exheusted'?' she starts off as the waiter brings us two

Martinis. But then to my relief she goes back to speaking in French.

'Don't you wish you were married? she asks me.

'I don't know,' I say, trying to react as if she'd asked me how I was liking Paris. 'It's not that I don't want to get married. It's just that I want a career as a hairdresser as well, as you know.' Maybe Marie Claire doesn't know.

'Ah, but to be married….' An ecstatic look has come over her face. Marie Claire is twenty eight. She must be very anxious. I don't know whether I should ask her if she's got a boyfriend.

'But you can be 'airdressair and be marrreed too, no?' She's gone back to speaking in English.

I shrug my shoulders. What I want to say is that it's difficult if you're a woman, you don't get the backing. As a wife your main job seems to be to be behind your man, supporting him and encouraging him. But I can see that what I'd be describing would be Marie Claire's idea of heaven so all I say is that it isn't easy for a woman having a career if she's married.

As I say this, in English, I notice a young man with curly brown hair standing beside our table. He's carrying a rucksack and wearing blue jeans so he looks funny amongst all these men in suits with their black brief cases. There's a spare seat and he's asking if he can sit there.

'I'm sorry to bother you but do you have a light?' he asks us in English as he fishes a battered looking packet of *Gauloises* from a pocket in his rucksack. He sounds as if he comes from Scotland. He does, and he's called Jack and he's going round the world, he tells us. I can smell B.O. ever so slightly coming from his armpit as he reaches out to take my Ronson lighter.

'How about you?' he asks us, so Marie Claire tells him that we both work at *Bertrand*. She waits a second for him to look impressed and then goes on

'Lucy is a verree verree good 'air cuttair,' She sounds as if she's really proud of me and I feel like giving her a kiss.

'You're a career girl, are you?' he asks me. He's obviously heard what I said about it being difficult.

'Yes,' I say. 'I'm a hairstylist. One day I want to have a salon of my own.' The Martini's gone to my head. 'I haven't actually decided yet whether my first salon will be in London or Paris.'

'Maybe you'll have one in each,' he says and we laugh and Marie Claire joins in.

'That's great, that's really great,' he says. 'So many women, the only thing they're interested in is men and getting married.'

I catch Marie Claire's eye.

'Yes, you're right,' I say, trying to look as if that's the last thing on my mind.

Jack's ordered a beer and I ask Marie Claire if she wants another Martini but she says she has to go. She hurries off and I know she's giving me the chance to get off with Jack but I have to go too as I said I'd baby sit for Monique this evening. Jack's leaving Paris in the morning but he says he'll be passing through again on his way back to Britain in September. I say I'm not sure if I'll be here in September but he asks for my address and telephone number all the same and we say goodbye.

There's a letter from Juan when I come in this evening. It's propped up on the table in the hall with the Italian stamp on it. It's been there all day, so now Monique knows that Juan is writing to me. Usually it's me picks up the post in the mornings but this morning it was late.

When I got back from Rome Monique had wanted to know all about my trip. We'd spent the evening finishing the box of *Baci* chocolates Angelica had given me. Before I left for Rome Monique had given me a little box of what she said were Juan's favourite sweets – sugared almonds – just in case I'd time to see him while I was there. Monique thought I'd gone to Rome to meet up with my friend, Carmel, I don't know whether she would have understood any better than my parents about my relationship with Juan. I showed her the postcards I'd bought of St Peter's Square and the building that looks like a typewriter and the cloisters where I'd sat with Juan. I told her Juan had taken us there.

'What a pity you didn't have a camera,' she said. 'It would have been lovely to have had a photo of Juan in the cloisters.' I'd closed my eyes for a second and imagined the photo I never took of him standing there, gazing at me.

I can hear Monique in the kitchen now with Daniel and Catherine but I've bought myself a baguette and some cheese and a bottle of *vin ordinaire*, so I can go straight to my room. I feel like being by myself.

It's not really a letter, it's just a postcard with a black and white picture of a statue on it, but he's filled the other side with his tiny handwriting, mostly about the picture.

The picture is of St Teresa, not the Little Flower but the one Juan started telling me about that

Wednesday evening. He discovered that there was a famous statue of her in a church in Rome and he went to see it. He says on the card that he wishes he'd known about it when I was there and we could have gone to see it together. It doesn't look at all like the statue of any saint I've ever seen in my life. Usually they're standing upright with saintly expressions on their faces but St Teresa is on her knees looking really reckless and abandoned and her face is tilted upwards with an expression on it as if she's in the middle of coming. It's certainly not the sort of picture you'd see in a prayer book at home.

    If we'd gone to see that statue would it have led to anything? Or would we just have stood there looking at it in the dark church, not saying anything, and then parting a short while later, him to go back to his seminary and me to that *pensione*? I feel uncomfortable looking at the picture now. I prefer the statue of the Virgin Mary with the dead body of her son in her arms that we saw in St Peter's. Or even a statue of The Little Flower with that pious expression like she's just said five decades of the rosary. In Rome, I didn't want anything to happen to change the way we were. I just wanted to be with him, to try to feel again the way I'd felt when we were in Paris together. I didn't even want to hold his hand. That was what was so good about it in a way, I just felt elevated, a bit like the Mother of God being raised into Heaven on a cloud with the choirs of angels singing. Not like St Teresa with that crazy look on her face.

    I want to write to Juan but I'm not sure what to say. I still feel sometimes that I could give up everything for him if he wanted me to, but he's never ever said anything to suggest he wants me to follow him to Mexico. His refrain about me being twenty five in two years time; that can only mean he wants me to settle down with some nice boy. I think that's why he read me *The Little Prince*, knowing that one day we will have to part for ever, that we can never ever be together in the same place, physically. But as long as we know that the other exists, that is enough, that's what the story is saying, he explained to me.

What he'd like, I suppose, and what my Mum and Dad would certainly like, would be for me to marry Andrew. When I left Manchester to come to Paris I knew my mum was thinking I was throwing away the best chance I'd ever get - a nice Catholic boy who worshipped the ground I walked on, she used to say. But I didn't think I'd ever feel I wanted to marry Andrew and I should have told him that before I left. I felt hypocritical, saying goodbye to him at the station, pretending to feel sad when I was all warm and excited inside with my new suitcase up on the rack. It was really cold, in fact it was snowing, and he was standing there on the platform, looking so miserable, huddled into his raincoat. The snow was melting off his hair and running down his face like tears. But then, just as the train started moving away, I found myself not wanting to let go of his hand.

'I'll be back in six months,' I called out to him as the train gathered speed and I had to let go at last. I shouldn't have said that. The arrangement is for me to spend a year in Paris, and, in any case, this was meant to be goodbye for ever sort of thing.

I owe him a letter. Should I write to him now and tell him we can never be anything but good friends? It's not fair, keeping him on a string like this, letting him think that one day soon I'll come home and we'll get married. I should be honest with him. *You have to be cruel to be kind*, my mother always says.

But maybe I'll change, maybe suddenly I'll discover that I do love him, that it's him and not Michel that I've really loved all along. Like Scarlett O'Hara realising it's Rhett Butler and not Ashley that she really loves. It would make my mother so happy. But then what about my career stuck in the north of England? And my life, with no excitement, no adventure, just the ordinary humdrum?

I put some water in the saucepan and plug in the little stove Monique has bought for me. I'll have a cup of coffee while I'm thinking what to say. St Teresa is there in front of me. I put her in the table drawer, face down, next to the medal with the word 'love' scratched on it that Juan gave me in Rome. I get my writing pad out of the drawer.

Dear Andrew, I write. He *is* dear to me. And then I remember he's got his Quantity Surveyor exams in two weeks' time. I couldn't break with him now, even if I wanted to, I couldn't upset him just before his exams. If he failed it would be my fault.

So instead I write to him wishing him luck. I tell him I'm very sorry but I won't be back in June. I tell him this marvellous opportunity has come up to work in a newly opened salon in Nice over the summer and that I'll probably go down there.

It occurs to me then that he'll wonder why I don't suggest him coming down to Nice to be with me there. I know he's longing for me to ask him to come over to France and I hate disappointing him. At the end of the letter I find myself writing *I'm thinking of going in for this hairdressing competition that takes place in Paris in the autumn. That's a long way away but you've got to get your name down really early. Maybe you can come over to Paris then and cheer me on - and up!!!*

I put the letter in an envelope and go out to post it straight away. On the way back I start wondering if I'm not making the situation worse, inviting him to Paris when part of me was on the point of telling him there was no future between us.

Marie Claire asked me if I wanted to have a drink with her again this evening but I need to be on my own. I've got to decide what I'm doing. I still haven't said anything definite to either Bertrand or Michel.

So here I am at a pavement café just ten minutes away from the flat. I've walked here from the salon. I didn't feel like going straight back home. I've got a large glass of red wine in front of me. I thought of asking for some peanuts as well - *cacahuêtes*, they're called in French. I remember the word because Monique's kids are always talking about having done *caca* - that's Number two. But they're quite fattening and I have to be careful. Everyone else in the salon's like a beanpole.

I get up to go home and I'm half way along the street when I hear someone behind me running. It's the waiter who served me my glass of red wine. He says I haven't paid, I've left without paying. He's waving the bit of white paper at me with the amount I owe marked on it. I'm sure I've paid. I left the money on the table, I tell him. But there was no money on the table when he came to collect the empty glass, he says. I pay again. There's a lump in my throat as I open my purse to get out the money. I go home, struggling not to cry as I put my key in the lock.

The phone is ringing as I go through the door. Monique and the kids are out. Claude has offered to take them for a meal in *The Drug Store*, which has just opened on the *Champs Elysées* - to make up for him going off on a business trip next week.

' 'Allo,' I say carefully, prepared to tell whoever it is that '*Madame n'est pas là*'. It's Alberto.

'Lucy, ma chérie, how are you?'

'Oh, Alberto!' I exclaim. It's so nice to hear a friendly voice that I greet him as if he was a favourite uncle I haven't heard from for a year. Am I free this Saturday? Or next Saturday? He would love to take me out to dinner. Saturday's always the worst evening of the week, the evening when I feel loneliest, when I'm all alone in the flat. Monique usually spends Saturday afternoon with a friend who has children the same age as hers and gets back late. I say I'm free this coming Saturday and we fix up to meet at the Porte Maillot. He knows a wonderful fish restaurant near there. I put down the phone and put on the record of *My Fair Lady* that Monique brought back from London last week. '*All I want is a room some where ....*' I take my shoes off and start dancing around the room on the soft green carpet.

Chapter 8

It's Saturday afternoon and I'm happy because I've got a date for this evening. I wonder if Michel will phone and no one will answer and he'll wonder where I am. I've left the salon early, my last two clients cancelled. I cross the river to the left bank by the *Pont de la Concorde*. I've never been the other side of the river before and I feel like a walk. I've got my black flatties on and my dirndl skirt with the splashy orange and yellow roses on it and a black top. And I've put my hair up and curled the chiffon scarf around it that I was wearing in Rome, the day I went out with Juan to the church with the cloisters.

    It's lovely and sunny and the trees are a nice fresh green. The only bother is all these men that keep following you wherever you go. It's a real pest. You're walking along, feeling good, swinging your handbag, when you hear this voice behind you - 'Vous êtes seule, mademoiselle?' 'Are you alone?' 'No, my guardian angel/my body minder/the ghost of my father is right here beside me,' I always feel like saying. The voice usually sounds quite respectful but you know that what they're hoping for is to end up in bed with you. The next question is always: 'Vous êtes anglaise?' This depresses me because the English have a reputation for being frumpish - cardigans and droopy dresses - so it's not much of a compliment to be taken for an English girl.

    Anyway, when you don't answer, they try Spanish - 'Vous êtes espagnole?' and then Danish, and Swedish and Italian and Dutch and German. This one today finally loses patience, he's been following me all the way across the bridge. 'Enfin, vous êtes un produit de quel pays?' 'you're a product of what country?' he bursts out, as if I were a tin of beans or something.

'Va t'en, go away,' I turn and hiss at him and he backs away. Thank Goodness. Though a little bit of me feels mean. He's got a dark face, he's probably North African and lonely like me.

I've not much idea where I'm going but I've got a map, and, in any case, as long as I follow the river I can't go wrong. But then I see these little narrow streets leading up onto what the map says is *Boulevard St Germain*, so I go up there. There are lots of pavement cafés crowded with people sitting at them drinking beer and wine. A lot of the women look as if they've never been near a hairdresser's in their lives - long untidy hair stretching down their backs that looks as if it could do with a good wash and brushing. And a good cut. My geometric hair style, it would really suit some of these faces. I'm longing to try it out on someone. I talked about it to Bertrand last week but he told me just to go on doing what I'd learnt to do during my training in England.

'The clients are very happy with you, Lucy. No need to change.' Maybe Nice was the place. I wouldn't just be going down to be with Michel.

My feet are killing me and I see a small café on a corner. Some people are just leaving, so I sit down at the empty table that's only inches away from the people passing along the boulevard. At the next table there's a girl with blonde hair in a pony tail and a skimpy white blouse. She looks the same age as me. She's with a small dark skinned man and a long thin man with pimply skin. They're talking in English. The man with the pimply skin is American but the girl's English. She has quite a posh voice. When the waiter comes they order more wine but I just ask for *un limonade*. I'm quite pleased I know the word but the waiter barks at me

' Une - pas un. C'est une limonade,' he says as he scoops up the dirty glasses.

I feel embarrassed but the girl beside me bursts out laughing and says how stupid the French are to be so fussy about their language.

'I'm Vinny and this is Bill and this is Meriche - he's Algerian,' she says. She asks me if I'm a student so I tell her I'm a hairdresser.

She seems a bit surprised at this, like she never met a hairdresser before in her life. When tell her where I work she gives a sort of shudder.

'It must be awful having to talk to all those bourgeois people all day long,' she says, taking a puff of her cigarette and then blowing the smoke slowly out into the air. They ask me what sort of women come into the salon and what they have done to their hair and how often. They're amazed when I tell them some of them come in every week for a shampoo and set.

'There's this old woman who's a duchess and all she's got is a little bit of wispy white hair left but she comes in every Thursday afternoon at three o'clock. She likes me to put it in pins so she can have tight little curls all over her head.' Actually I'm quite fond of the duchess. And she's very generous, not like some of the others. As I help her on with this black astrakhan coat she seems to wear winter and summer she always puts her hand deep into the pocket and brings out a note smelling of face powder and whispers to me to go away and buy something nice for myself. She has a way of saying this which makes me think she's hoping I'm going to spend it on naughty underwear.

It's really nice sitting in the sunshine with them, talking in English. I've never spent time just sitting at a pavement café like that before. The ashtray's filling up. We're all puffing away. And I've begun to imitate Vinny's way of smoking. I ask them if they're students and they say 'sort of' - except for Meriche who works, he's a plasterer, Vinny tells me. Meriche doesn't say anything, he probably doesn't speak English but he doesn't seem to mind just sitting there listening and laughing when everyone else laughs. They order more wine and this time I have a glass too, white wine. And then Vinny says she'd better be going.

'We're having a party this evening. Come along if you like'

I've fixed up to meet Alberto but I'm so glad to be meeting people of my own age that I can talk to. I don't want to just say goodbye and that will be that.

'Where do you live?' I ask. She says it's about a thirty minute walk from the café.

'You walk along the *Boulevard St Germain* till you come to the *rue Saint Jacques* and then you keep walking up the *rue Saint Jacques* till you come to this little street.' She squiggles the address on a scrap of paper. I say I'll have to go back home and change but Vinny says I'm fine the way I am. As they get up to go, Bill bends down to pick up a stick.

'I've got a wooden leg,' he says, rolling up his trouser leg to show me. I don't know what to say. I push the table to give him more room to get out.

What should I do about Alberto? I was really pleased when he asked me out for this evening. But he had said either this Saturday or next. I decide I'll phone him to put him off. If I don't turn up at the party this evening I'll probably never see Vinny again.

I go down the narrow corkscrew staircase inside the café, following the sign that says *Téléphone Toilettes*. There's quite a smell down there of pee and there's a man coming out of the toilet doing himself up and leaving the door open. I can see that there's no lavatory bowl inside, only a hole in the ground and two kind of raised bits where you're supposed to put your feet. I'm badly in need of a pee so I go in, only when I close the door I'm in complete darkness and I can't find the light switch. I try to remember where the raised bits are. When I've finished, my eyes have got used to the dark and I can just make out the string you have to pull to work the flush. So I pull and the next moment I've got all this water coming up over my shoes. I get out as quick as I can, with the water coming after me as far as the door practically.

I've never used a public phone before. I stand looking at it, searching in my purse for some coins. A man who's going into the lavatory says something to me and points up the stairs. A woman coming down the stairs tells me in English that what I need to use the phone is a *jeton* which I have to buy at the cigarette kiosk on the way in. So I go back up the stairs again.

I try to sound as nice as possible to Alberto when I finally get through to him so that he won't give up on me completely. He didn't seem to mind when I said I couldn't make it after all. I've fixed up to meet him next Saturday.

I have some time to spare before turning up at Vinny's - she said things wouldn't start warming up till after eight. So I decide to have a look at Notre Dame.

It's only a short walk from where I am, I can see on the map, half way across the river.

I'd seen postcards of it but actually standing there in front of it I'm completely unprepared for how big it is - or how dirty. There are lots of people standing around, taking photos. Lots of young couples, girls the same age as myself. They don't any of them look as if they're involved with a married man or a priest or an elderly seducer.

Inside it doesn't feel all that different from all the other churches I've ever been in, apart from the huge pillars and the incredibly high ceiling. The same rows of candles and holy pictures of the Sacred Heart on the way in, and leaflets about pilgrimages and women in headscarves blessing themselves and lighting candles, and dark confessional boxes further along the side aisle. One of the women waiting to go into Confession reminds me of my mother, who's probably at this moment going to Confession at home ready for going to Holy Communion tomorrow morning. I can't imagine what she can have to confess. Like me before I started committing mortal sins, trying to think of things to say to the bowed head listening the other side of the curtain. 'Please Father I have missed my morning prayers three times, I have told lies five times, I have been disobedient to my mother and father four times.'

I walk down the central aisle to have a closer look at the statue of the Virgin Mary you can see in the distance. She's standing upright holding the Infant Jesus in her left arm and she's wearing a crown and looking very dignified. The statue is like the one in St Peter's, it's not painted, not like the statues at home. I wonder how Juan is getting on in Rome. He won't be coming back to Paris for another month. I should write to him, reply to his letter, but I'm not sure what I can say to him. If I decide to go to Nice I'll have to write and tell him that. But I won't tell him it's because of Michel.

I sit down on one of the benches at the back. A priest is appearing and the organ is starting up. There's going to be an evening Mass. I don't feel like joining them in the front. I slip my feet out of my pumps and wriggle them about. It's a long time since I walked so much and I've got this other walk in front of me as well, up to Vinny's flat. I wonder if I want to go. I'm not going to know anybody and they'll all be students and I won't know what to talk to them about.

Vinny's flat is at the end of a long passage way. You have to cross a small courtyard to get to it. It's easy to know which one it is because of the music coming from it. It sounds like an awful din to me. I push open the door. There's a fat girl just the other side who looks at me in a very sulky way. She's dressed in black and she's got hair falling all over her face. I ask her in French if this is Vinny's flat. She answers me in English but with a bit of an accent. She doesn't actually say it's Vinny's flat, she just says there's bottles over in the corner if I want a drink.

There are two men who look Chinese standing by a table with lots of bottles on it. They're friendlier than the fat girl, they give me big smiles and ask me what I want to drink in sing song voices in a funny sort of French. I ask them where they're from and they say they're from Indochina. I think that's where Michel said his eldest brother got killed. The French were fighting a war there. Anyway they're very nice. They hold out a plate of what look like rolled up pancakes with bits of grated carrot and things hanging out the end. They're very good. I haven't eaten anything since this morning, except for a sandwich at midday.

'He's Han and I'm Tan,' the one nearest to me says. I'm never going to remember which is which, supposing I ever see them again. They have a restaurant in the Latin Quarter and they've brought lots of food from there for this evening. Vinny's suddenly beside me. She's exchanged the skimpy blouse for a skimpy flowery dress. She's got nice legs and she's holding a cigarette holder - like the peroxide blonde in *La Belle Ferronnière*, only her one was gold and Vinny's is black.

'It's nice that you're here,' she says to me with a bright smile. 'Come and meet Steve.' I follow her as she glides her way across the room, her blonde ponytail bobbing. There are lots of people here, a bit like the ones I was seeing this afternoon, nearly all of them in black, the men as well as the women. They're talking in loud voices, mostly in English about this person's paintings and that person's sculptures and 'Did you read this article?' and 'Did you read that article?'

'Did I tell you I went to hear Juliette Greco the other day?' one of them is saying. I recognise the name. I've seen it on posters beside a picture of a woman in black with hollow cheeks and straight hair. 'Do you know who was sitting at the next table?' They mention the names of two people I've never heard of but everyone is exclaiming 'Really? Did you hear what they were talking about? Was she wearing her turban?'

'This is Steve,' says Vinny. Steve stops playing his electric guitar for a second and bows to me as if he's on the stage. He's with three other men - two of them have guitars like his and the other one's sitting in front of drums.

'Let's play a song to Lucy,' says Steve, and they start playing this music which doesn't sound like jazz only it doesn't sound like the sort of music I'm used to either. They're making it up as they go along. *Lucy, don't crucee- fy ai ai me ... .*' I stand there feeling stupid till it comes to an end. Vinny has wandered off.

'Can you play any Elvis Presley?' I ask them. They laugh, making me feel even sillier. Steve is very good-looking. He's tall and lean and has good bone structure. He could wear his hair any way he liked. At the moment it's longish and no particular style, it just hangs round his face like Jesus's. He has a vague look in his eyes though. He's reaching out for his lighted cigarette that he's balanced on the end of a chair. He takes a long pull and holds it out to me.

'No thanks,' I shake my head and manage a smile and then move away. It's pot of course and I'm not into pot. I prefer sticking to cigarettes. I take one out of my bag.

'Oh, 'ave you got fire?' A nice looking man with reddish hair. 'You are a friend of Vinny? You are a student in art?'

I tell him I'm a hairdresser and he says that hairdressing can be very creative. I agree, that's exactly how I feel, and I'm about to tell him about my idea for a geometric style that doesn't need any of these silly rollers and all this business of perms and sets. But he's going on about how hair is very important for a woman and how it can make all the difference, how it can make women look beautiful. Look at the Mona

Lisa, her lovely hairs falling round her face. He pulls on the sleeve of a couple standing next to us.

'Jean Pierre … Loulou …..Lucy eez an 'airdresser. Look at 'er lovely 'airs. Lucy, you can make cutting Loulou's 'orrible 'airs?' He starts pulling on Loulou's long, frizzy auburn hair that she's obviously been dyeing herself with that stuff that comes out of a tube. She puts her arms around him. 'Frédéric' she's murmuring as she drags him over to where people have started dancing. Her skirt is nearly falling off of her.

I'm left with Jean Pierre, who's looking very put out at Frédéric going off with Loulou. He's not even looking at me. I see a girl with very dark eyes sitting over in the corner. She gives me a smile so I decide to go and talk to her. It turns out she's Russian and she doesn't speak much English or French, she just goes on staring into space, smiling and repeating something in Russian.

The music's getting louder and louder and there are a lot more women than men so there's not going to be much chance of anyone asking me to dance. I'm beginning to feel like I used to feel at the first hops I ever went to in my home-made taffeta dress when I was sixteen and you'd be sitting there all evening, waiting for a boy to come up and ask you to dance.

I look at my watch, it's getting on for eleven, I feel like going home. I look round for Vinny. She's over the other side of the room, dancing with two men at once - Bill, who's sort of throwing himself around, and a short man who looks different from all the other men because he's wearing a bright yellow polo neck. She's swaying and waving her cigarette holder about.

You can tell that what she's smoking is marijuana, she's got that dreamy look about her, the same as Steve.

There's no sign of Han and Tan so I just leave. In the courtyard I see Meriche coming towards me carrying two enormous saucepans. He puts them down and lifts off the lids.

'Couscous,' he says. I peer inside. One saucepan is full of chunks of meat floating in red sauce and the other has something that looks like semolina with not enough milk in it. I'm hungry, but I don't feel like going back in.

'That looks very good but I have to go,' I say. 'Next time,' I add. I really would like there to be a next time, with just Vinny and Meriche and Han and Tan and maybe Steve.

Chapter 9

I'm in my room, looking at myself in the mirror, waiting for the doorbell to ring. I'm wearing a dress and matching coat that I made myself. Parisians all seem to dress in the same way. Now that spring's here most of them are in short brown suede jackets and straight brown or beige or grey skirts during the day and neat little black dresses in the evening. But I bought yards and yards of a lovely Indian cotton material I found in a shop called *Boussac* in the Champs Elysées – dark reds and greens and blues – and also a pattern. The instructions were in French so I had to get Monique to help me out and also she lent me her sewing machine. I really enjoyed sitting there this week, sewing, listening to Radio Luxembourg.

Anyway I just finished it yesterday evening, though I can see I still haven't managed to get the shoulders of the coat right. It's what they call a duster coat, I don't know why. The dress is quite fitted so it shows off my 'hour-glass' figure. I wish I didn't have an 'hour-glass' figure, I'd much prefer to look boyish like Audrey Hepburn.

Monique offered me a label from one of her expensive dresses so that when I take the coat off in the restaurant they'll see *Dior* written across the back of it. I'm sure they'll guess it's not from *Dior* with all the seams unfinished but maybe Alberto will be taken in. I'm wearing it with some dangly earrings in the same shade of red. Alberto's supposed to be picking me up at seven. I'm feeling a bit apprehensive.

I can hear Monique reading a bedtime story to Daniel and Catherine. *'Bonne Soirée!'* she calls out to me as she hears the doorbell. Alberto's in a grey suit, white shirt and blue tie and his grey-black hair is sleeked back with expensive hair oil. He holds his arms out wide at the sight of me like he's about to take off, and then he brings them round to enfold me. He's drawing me to him. 'Hold on a bit,' I think and back away. He's put some sort of cologne on or else it's the soap he's using. I'm trying to figure out what the smell reminds me of.

'I'll just get my bag and gloves,' I say. I've bought beige cotton gloves to match my beige bag and shoes. In the bag I've got my ciggies and lighter, lipstick and powder compact. I step into his white *Giulietta* feeling a bit like Audrey Hepburn in *Roman Holiday* and we set off for the *Porte Maillot*, for the fish restaurant he was talking about.

'You like oysters?' he asks me as we drive around the *Étoile*. There's quite a lot of traffic as it's Saturday evening and we're caught up in the swirl, but as he turns into the *Avenue de la Grande Armée* he slows down. He stretches a hand across to touch me lightly on the leg just above the knee. For a moment I think he's going to run it up along my thigh. I pick my handbag up and put it on my lap so that, if he tries again, he'll find a bulky bit of imitation leather. I open it to get my cigarettes out, so it doesn't look too obvious why I put it there in the first place, and I offer him one. But he notices the cheap *Raleigh* packet and says if I put my hand into his jacket pocket I'll find some *Philip Morris*.

The restaurant's very full but he's booked a table in the far corner from the door. It's not that different from the restaurant he took me to in Rome, chandeliers and old wood and candles and white table cloths down to the ground. The women all seem to be in little black dresses here too with lots of gold chains and bracelets, and shoes with spindly heels and very pointed toes and *Hermès* bags by their sides. I'm beginning to feel like a peasant in my home-made clothes. Alberto hasn't commented on my rig-out, though I thought, being Italian, he'd have liked the bright colours.

He tells me the best thing to have is what's called a *plateau de fruits de mer*. That's a tray with all sorts of things arranged on it on a bed of sea weed - sea urchins, clams, lobster, prawns and, of course, oysters, two different sorts. It's strange to have a smell of the sea mixing with *Shalimar* and *Jolie Madame* and *Chanel 5*.

Monique told me oysters were an aphrodisiac, that means they make you want to make love. A bit of a waste since Alberto doesn't seem to be in need of any aphrodisiac and all I'm here for is a nice friendly night out. What sort of girl would I be turning into if I went to bed with an Italian colonel I hardly know? But to judge by how fresh he was getting in the car he's maybe thinking I am that sort of girl. I'm beginning to feel more and more uncomfortable. I'm not sure how much I even like him. I keep thinking of what he said about bombing Republican Spain. I asked Michel about that and he said they were fascists, the same as Hitler, the ones that won the Spanish Civil War, and the Germans and Italians that helped them. In that case maybe I shouldn't have accepted his invitation in the first place. And all this must be costing him a bomb. Is it going to be worth his while if all we do is sit here talking?

'Lucy, you are looking lovely,' he says as he pours me a glass of wine. I give him a warm smile.

Well, maybe it will be enough for him to have the pleasure of being seen out in animated conversation with a lovely young girl.

He starts talking about the people at the salon. He's known Bertrand for years.

'You know he was married with a friend of mine – an Italian lady? Only they are not living together for many years. She is a painter, she is living in Tuscany.'

How can people be together and not be together? If I could be with Michel all the time I would never want to spend even part of the year somewhere else without him.

He starts talking about Marie Claire. I wonder if he's ever taken her out to dinner.

'Has Marie Claire got a boy friend,' I ask him. He shrugs his shoulders, and hesitates and then he says

'You hadn't noticed? She is madly in love with Bertrand, she has been in love with him for years.' Was that why she wanted to have a drink with me after work? Would she have told me about Bertrand that evening in the *Pampam* if Jack hadn't appeared?

'What about him? Is he in love with her?' Alberto raised his hands like I'd asked a stupid question.

'Who wouldn't be in love with a beautiful woman like Marie Claire?'

'But Marie Claire wants to get married. She told me so.'

'Then she is wasting her time. In Italy there is no divorce. In any case Bertrand's wife is a devout Catholic. And also Bertrand is still loving his wife, I am sure.'

'Poor Marie Claire,' I say and he nods and sighs and looks sad. He thinks the best thing she can do is to find a job somewhere else. He will maybe say something to Bertrand about this.

'And you, you 'ave a boy friend?' He looks into my eyes and I feel myself beginning to blush. He pours me another glass of wine.

'Not really,' I say. What sort of answer is that? I realise I've made a mistake. I should be making it clear to him that there is no hope whatsoever of me going to bed with him. I am wholly and hopelessly in love with another man. I am a devout Catholic saving myself for my future husband. I am not in the slightest bit attracted to him.

We look at the pudding menu. There's *crème caramel* and an Italian thing which they have on the menu this evening especially for Alberto called *Zuppa Inglesa,* so we order that. There's nothing English about it at all, they've drenched the sponge cake in some sort of alcohol, which gives it a really nasty taste. I just eat the cream. I don't actually like cream but I don't feel I can leave the whole thing untouched.

He asks me about the people I'm living with so I tell him about Monique and how I often eat with her when Claude's away or out on business. So he asks me if Claude's away this weekend and I tell him that he is. Maybe he's thinking that Madame's a *femme du monde* and that she wouldn't mind having a middle aged Italian army colonel creeping into the flat late at night to bed whatever attractive young girl she happens to have staying under her roof. A gleam seems to have come into his eye and I wonder whether he isn't also developing an interest in Monique as well, as the abandoned spouse.

Back in his car, he turns on the ignition and moves out onto the wide avenue. He doesn't ask me where I want to go so I suppose he's driving me home. I'm a bit put out that he's not going to make a pass at me. Does he not find me attractive? But, as we get near to the *Etoile*, he stops the car and starts putting his arm around my shoulder. '*Chérie*,' he whispers. He starts kissing me, and, not sure what I'm doing, I'm starting to respond.

'Come back with me,' he whispers in my ear.

I say No, no but maybe the choice is being taken out of my hands. If he goes on being so insistent. He must sense that I'm wavering, that No, no is becoming maybe ... I don't know ... I shouldn't ... But I'm embarrassed because I haven't got my cap with me only I can't possibly tell him this.

'I have nothing ... ' I start off mumbling. He understands immediately.

'Do not worry,' he says, giving me a squeeze and a quick kiss, this time on the cheek. The next moment he's turning the key in the ignition and we're away around the *Etoile* and down *Avenue Marceau* and across the *Pont de l'Alma*.

His flat is big and full of chairs upholstered in dark gold velvet, and there are gilt mirrors and heavy brocade curtains. There's a view out from the window of the Eiffel Tower. I stand pretending to gaze at it but I'm trembling. He slowly unzips my dress and runs his hand over my knickers and then down inside them. He's gradually working his hand around to the front.

'*Viens, chérie.*' He's leading me into the bedroom with the cream satin cover on the bed. He presses me down gently onto it and finishes undressing me.

I'm lying there, feeling excited but also anxious. I don't want to get pregnant. He told me not to worry but I hope that means he's got something he's going to put on. And I'm also thinking of Michel, because it's Michel I'm in love with, so why am I here?

He's turned away and he's taking something out of his wallet. I hear the slight snap of the rubber. And now he's over me, caressing my breasts.

I'd assumed we'd be spending the whole night together. I was imagining him in the morning making Italian coffee and going out to buy croissants and me wanting to get away but not wanting to seem rude. I'd have to phone Monique with some excuse or other because often on a Sunday morning Daniel and Catherine come into my room.

But after we'd lain there for a while he disappeared into the bathroom and I could hear him splashing around. Then he came out rubbing himself with this large white towel and standing there, sort of suggesting that now it was my turn to go into the bathroom. He was starting to dress.

He'd been washing himself in what they call a *bidet*. I'd asked Michel once what it was for - I'd never seen one before coming to France - and he told me the joke about the English woman in some Paris hotel asking the chambermaid if it was for washing the baby in. And the chambermaid had said 'Oh no, Madame, it's for washing the baby out.'

I was glad I didn't have to sit in it now, hoping the baby was being washed out. I was feeling a bit low. I didn't like the way Alberto seemed to have got so detached and down to earth. It was just getting light as we got down into the street and walked towards the car.

He drove me back to the flat with the new yellow sun blinding me through the windscreen.

When we said goodbye I thought he was going to ask me when we could meet again. I suppose a bit of me was hoping he was going to tell me that he could hardly wait before we were together again. Instead he touched my cheek lightly, whispered 'Au revoir, chérie,' and waited for me to get out of the car.

I'm sitting with Monique in the kitchen of their flat. We're sharing a bottle of red wine. The two children are tucked up in bed. Monique tells me it's Bordeaux wine from near where she comes from. Bordeaux wine comes in a different shaped bottle from Burgundy. I say it has a light, soft taste to it and she says I'm developing a palate.

'Smell it before you drink it,' she tells me 'and then keep it in your mouth for a few seconds before swallowing it.'

I think she's feeling particularly down this evening. Claude has just told her he's going to be away next week, somewhere on business. I think she knows that's an excuse. I saw him at the beginning of the week coming out of a restaurant round the corner from the salon with a tall redhead. He's short and dark. He looked funny walking beside her, even in the expensive cashmere coat with wide shoulders he'd bought himself. She looked very glamorous, like one of the models you see stalking around that district - out of Dior or Balenciaga, or Chanel just down the road.

I think it's not the moment to tell Monique I'm probably leaving Paris in a month or so. She doesn't know about Michel, I haven't talked to her about him. If I tell Monique about Michel that would mean telling her he's married. Then for her I'd be *the other woman*, just like the tall redhead. Monique has never let on that she knows Claude is being unfaithful to her but she must know. We don't talk about these things. She tells me she's just bought a new hat.

'Come and I'll show it to you,' she says and we go into the bedroom, hers and Claude's. Twin beds. This looks odd to me. I thought people who are married are supposed to sleep in a double bed, they become as one flesh, like it says in the marriage service. It's only when you're carrying on an illicit affair like me and Michel that you have to make do with a narrow little bed like the one on the sixth floor.

Monique takes the hat out of its shiny hat box with *Franck* scrawled across it in gold. Black felt with a wavy brim and with a white rose on the side.

'Very chic,' I say. I've learnt to pronounce it in the French way. This gives me a funny feeling like I'm changing into a different person.

She's tumbling other hats out of other boxes.

'Do you think your mother would like this one? And what about this one with the matching scarf? Or this one with the mink trim?' I've told her my mother loves hats and she said when I next went home I should take her some. She has far too many, never wears half of them and my Mum likes shining out in style on Sundays for Mass.

We go back into the kitchen to finish the wine. One of the children starts calling '*Maman. maman*' and Monique hurries in to attend to her. I go down the corridor to my room. Monique has lent me a couple of magazines but they're all in French - *Paris Match* and *Noir et Blanc*. I stare at the pictures and think about Michel and feel really lonely and wonder if I won't phone him at the salon. He said in one of his letters that he stayed on late most evenings doing paperwork. Usually it's him phones me, once a week on a Friday evening. I don't like using the Marcels' phone too much, except now and again to phone my parents if it's one of them's birthday or something.

The phone's in the library. I stand there waiting to be connected. The library reminds me of Juan and sitting there in the deep leather armchairs. The phone's on a huge mahogany desk and behind it there's a wall of posh looking books. The only books we had at home were *The Family Doctor* and an *Encyclopaedia Britannica* my Dad got talked into buying once. And then there's the record player that nobody ever plays much, except for Claude when he's here, when he puts on classical records really loud so the music's blaring out all through the flat.

'The line's engaged,' the operator says. It suddenly occurs to me that Michel's on the phone to Jeanne. That's probably why he stays late at the salon, so he can talk to her and Charlotte. I hadn't thought of that before. I imagine Charlotte talking to Michel, telling him about what she's been doing at the *maternelle* during the day, blowing him kisses down the phone and him blowing her kisses back, and to his wife too. I hang up and go back to my room. Monique brought me back a poster from somewhere that I've pinned up on my wall. It's of a girl standing in the middle of an incredibly untidy room saying 'Some day I'll get organised'. I liked it when I first saw it but now I'm beginning to find it depressing.

Chapter 10

We always go to the same restaurant for lunch - *Chez Gilbert*, which is in a small side street just a few minutes away from the salon. My first weeks here it was really strange being in such a noisy cramped little place with all these French people pushing food into their mouths and talking at the same time. And the two waiters rushing up and down, shouting out as they took orders or put plates down on the tables: Un bifteck frites, deux poulets rôtis, une escalope viennoise et bon appétit, Messieurs Dames.

When you ask for your bill the waiter just scribbles the amount on the paper tablecloth. Then, as you get up to go he carts away the wine glasses, the empty carafe, the plates and the bits of bread, whips off the sheet of paper and lays down a nice clean one. Before you've put your coat on and are out of the door the table's ready for the next customers, who are already installing themselves and looking at the menu.

I've come to really like this restaurant with the menus written out in slanting handwriting and runny purple ink, a different menu every day but with always things like *Carrottes rapées* and *Crudités* and *Salade de saison* and *Tarte maison* on them. But I didn't like it at all that first week, I felt really out of place and homesick. At home we only had a half hour lunch break so we used to go to the place on the corner, which was a big self service café with lots of tables with grey Formica tops and metal trays. I always had either soup and a roll or cheese and cream crackers and milk with a dash. The others usually had beans on toast but I hate the way the beans make the toast soggy. Now and then if it was very cold outside I used to have fish and chips or steak and kidney pie but that didn't happen very often as that sort of food's quite fattening.

But now I've got used to *Chez Gilbert* I really like the noise and the friendly atmosphere, though, since Michel left, I also find it a bit sad too. There's an older waiter who's short, with his head sort of hunched into his neck like he's frightened someone's going to throw something at him. He's called Mario. And then there are two much younger waiters, quite attractive looking. One of them's called Francis and the other's Etienne. Etienne always says '*Ah, voilà la belle anglaise*' when I come through the door now.

There are the same people there every day and we always sit at the same table. At the next table there are these three elderly men who look as if they're retired. They're always discussing politics, arguing all the time, waving their arms about and banging on the table. Michel says they have the same argument every day. He gets quite angry. He says there's a war going on in Algeria but they never talk about that. Mind you, we don't talk about the war in Algeria either now that Michel's not here.

Apparently the one with the droopy grey moustache is always going on about 1936 and the *Front Populaire*, and the other two keep telling him that we're no longer in 1936, that this is 1961. And the one with the thin face and the glasses and the hair that sticks straight up is always on about *les radicaux*, which means the radicals, whoever they are. The third one, who's very fat - he has to sit by himself on one side of the table - is a Communist, Michel says.

'How do you know?' I asked him. I'd never met any Communists in England. At school the nuns were always going on about how wicked they were and how they were the great enemy of the Church and I wondered if there was some way you could tell just by looking at them. I thought the fat Communist in *Chez Gilbert* had quite a kind face.

'It's not difficult,' said Jean François. 'He has *L'Humanité* sticking out of his jacket pocket always.' *L'Humanité*'s the Communist newspaper. I don't think Jean François likes Michel very much. I think he thinks it's he who should have been asked to go down and start up the Nice salon. Jean François is a good bit older than Michel, he must be at least thirty. He's not bad-looking, I suppose, but he has a miserable look about him most of the time. He's always having unhappy love affairs. He fell in love with two girls in the three months he was in Manchester.

At the other table there are always two middle aged women who work at Dior. Jean François says they're in the Accounts Department there. They have very long painted nails and the only thing they ever eat is *salade niçoise* and they always drink Perrier water with a slice of lemon in it. They sit up very straight in their tailored jackets with their silk scarves carefully arranged around their necks. They don't talk very much but, once they start, they lean forward and drop their voices so that all you can hear are things like *'Ecoutez, je vais vous dire quelquechose.'* 'Listen, I'm going to tell you something.' And then *'Ah non!' 'Jamais!' 'Ca alors!'.. 'C'est incroyable!'* – No! Never! Really! Incredible! And they shake their heads a lot and roll their eyes and purse their lips and then stare at each other meaningfully. The first weeks I was here, one of them had dyed blonde hair but she's decided to go grey because the part that was blonde is now dyed to match her grey roots. I don't know why she doesn't just have it cut very short so all she's got are her grey roots. The other one looks as if she could be Spanish, she has this very dark hair drawn back in a chignon with a black satin bow.

The menu has a different speciality for each day. On Mondays it's *boeuf mode* - a sort of boiled beef, Tuesdays it's rabbit, Wednesdays *coq au vin*, Thursdays *escalope* and Fridays always some sort of fish.

It's Wednesday today and I'm sitting just with Jean François, missing Michel as usual. I'm eating the *coq au vin*, mopping up the sauce with my bit of bread like they do here. Some of the sauce splashes on to my blouse so I'm busy soaking my serviette in water to rub it off but Jean François doesn't notice, he's busy telling me about this girl that gets the same bus as him in the mornings - the Number 63 from *Passy* - that he thinks he's fallen in love with.

It's because of Jean François that I'm here in Paris. He was over in Manchester last year, working at the place where I was - *Alexander*. He'd been telling me he was sure Bertrand would be glad to have me in their salon in Paris. It wasn't because he'd designs on me - there's never been anything like that between me and Jean François - it just meant he thought I was a good hairdresser. I'd come top in the competition for the north west that year and customers were always asking for me. I'd been dithering about whether I should accept or not. I was a bit frightened of leaving home - I'd never been out of Manchester before - except for day trips to Blackpool, and once to London with the school, and twice to Ireland with my Mum to see my grandmother. And then part of me didn't want to leave Andrew. But after that Sunday afternoon in the café I realised I had to get away.

'She's so elegant and so young. She can't be more than nineteen,' he's saying, 'Today she was wearing a very chic ensemble - a sort of powder blue linen - and she had this *Hermès* scarf with the same shade of blue in it draped round her neck and then her *Hermès* handbag.' Listening to him I begin to feel really dowdy with my home made corduroy skirt and my cheap Marks and Spencer's bag.

'And she actually came and sat down beside me today. I gave her a smile as I made room for her,' he said. 'She was reading Pierre Daninos in the *Figaro*. You know, he's that funny man that writes a column on the front page every Wednesday. I actually said to her that Daninos was the first person I read on a Wednesday too. We had quite a conversation about Daninos after that.'

When Michel was here we hardly ever got to be just the two of us eating, there was nearly always at least one of the others - Bertrand or Marie Claire or Jean François or one of the apprentices. But just having him there, looking across at him, holding each other's eyes for a few seconds. We always tried to fix it so we were opposite each other and sometimes I'd slip my foot out of my shoe and start sliding it up his leg. Or I'd feel his foot nudging my skirt. Once he nearly overbalanced and he sent Bertrand's glass of wine flying. 'What on earth do you think you're doing?' Bertrand had said. Another time I started giggling because his foot had got caught in my suspender. Marie Claire asked me what the joke was in quite a snappish voice, she was really in a bad mood that day. She's probably depressed about her love for

Bertrand going nowhere. I'm sure she's hoping that one day he'll divorce his wife and they'll get married but Alberto doesn't think this will ever happen. And Marie Claire's nearly thirty so she's leaving it a bit late as my Mum would say, she hasn't got many years left if she wants to settle down and have children. She shouldn't be wasting her time on someone like Bertrand. Like I shouldn't be wasting my time on Michel either, with the best years of my life slipping by.

'That's really good that you got to talk to her this morning,' I say to Jean François. I hope he's not going to start on his other love affairs that also promised so well at the outset and then came to nothing. 'I've already told you about Brigitte, haven't I?' he'll say and I'll say 'Yes,' very quickly, though I'm thinking - I thought her name was Chantal. But maybe that was some other time he told me about Chantal.

I'm beginning to think it's funny that I seem to be spending so many lunch times just with him. Today Marie Claire had to take stuff to the dry cleaners and the other day it was Bertrand who said he was having lunch somewhere else with a friend. Maybe they're trying to pair me off with him. Maybe that's Bertrand's idea, to get me away from Michel.

I think some of them in Manchester thought it was because Jean François fancied me that he wanted me to come to Paris. The time I took him out to meet my parents, they were so thrilled because he's very gentlemanly and quite distinguished looking and, of course, being French, he's a Catholic, though he never goes near a church but they didn't realise that.

'I suppose you go to Mass at *All Saints*,' they said to him, 'It'll be Father Moran, the priest there,' and he just said 'Yes, a very nice man.' He's really smooth. But I don't think he's ever been keen on me. I'm obviously not his type. And I don't fancy him either, there's something about him that gives me the willies, if I'm being honest. He's got frizzy hair and a really unhealthy colour, as if he had a bad stomach. But what really puts me off is that he always looks so doleful.

That's what I think I love most about Michel, he always seems happy to be alive. People always brighten up when he's around, he makes them laugh, he makes them feel good. And it's not just the women customers that are charmed by him, that are all there telling him their life stories. Francis and Etienne like him too, they're always asking after him. They say to Bertrand '*Et Michel, comment va-t-il?*'. I wish they'd ask me about him, say something that would let me know that they know he and I are in love with each other. But it's always Bertrand they ask.

Back in the salon Madame Chénier's just arriving. Every time I see her I think of that morning in early March, the day of the Metro strike. All the others were late getting in and there was just me and Michel there. And Madame Chénier and this young fashion model from Balenciaga called Simone something or other. I'd just put Madame C. under the dryer and Michel was finishing off putting *bigoudis* into Simone's hair. He sort of gave me a nod in the direction of the cloakroom and I suddenly realised what he meant, that with those two under the dryer and nobody else around ... . I gave Madame C. the control thing so she could set the temperature to whatever she liked. Once in Manchester I'd set it too high and the client had almost gone on fire.

Then I rushed into the posh *toilettes* that the staff aren't normally allowed to use. There's expensive soap and handcream - *Roget et Gallet's Gardenia* - in there, and mirrors with soft lighting. I stared at myself. I undid the clips which I put in to keep my hair up, away from my face, and I gave my head a good shake so that my hair was all falling over my eyes and I ran my fingers through it. My eyes were dancing back at me and my lips had still got the fresh look of my newly applied lipstick, coral rose. It was a pity to mess it up but I got some cotton wool and rubbed it all off. My lips still looked lovely and pink after the scrubbing they'd had, and now there wouldn't be a coral rose trail as my tongue travelled over Michel's face and I licked the space between his eyebrows and then his eyelids and then his ears and finally his mouth.

I decided to take my knickers off. They were cream celanese that I'd bought cheap in a sale. It would be awful to have Michel running knickers like that down over my knees to my ankles and then lifting each foot in turn so that I could step out of them. I'd never have put them on this morning if I'd known. My bare skin against the slippery satin of my slip excited me, made me feel luxurious. I lifted up my skirt and stared at myself, at the black band of my suspender belt, at the tops of my stockings. I smoothed some of the cold hand cream onto my curly red-brown patch of hair down there.

'Lucy,' I heard Michel whispering at the door. The way he pronounces my name makes it sound like a kiss.

I dropped my skirt and opened the door and the next moment our lips were fastened together and we were backing towards the cloakroom. There wasn't much room, my head was pressed against the cold metal coat rail and the coat hangers were clattering to the ground. The phone started ringing. 'Merde,' said Michel, hitching his trousers up. It was a client cancelling. 'That's okay,' I heard Michel saying. 'We look forward to seeing you another time.' I heard Madame Chenier calling to him about something.

'She was just wanting the latest *Vogue*. You'd given her last month's,' he said as he came back. 'And I've left the phone off the hook,' he whispered and started running his hands up inside my skirt. 'Merde,' he said again but this time it was because he'd discovered I didn't have my knickers on. Suddenly he was in a hurry and we were on the floor and he was fishing a French letter out of his pocket. We heard Simone calling. 'Michel, Michel, vous êtes là?' 'Yes, he's here, he's here,' I breathed, holding him tight to me.

I'd completely forgotten to pick up my cream celanese knickers from the floor of the toilets and push them up my sleeve, I realised a while later as I saw Madame Chenier disappearing in that direction. When she came out again I tried to smile and look relaxed. I helped her on with her coat and she paid her bill and then I rushed into the toilet. They were still on the floor where I'd dropped them, she hadn't touched them but she can't have missed seeing them.

All this is going through my head now as I say 'Bonjour, Madame,' and hold out the pale pink gown for her to slip her arms into. What was I doing taking my knickers off in the customers' toilet? Maybe I'd been thinking of washing them in the hand basin and then got distracted. Or I'd bought a new pair, a fancier pair, on my way in to work. I run my hands through her wiry grey hair that has had too many perms. I look across at Bertrand. He's combing out the long silky black hair of one of the models from Dior. She's tilting back her head and laughing at something he's saying, showing perfect teeth. She's the sort of woman who makes me feel like the girl in my class at secondary school we used to make fun of because her dresses were always too long. I'll talk to him at the end of the afternoon. I'll tell him I've decided to go down to Nice. I've had enough of snipping at over permed hair.

Chapter 11

Dear Mum and Dad,

I hope you are well. I am very busy at the salon at the moment. We were working till eight this evening and I've only just got home.

Monique's out so I'm not eating with her in the kitchen. I've just opened a tin of sardines and made a sort of sandwich with the funny bread they have here. In the kitchen with Monique we usually eat the leftovers from their lunch. Lunch is their main meal of the day, so often it's something like roast beef. They have lettuce every day too, with something they call vinaigrette poured over it instead of salad cream. I watched Monique making it once - it's a mixture of olive oil and vinegar, only it's red coloured vinegar made from wine, not the sort you put on fish and chips. And the olive oil they have here they buy in the grocer's in big bottles.

There was a film star came into the salon today who's apparently very famous but you wouldn't have heard of her because she's only been in French films. She's called Simone somebody or other. Her hair's dyed a pale blonde and it's only about two inches long all over but she wanted Bertrand to cut it so it was only one inch. Marie Claire asked for her autograph and after she'd finished signing it she asked me if I wanted her autograph too so I had to say Yes, though I wasn't bothered, seeing as I'd never heard of her before she walked into the salon this afternoon.

It looks as if I will definitely be going down to Nice at the end of June for most of the summer. Bertrand is very keen for me to go. He thinks it will be very good for my career to be down on the Riviera. There's not much going on in the Paris salon in July and August so they don't need me there. I'm sorry this means I won't be able to come home but I will try to manage a week in September. I'm sure there'll be lots of nice young men down there, Mum! Maybe I'll bring one home!!

Lots of love to Jim and Helen. Isn't it exciting that Teresa has said her first word. Tell them to send me some photos. I got a letter from that friend of Helen's, by the way, that woman who works in the post office, asking if I can put her up if she comes to Paris. I think she has a cheek. I hardly know her. I wrote back giving her the name of a hotel - a long way from the Marcels' flat. What's happening about your knee, Mum?
Love from Lucy.

I haven't actually had a chance to talk to Bertrand yet. I haven't told Michel either. I wanted to phone him this evening but he said he was having dinner with someone who wants him to sell beauty products in the salon and maybe open a beauty clinic as well, make up and manicures mostly. Michel thinks that wouldn't be a bad idea, it would mean more business. I'll phone him tomorrow.

I haven't phoned Michel. Something awful happened in the salon this morning. It was about eleven o'clock and I was just thinking that, if I was in England, I'd be having my tea break now in the little place in the back and getting to hear all the gossip. I can't get used to working right through the morning like we do here without a stop for a cup of tea or coffee.

Anyway, I was just thinking how I'd like a break when this girl walked in - very slim, with an elfin sort of face and brown hair done up in a chignon. She was wearing quite a clinging accordion-pleated beige skirt and pale pink sweater with the sleeves pushed up. Not the usual sort of customer; she looked a bit lost. Marie Claire had disappeared and I looked around to see if one of the other girls could help her. I was taking Madame Gibb's rollers out at the time. Madame Gibb - the way they pronounce it, it sounds more like *Sheeb* - was just telling me she was married to a Mr Gibb from Manchester. She spends half the year there and half the year in Paris where she has a little apartment.

'I couldn't possibly live the whole year in England,' she was in the middle of saying when Marie Claire emerged from the back.

'Oh, here's Michel's wife come in to see us! Bonjour, Jeanne,' I heard her exclaiming. I was suddenly in a turmoil inside myself, like the time I discovered my handbag had been stolen. Marie Claire was jabbering away, asking her how Michel was getting on, saying how much he must be missing her and his little girl and when was Jeanne going down to see him.

'That's Lucy over there, you haven't met her, have you? Lucy's from England. 'Lucy,' she called out, 'this is Michel's wife.' I'm sure Marie Claire was doing this on purpose, introducing me.

'Bonjour, Lucy,' Jeanne called out. She said this in quite a normal voice and gave me a smile and I had to smile back. Then I saw my face in the mirror and I saw Madame Gibb staring at it as well. I was all red and embarrassed-looking, as if I was about to start crying. I'd turned my back on Marie Claire and

Michel's wife but they'd still be able to see my face in the mirror too if they looked across. That's the trouble with a hairdresser's, all those mirrors. Madame Gibb gave me a really nice reassuring smile as if she understood, which made me feel a bit better but not a lot.

Marie Claire's a real hypocrite, though. She was all over Michel's wife while she was there but in the toilet afterwards she said to me

'Did you see she had a ladder in her stocking and her seams were all crooked? And why wasn't she wearing lipstick? It's very stupid, women letting themselves go like that.'

Or maybe Marie Claire was just being catty about Jeanne in order to make up to me, knowing there was something between Michel and me. I'm sure she does know, or at least suspects. I just said that I thought Jeanne looked very nice. Though it's true, it was a bit funny coming into the salon with a ladder in her stocking and without any lipstick.

'She has a lovely figure,' I said 'And she has a child, doesn't she?

'Yes, a little girl called Charlotte,' said Marie Claire. As if I didn't know.

I'm sitting now in my room, trying to get Jeanne out of my mind, when the phone rings and it's Alberto.

'How are you, *chérie*? When are we going to meet, *chérie*?' he asks in that tender, intimate way he has.

I'm certain that I don't want to go back to his flat again but I end up agreeing to have dinner with him all the same. He'll try his best to persuade me, no doubt, but I can tell him I have my period, or at least I can say something that will make him think I have. I'd be far too embarrassed to ever come out with the word. Not like the girls at work. In French they call it *règles* which means *rules,* which is a bit funny. They're always talking about their *règles* among themselves, borrowing sanitary towels off each other or worrying because they're late and they're not needing to borrow sanitary towels. Christine, who's married to this bloke who sells cars, is always in a panic every month. She's a very devout Catholic so they practise what they call the rhythm method, which is apparently not all that reliable. In any case the others say her husband is a real pig who never lets her alone, he doesn't care what time of the month it is. We fix up to meet this coming Saturday.

'I will come to your apartment at seven.'

There's something about the way he says this which suggests he might be planning a seduction scene in my room. I tell him it would be nice to meet at a pavement café somewhere on the *Champs Elysées*. I'll wear my new summer dress with the big blue and orange flowers and the cinched-in waist that I bought in *Galeries Lafayette* last week.

We're sitting having Martinis in this large café in the *Champs Elysées*, called *Fouquet's*. Monique said it's quite a famous café, which is maybe why the drinks are so expensive - the price is on the bit of paper Alberto has put under the ashtray so it won't blow away. There's quite a wind blowing and it looks as if it might rain but I like it here on the terrace, though I'm glad I'm wearing my blue jacket. Not a cardie, I've been careful not to wear a cardigan ever since Marie Claire said that's what all the *anglaises* wear in Paris in the summer, cardies and comfortable sandals.

I hope there's not going to be too much walking involved this evening. It's my first time wearing this pair of navy blue court shoes that I got to match the bag I bought before I went to Rome. Alberto says he wants to take me to an Italian restaurant he knows in the Latin Quarter.

His car's just round the corner, fortunately. We drive down the *Champs Elysées* and round the *Place de la Concorde* and then along the *Boulevard St Germain*. We pass the café where I met Vinny. There are lots of people who look like students sitting at the tables but I don't see her. I'd thought of going back to her place one weekend, but maybe I could just turn up at the café one Saturday afternoon like last time. And they'll be there, and if they haven't forgotten who I am I'll sit down at the table with them. It was nice sitting with them there in the sunshine, drinking wine. Maybe next time I'll have a puff of one of their cigarettes, not that I want to get hooked on marijuana. It's bad enough being hooked on ordinary cigarettes, having my brother and sister-in-law being on at me all the time.

The Italian restaurant's upstairs and we've got a window seat overlooking the Luxembourg Gardens. Alberto has ordered a bottle of *chianti*. He gives my hand a squeeze before he takes up the bottle to pour me a glass and I smile at him and feel happy. He has these crow's feet round his eyes and his hair's quite thin on top but there's still something attractive about him.

I'm thinking now that I may go back with him after all and I'm glad I put that stuff in the bottom of my handbag just in case. At the end of the evening we'll go back to his empty flat where he lives all alone and I'll feel at home, it won't feel strange like last time. It was really upsetting seeing Michel's wife in the salon. I hate her, I hate the idea of her sharing everything with Michel. It never bothered me before. Before I used to think their life together must be really boring. Sunday mornings on my way back from Mass I used to notice these families doing their shopping together and I'd imagine Michel and Jeanne going to the market at the *Porte D'Orléans* with Charlotte, choosing a melon, telling the *charcuterie* woman to give them *une belle tranche* of *pâté*, filling brown paper bags full of cherries, and then going to the *pâtisserie* for a shiny strawberry tart because it was Sunday. I wasn't the least bit envious. I was lonely for Michel but not for all that domestic stuff. But now I've seen her I can't get it out of my mind, her sharing everything with him. I bet she and Charlotte will be going down to Nice next week end, he said something on the phone the other day about it, didn't actually say he was looking forward to them coming but didn't say he didn't want them to come either.

    Alberto leans forward and places his hand over mine.

    'What are you thinking about?' he asks me. He looks quite concerned about me. I must have been looking far away and unhappy. I start telling him about Marie Claire's efforts to win Bertrand. He shakes his head and says how sad it is. Bertrand will never marry and Marie Claire is wasting her precious youth.

    He tells me about this woman who was chasing him last winter. She phoned him one evening to say that in five minutes she'd be in her car down below in the street, waiting for him. He didn't want to go down. He'd slept with her once - she's a mannequin at Chanel's and he'd been smitten by her looks. 'But naked …' - he raised his hands and turned them palm upwards to express his disappointment - 'she was so thin. She was just bones. When her clothes were off there was nothing. Not like you, *chérie*.'

He reaches out to stroke my cheek and his eyes are on my breasts. I'm self-conscious about my breasts - they stick out much more than I want them to, I wish I were flat-chested like Audrey Hepburn - but most men seem to like big breasts. There's a calendar at work called *Masterpieces from the Louvre* and the woman in the picture for May has these enormous breasts, bigger than mine, the colour of peaches. They're spilling out of a very low cut long red gown. Bertrand was in ecstasies when he turned over the page and saw that's what he'd be looking at for the whole of May. Marie Claire went out and bought herself one of those pointed, sticking out bras like Jean Seberg wears in that French film that's just come out.

Anyway Alberto finally gave in to the pleas of this mannequin and went down and got into her car. She had a fur coat wrapped around her but, as he got into the car, she threw it open and she was completely naked underneath.

'A fur coat and completely naked underneath,' he keeps repeating. He doesn't say what he did next and I don't ask, though, since he said how awful she looked naked, this should have put him off her completely.

There's a woman at the next table with a beehive hairdo. I begin to explain to Alberto how you create a hairdo like that and how ridiculous it is and how people say that you can get cockroaches nesting inside beehive hairdos. Only he doesn't understand 'cockroach' and I don't know the French for it, so he doesn't scream like people do when you tell them that.

Alberto thinks the woman in the beehive looks very beautiful, very feminine.

'That would suit you, Lucy,' he says. No thank you, I think to myself.

I brought a design for a haircut into the salon the other day, and I said to Bertrand 'Can you cut my hair like that for me?' It was an adaptation of my geometric cut to suit my curly hair. Bertrand's a good cutter, but I was nearly sure he'd refuse. He's got very old-fashioned ideas, and not just about hair but about women too. If he knew the expression in English he'd be talking about hair being a woman's crowning glory and things like that. Anyway he thought it would be a very bad advertisement for the salon to have one of their leading stylists with a hair do that looked as if it had been cut by a peasant. I was disappointed but it was nice to hear him calling me a leading stylist.

We've finished our meal and Alberto has ordered a *grappa* for himself and a green Chartreuse for me. I've chosen that deliberately because it's what I drank that time with Juan when I told him about Michel. Now it makes me feel slightly sacrilegious drinking it here with the man I'm going to spend the night with who's not even Michel.

We're not saying very much, just looking at each other. Earlier on, when he looked so concerned about me and asked me what I was thinking, I was on the point of telling him about Michel but now I'm glad I didn't. Now I just want to forget about everything and have a simple, happy evening with Alberto. As long as I don't start expecting him to phone me tomorrow saying he can't live without me.

He really does look as if he's thinking he can't live without me at the moment. He gets the bill and then we're in the car. He runs his hand down the back of my head and caresses my neck, just inside the collar of my dress, but then he puts the key in the ignition and we're off down the Boulevard St Michel and then along the banks of the Seine.

He seems to be taking it for granted that we're going to end up in his flat together. I wonder about making a show of pretending I have to go home, but the wine and the Chartreuse are making me feel indolent and abandoned like the woman in the calendar on the wall of the salon.

'Bonne nuit, Madame,' he says to the concierge who's in the doorway of the block of flats when we arrive - a stocky woman in an overall who looks like Madame Pie, the Marcels' concierge, with her grey hair tied back in a bun. Alberto doesn't seem the slightest bit embarrassed. Is she used to seeing him bringing women back, spying on him as he goes past with his different girl friends? I imagine her shaking her head as we disappear into the lift. 'Ah, ces messieurs, c'est quelque chose.' These men, they're quite something. And me no better than I ought to be, she's probably thinking too.

This time I'm prepared. I have my rubber cap and the cream, and the sort of bicycle pump thing to squirt the cream up inside, once the cap's in place. But I'm wondering how I'm going to manage to put the cap in as, once we get inside the door, Alberto's going to be concentrating on taking the clothes off me. It's a bit awkward, interrupting an urgent kiss to say you want to use the bathroom. But it turns out to be easy. He gets as far as taking my dress off and fondling my breasts and then he whispers that maybe I want to use the bidet.

I feel a bit silly, in my dusky pink satin slip and my bare feet, grabbing my handbag and taking it in with me and getting the stuff out of the bottom of it. I hate the cream, it has a smell of dispensaries, not at all the sort of smell you want to have when you're making love. At the bottom of my handbag there's also a little bottle of perfume that Andrew gave me before I left. *Je t'adore*, it's called. That means *I adore you* the girl in *Boots* had told him. I wonder about dabbing some of it down there. Suddenly I feel sad.

This time I do actually stay until morning. It's broad daylight when he drives me back to the *rue Galilée*. As we arrive part of me's wanting to ask him when I'm going to see him again. But another part of me's thinking that I don't want to see him again ever. There's something a little foolish about his face as he drives up the *Champs Elysées* in the light of morning.

'When are you going back to Rome again to see your wife?' I ask him out of spite. He smiles benignly and reaches out to stroke my knee.

'Chérie,' he says, and a few minutes later he's giving me a light kiss on the cheek.

'Ciao, chérie.' His lips are very close to my mouth but they don't actually get there.

'Ciao,' I say back, trying to sound breezy but it comes out more like a snarl. I give him a sweet smile to make up for this and I stand on the pavement, waving, as he zooms off. This mustn't happen again, I'm saying to myself.

People are returning from Mass, including Monique. I see her and the two children approaching from the other end of the street. It's not often they go to church. The French are much more casual about this, as if they didn't care they were committing a mortal sin. I feel embarrassed. This is really bad timing. I'm still in the things I was wearing when I said goodbye to them yesterday evening. I try to look as if I'm coming back from Mass too.

'I knocked on your door, Lucy, but you didn't answer,' says Catherine, making large reproachful eyes at me.

'I was probably still asleep,' I say. She's standing there with her arms out for me to pick her up. She's quite a weight.

Inside the flat Monique takes the *tarte aux pommes* that she's just bought at the *pâtisserie's* out of its white cardboard case. She's noticing that some of the apple still has bits of core left in it.

'That's the last time I'm going to go to that *pâtisserie*,' she says. She looks tired, as if she hasn't slept much. Where's Claude? He's off somewhere playing golf for the day. She asks me if I want to have lunch with them but I'm not hungry. In any case, in the afternoon they're going to be meeting up with her friend and her children in the *Tuileries Gardens*. I decide that I'll go over to the Latin Quarter and see if Vinny's there. I'm badly in need of a change of scenery.

Chapter 12

It's a relief to get out of my court shoes. I take my stockings off too but my legs look awful. I read in a magazine the other day that you should only go without stockings if your legs are smooth, hairless and brown. Mine at the moment are rough, hairy and white. I decide to go out again to the *Pharmacie* on the corner and buy some of that evil-smelling hair-removing cream and some liquid stocking, otherwise known as gravy browning.

    An hour later and I'm setting out for Vinny's with my black pumps on and my bare legs smooth, hairless and a sort of yellowy orange. It's a warm sunny day and it's quite nice standing at the bus stop, watching people emerging from the posh restaurant the other side of the road - *Les Oliviers*. Just as well, as there's no sign of a bus. When one eventually arrives there's a grumpy looking woman sitting in it who stares at me as if I was part of an invading army. She's all alone except for an elderly gentleman across from her with a carnation in his buttonhole and a bunch of white roses in his lap. He gives me a big smile and looks as if he'd be very pleased if I sat down beside him but I go right to the back. It's lovely having an empty bus so you can sit there looking out of the windows either side. I get off along the *Boulevard St Germain* at the stop close to the *rue Saint Jacques*. Looking across, I can see *Notre Dame* through the trees down by the river.

    Vinny's is further than I'd remembered and as I trudge up the hill I'm wondering what I'll do if they're not there. But as I knock I can hear music from the other side. It's Steve who answers the door, holding his guitar and I feel silly standing there. He looks very intimidating, maybe because he's so tall and confident looking with his thick straight brown hair which today is tied back in a pig-tail. I feel even more intimidated when he tells me that Vinny isn't there, he's all alone.

'I'll make some coffee' he says and disappears into the kitchen where I can see piles of dirty plates and a torn bit of curtain on the window. We sit on cushions on the floor with our cups of coffee without saucers, and I'm noticing how my legs have gone all streaky. I've got this short tight skirt on so I can't pull it down much below my knees to hide them. I start asking him about his music. I'm quite good at asking people questions about themselves. That comes from being a hairdresser, though most hairdressers, you hear them always asking the same questions. 'So, have you any plans for the summer?' and 'I suppose you've all your Christmas shopping done' and 'Did you have a nice holiday?' depending on the season. Really tedious.

Though often this gets them on to talking about their personal lives. I had one woman started crying once, just as I was about to put her under the dryer. Her husband had walked out on her without any warning a few days before. That's always happening - I mean women telling you that their husbands have just walked out on them. They say if your husband leaves you, you should go out and buy yourself a new hat, but they also seem to feel the need to come and have their hair done. You get these grey-haired women whose husbands have gone off with blondes asking you if they'd suit having their hair dyed - a sort of gentle ash blonde, they say. It's sad. Usually it wouldn't suit them at all. I try to tell them they'd be better keeping it grey but having a really jazzy cut, like my geometric style. Or a bob or a bingle or a shingle or anything for a change, to make them feel different.

I've asked Steve the right question anyway. He's talking non-stop about his career as a rock musician. He also writes poetry and sets this to music. He's playing me something now about *if words were birds* and, as I sit there listening, it's reminding me a bit of being with Juan. It's in some ways like Juan playing me Mozart and talking to me about *The Little Prince*. Only it's also different. Steve's Australian but he used to be part of an American band that he says is quite well known. When he tells me the name, expecting me to be impressed, I tell him I've never heard of them. And that's when I realise that this is different from being with Juan. With Juan I'd probably have felt I had to pretend I'd heard of them.

I'm quite sorry when the door opens and there's Vinny with Han and Tan in tow. I told Michel in a letter that I'd met two Vietnamese and he'd written back saying how his brother had been killed in the last few months of the war there, that was about six or seven years ago. He said that more than 35 000 French soldiers had been killed in that war. But then the French shouldn't have been there in the first place, he said. A lot more of the Vietnamese had been killed, and they'd no sooner got rid of the French than the Americans started moving in, stirring things up. And they're still there, the Americans, he said. I'm thinking of this as I shake hands with Han and Tan but they always look so smiling and happy.

Vinny seems really surprised and pleased to see me, though I also thought that there was a slight look of unease in her eyes as she came in and saw me sitting side by side with Steve on the floor. She really doesn't need to worry, my life's complicated enough without getting involved with a rock musician. Besides, the person I want to get friendly with is Vinny.

She says she's starving, which suits me as I only had a bit of bread and cheese before I came out. We go into the kitchen and she gets a packet of Beef Vesta Curry out of the cupboard. This makes me feel really at home as this is what we always ate whenever I went round to see my friend Carmel, in Manchester. It's all in sachets - you don't have to do anything except heat it up. Han and Tan start laughing as they watch us.

'We will cook for you one day,' they say to me. 'We will show you how to make very nice food. That is not good what you are eating.' They shake their heads. It's just as well they're not interested in sharing it with us as there's only just about enough for two in a packet anyway. Vinny finds a bottle of vin ordinaire on the floor in a corner and we go back into the room and settle ourselves on the cushions.

Steve has started playing his guitar only it sounds weird. He's got a tape recorder on the floor and he's making a tape which is a loop, he's explaining. This means that the same bit of music just goes round and round. They're all listening, thinking this is great.

'Is this like music in your country?' I ask Han and Tan but they just laugh without answering. I'm wondering if they're brothers but they look about the same age. Maybe they're twins. I notice they're smoking and Steve too and judging by the smell and the look on their faces it's pot. I'll have to decide if I'll join them but for the moment I'm happy with my curry and glass of wine.

I'm about to ask Vinny what she does with her time, when she starts asking me about hairdressing. I remember how they'd all laughed, the other time, when I told them I was a hairdresser but now she seems interested in knowing about it.

'Don't you find it boring standing around all day, fiddling with other people's hair?' she asks me. She's got this smart south of England accent and normally I'd feel like crawling into a corner having someone ask me something like that. I know what she's meaning. She's thinking of all those girls who work in hairdressers who look like zombies, sweeping up all that mess of other people's hair from the floor and standing handing rollers and pins to the boss who's showing off to the client and ignoring them completely except to say 'Mandy, I think Mrs Scunthorpe's done, Mandy, could you hand Mrs Braithwaite a magazine? Mandy, you could maybe open a window, it's getting a little stuffy in here?' But it's not like that when you're a top stylist, I try to explain this to her.

'But the customers still don't let you do what you want, do they? They just expect you to do their hair the way they tell you, or the way the magazines tell them, so you end up giving them all the same boring hairstyles.'

When you've got a reputation, then the customers just put themselves in your hands and you do what you like with them, I want to say, but she's right, most of the time it's like what she says. At *Bertrand*'s, anyway. They come in and they say they want this and that, and that's what you have to give them. Sometimes, they show you pictures of film stars like Marilyn Monroe and they want a hairstyle like hers, though they may be fat and fifty. To tell the truth I'm a bit disappointed in Paris in that respect. I thought they'd be swanking in on their spiky heels saying 'Transform me! Create a new me.'

There are all these pictures propped up against the walls here, bright colours and all portraits of women but they're not like any women you'd ever meet walking along the street, they all look completely exaggerated. At the same time, they still manage to look like real women, they've all got something about them. Looking at them I suddenly think: that's the sort of women I want to create. I bet the women in these pictures looked at them when they were done and said 'But that's not me!' and then they'd look again and think, well, yes, that *is* me, he's discovered something about me that I didn't know was there.' I want to be like that, a sort of portrait painter.

I'm getting quite carried away by the idea. Maybe it's because Steve has handed me this cigarette that he's rolled specially for me, he says, as he puts it between my lips.

'You've got to breathe deep. Let it get right down.' He breathes deep himself to show me how. I'm being transported. A portrait painter, yes that's what I want to be.

'I'm going to be a portrait painter,' I turn to Vinny and say. She's looking at me with those amused eyes of hers and the next moment I'm feeling her hand between my legs, moving up, and she's pushing me gently back onto the cushion, and her hair is falling into my eyes.

But I'm still in the middle of thinking about how I'm going to become a famous hair artist, and what I'm wanting is to grab hold of one of those paintings and dance round the room with it. I struggle to get into a sitting position again, as if all this is part of a dream and the next move is for me to get up. I grab Vinny by the hand and pull her up with me. 'Let's dance,' I say and we move round the room like we're in a trance. She's got her cool hands loosely around my neck and her hips are swaying and her lips look as if any moment they're going to touch mine.

Han and Tan are leaving, they have to get back to the restaurant. They wave at us as they go out the door and we call out 'Au revoir', wailing it out so that it sounds like the wind in some horror film. We start giggling.

And now Steve's coming back into the room and there's a grin on his face as he watches us. And then he starts dancing too, separating Vinny and me to dance first with me and then with her. And then we're each dancing alone, moving around the room as if we're sleepwalking. Vinny starts making this eerie sound again, and I join in. It's reminding me of something, and then I think *cats*, we're like the cats at home on the walls at night calling to each other.

I'm thinking that I want this to go on and on, the three of us flitting around the room and me looking at these portraits jumping up and down before my eyes. But now Steve's stopped dancing and he's doing something with the tape recorder. He's turned off the music but he tells us not to stop.

'Go on, that's a great sound.' He's excited. 'Try it a bit higher, a bit softer. Do a whisper. And now imagine you're pigeons on the roof. Come closer to each other. And now that wail again.'

He's picked up his guitar and he's playing as we dance and wail and whisper and coo. But it's no longer the same. I'm beginning to feel like a film star on a set being ordered about, wondering if I'm getting it right.

'Come and sit down and listen.' He's rewinding the tape. We hear these strange noises, I can't believe it's me helping to make them, I think I sound horrible, daft.

'That's amazing, isn't it, Vinny?' Vinny's busy rolling joints.

'I think I'll go back to my *Raleighs*,' I say, looking round for my handbag. I stand there holding it and feeling like a square. I get a Raleigh out of the packet and light it and take a few puffs. I've turned into a tourist who's been shown round some strange, exciting place but now it's time to go home. Steve has put the loop back on again and he and Vinny are moving around the room in a trance.

'Maybe it's time I went,' I say. They don't seem to hear.

Out in the street the sun is still shining but it's cooler and I'm practically floating down the *rue Saint Jacques*. I can see the towers of *Notre Dame* in the distance. I've never missed Sunday Mass in my life and I still haven't been to Mass today. It crossed my mind this morning to say something to Alberto because he's Italian, he must be Catholic, but it would have been funny going to Mass with him. It wouldn't have been right at all, not because of what we'd been doing together - I'm, in a way, really surprised at how I don't feel guilty about that at all, though, if there are degrees of mortal sins, surely that's worse than missing Mass, which I *would* feel guilty about. But being in church with Alberto would be as odd as going to the pictures with the nice old duchess I see every Wednesday afternoon in the salon. As we were drinking the coffee he'd made with his espresso machine this morning I realised I was going to be too late for eleven o'clock Mass in the church across the road from the flat but I knew there was an evening Mass at seven o'clock. But now it occurs to me I could go to Mass in Notre Dame. If it starts at six I'd better hurry. I start to run.

There are lots of people hanging around outside eating ice creams and inside there are others staring up at the enormous stained glass window on the end wall and wandering around, but up at the front I can see rows of people kneeling and a priest at the altar. I find a space just close to the statue of the Virgin Mary with the Infant Jesus in her arms. She looks so serene and confident, smiling at her baby. She even has the beginnings of a double chin, I'm noticing.

The priest is climbing up into the pulpit, a big heavy man. The sermon's going to be in French of course so I'm going to understand hardly anything at all. That's the great thing about the Mass - apart from the sermon. Wherever you are it's in Latin so you can feel at home. *Introibo ad altare Dei ... Dominus vobiscum... In principio verbum...* I know quite a lot of bits by heart. But that man up there declaiming to us in French, I haven't a clue what he's on about.

I start thinking about Vinny and that pass she made at me. I'm really not into that sort of thing. I want to be friends with her, I don't know anybody else here of my own age that speaks English and I like her. But the idea of kissing her in the sort of way I was kissing Alberto last night, well it doesn't actually disgust me but it doesn't attract me either, in the slightest. And what would Steve have done? Would he have gone on playing his guitar, watching us. Maybe he'd have joined in.

But I'm glad I went there today because I do like them, they make me feel light-hearted, they make me feel like I can do crazy things. Like dancing with a painting of a woman with hair flying all over the place. I'd never have seen the pictures of those women if I hadn't gone there today. And if Steve hadn't been the way he is, sort of free and creative, I wouldn't have started feeling inspired by them. I wouldn't have started getting the feeling that I had the power to create too, like the bloke that painted those pictures whoever he was, and like Steve with his music.

I must pluck up courage and get to work on some of these women who come into the salon, I'm thinking, as the priest comes down from the pulpit and returns to the altar for the reciting of the Creed. *Credo in unum deum* …. The man next to me is bawling it out from his missal, which he's holding out about a foot away from his eyes. I don't have my missal so I just do a sort of murmur under my breath.

I give the statue of the Virgin a little wave as I leave my seat. People shuffling their way out who see must think I'm fancying myself as a second Saint Bernadette but I don't care.

'She'd look more the part if she was wearing a black mantilla instead of that multi-coloured bit of chiffon she's draped over her dyed hair,' they're probably thinking.

In the bus going home it occurs to me that maybe I looked to them more like a reformed Mary Magdalene. Except that I don't feel very reformed. I start thinking of Michel. I'm wishing we were back in March, the morning of the strike, making love in the little cloakroom with Madame Chenier under the dryer just a few yards away. But the thought of Madame Chenier depresses me. She doesn't look right, somehow, she looks like someone who's being forced to be the way it doesn't really suit her to be, deep down. Suddenly I'm seeing her without that perm, shorn, with a coppery tint to the ends of her grey hair, looking like a warrior queen. As the bus driver accelerates across the *Pont Alexandre III* I'm seeing those portraits again. I decide I must get to work on Madame Chenier.

As I open the door of the flat I hear the sound of laughter coming from the kitchen and then, unmistakably, the sound of Juan's voice. I stand stock still, hardly believing my ears. He'd said in his last letter that he would be back in Paris soon but I'd imagined him writing again to say he must see me. I'd have written back 'Let's meet in the Trocadéro Gardens.' They're just a ten minute walk away from here. He would be sitting on a bench under a shady tree, looking at the ornamental fountain and waiting for me. And I'd come strolling along in my Indian cotton, with my chiffon scarf draped over my hair. I'm a bit put out that he's already in Paris and I didn't know.

    At the same time my head is full of Madame Chenier and my plans for her. I'm wondering if I want to meet him now with all the others there.

    'Have you met Juan, Lucy? I can't remember,' Claude will say. Monique, on the other hand, will remember. She knows I met him in Rome and she saw the envelope with the *Roma* postmark on it after I got back, the envelope with the picture of St Teresa in ecstasy inside.

I pluck up courage and go along to the kitchen. Juan says 'Hello, Lucy,' letting those brilliant eyes of his rest on my face for just a fraction longer than normal. But then he goes on talking to Daniel and Catherine. I notice his copy of *Le Petit Prince* on the top of the phone book just as you come in the door. He's been showing it to them too. He seems a little leaner than he was at Easter and maybe a bit tenser. He's being ordained in a few days, that's why he's here, and then it's goodbye Europe and back to Mexico.

Claude is busy making pasta. Claude is either totally absent from the flat or he's there and occupying every corner of it. Pasta is what they have on Sunday evenings when Claude is around, and he makes it. He's very proud of being able to cook pasta just like they do it in Italy. He always spends ages making the sauce - a mixture of olives and anchovies and capers and things - and then the great moment arrives when he puts the pasta in the boiling water. And in exactly seventeen minutes we've all got to be sitting down at the table because it can't wait.

We're all sitting there now and Claude is doling out this stuff which is like macaroni only much bigger. Juan has Daniel on one side of him and Catherine on the other. They're on their best behaviour because *Monsieur L'Abbé* is among us. I'm sitting opposite him.

'How are you Lucy?' he asks me as he picks up a fork.

'Lucy didn't come back last night,' Catherine pipes up. 'I went up to her room and she wasn't there.' I feel myself blushing.

'Be quiet, Catherine, it's no concern of yours,' says Monique. Claude looks across at me, he seems suddenly interested.

'Will you be able to come to my Ordination next week, Lucy?' Juan asks. 'You were included on the invitation I sent to Claude and Monique.'

'Oh, yes, you wrote something on the bottom of the card,' said Monique. 'I'm sorry, Lucy, I meant to say. It's next Wednesday at ten in the morning in *Notre Dame*.'

'I'll be working then,' I say. I wouldn't have wanted to go anyway.

'Lucy,' he says as we finish the pasta ,'Come with me for a moment. I want to show you a picture in a book in the library. It's of the statue we saw together in Rome.' I follow him out of the kitchen. Catherine wants to come too but Monique tells her to stay where she is.

In the library Juan puts his two hands up to touch my cheeks.

'I've missed you, Lucy,' he whispers to me. He doesn't want to show me the picture, that was an excuse. He just wants a few moments with me alone.

'When can we meet?' he asks. 'When can we be alone together?'

'The Trocadéro Gardens,' I say, 'on the bench overlooking the ornamental lake. Saturday, at four o'clock?'

He gives me a radiant smile and nods his head. And then we make our way back to the kitchen for the rest of the meal.

'What was the picture?' Daniel asks.

'It was a picture of a beautiful woman,' says Juan quickly, smiling across at him.

Chapter 13

I must admit, as I'm standing behind Madame Chenier a few days later, I begin to feel nervous about the big change I planned for her as I sat on the bus crossing the *Pont Alexandre111*.

'Alors,' I say to her with the nicest smile I can muster, as I stand behind her, my hands resting lightly on her hair. It always gives me the creeps to touch her hair - it feels like brillo pads - but they're always telling you how important it is to make the client feel valued. Men hairdressers have to be careful the way they manage this. It's trickier for them. Most of the clients like to flirt a bit with their hairdresser if it's a man, they like to feel cherished as women. But they don't want to feel they're being taken advantage of either, sitting there all helpless, with this man taking liberties. That's why a lot of the men act as if they're queer, I suppose, even when they're not, so the women don't feel threatened. It's different for me, as a woman. Though after Vinny on Sunday I'm beginning to wonder about this.

A shampoo and set is what she's wanting, of course, as usual, and, next time she comes in, just a few centimetres off the ends of the perm. She's not due another perm for a month.

'Next time,' I venture 'maybe I could cut a lot off. Beaucoup!' I demonstrate by holding the scissors just an inch away from her scalp. She thinks this is a joke and she looks a little shocked, like as if I'd told her I was dating an Algerian.

'You have a face like Joan of Arc,' I tell her. 'A strong, interesting face.' I've no idea what Joan of Arc looked like but she must have looked more interesting than Madame Chenier the way she looks at the moment.

'And you could have just a touch of a tint to bring out the colour of your eyes.' Her eyes are quite a nice warm hazel. 'Think about it and maybe next week you will become a different person,' I say gaily. I get the feeling I'm talking her round.

I have lunch with Jean François. It's some time since we had lunch together just the two of us. It's Wednesday so the menu reads:

Hors d'oeuvres: terrine du chef, carottes rapées, choux rouges, hareng pommes à l'huile

Plat du jour: boeuf mode, escalope viennoise, quart de poulet Bressoise

Légumes: purée, pommes allumettes, salade de saison

Fromages: camembert, carré de l'est, chèvre, bleu de Bresse

Désserts: tarte maison, gâteau de riz, compôte, fruit

I'm beginning to know the menus by heart. I have the *carottes rapées* and the *escalope* and Jean François has the herring and the chicken. He's made great progress with the girl on the 63 bus. She's called Sylvie. She came into the salon last week to have her hair done by him and I have to say she looked quite stunning when she walked out. She has very straight, very black hair and he cut it in a sort of helmet. He introduced me to her but we just said 'hello', she was all the time looking up at Jean François, thinking that everything he said was very funny. It's true he's brightened up a lot since she came into his life. I'm in the middle of thinking that having lunch with him is much more fun than it used to be when he says

'I'm trying to persuade Sylvie to come down to Nice with me one week end. I must fix it up with Michel - one weekend when Jeanne and Charlotte are not there.'

Fortunately Francis was just bringing me my *escalope* when he came out with this. It's not that I didn't guess they must be going down there to see him, I just didn't want to think about it. I look down at the plate so he doesn't see me going red. I feel like getting up and rushing out of the restaurant and just walking somewhere, anywhere. Jean François looks at me as if he's suddenly realising something. What's surprising me is that he didn't know already about me and Michel. But the last thing I want is to start having a heart to heart with him here over lunch.

'That sounds like a good idea,' I say, 'I still haven't decided if I'm going to go down there to work over the summer. I may just go back to Manchester. Andrew is getting a bit fed up with me being here and him there.'

Jean François met Andrew when he was in Manchester so we start this conversation now about me and Andrew while all the time inside me I'm churned up about Michel. He starts on about what a nice guy Andrew is. He'll make a very good husband is what he's no doubt thinking. And what sort of job will he get when he's finished studying, and does he want to stay in Manchester? There must be good opportunities everywhere for quantity surveyors.

'And hairdressers, too,' I interrupt. 'But I'm probably best staying in Manchester where I have contacts.' He looks surprised at this as if he'd been taking it for granted that my career would come to a stop when I got married to Andrew. This annoys me so much that it almost takes my mind off the thought of Jeanne and Charlotte with Michel.

My appetite's even returning and I find myself wiping my plate clean with a bit of bread. I'm wondering if I won't have the *gâteau de riz* when Jean François tells me that Sylvie never eats lunch because she's terrified of putting on weight.

'She is so slim, so slim.'

As we walk back to the salon I tell him about my designs on Madame Chenier. He shakes his head and says he thinks this wouldn't be a very good idea. Madame Chenier has a husband who likes throwing his weight around. Jean François saw him having a row with a policeman down in the street one day when he'd come to collect his wife. Oh, là là... Jean François shakes his hand up and down. Why don't I heed this warning?

The phone is ringing as I come through the door that evening. Monique answers it and calls me.

'It's for you, Lucy.'

It's Michel. He usually rings on Fridays and it's only Wednesday. He's written me a long letter - long for him is a whole page. He didn't have a letter from me this morning and he was worried something was wrong.

I'm wanting to be nasty, to lash out and say 'You have Jeanne and Charlotte coming down to see you. You don't need me and my letters.' Though I also realise I'm being unreasonable. So, instead, I tell him about my visit to Vinny's and about the paintings propped up against the walls.

'There was this one of a woman with her hair swept up but with lots of loose bits coming round her face. She looked very sophisticated and at the same time a bit wild,' I said.

Down where he is they're all wanting their hair cut short for the beach. So then I say about how I've been talking Madame Chenier into getting rid of her perm and having her hair cut very short. Michel sounds as doubtful about this as Jean François.

'Be careful, Lucy. That could be dangerous,' he says.

'It is five weeks and two days we have not been together,' he says then. 'I am counting the days. Only two more weeks. Bertrand said there would not be a problem. I told him I need you here and he thinks it will be very good experience for you to come. Lucy, it will be wonderful being together again.'

'Lucy,' Monique calls out as she hears me put down the phone. She's in the kitchen with a big plate of bright coral-coloured lobster in front of her and a bottle of white wine open.

'Come and have a glass of wine and help me eat this.'

Easier said than done. It's bad enough getting the bones out of kippers and herring but they're nowhere near as complicated as lobsters with all those broken legs and claws looking as if they've been in some road disaster. On her plate Monique has a pair of pliers, and a thin rod. She's poking down one of the legs and about a quarter of an inch of flesh is emerging at the other end. Privately I don't think it's worth the bother but it's nice being here with Monique.

'It was lovely seeing Juan on Sunday,' she begins straight away.

'Yes,' I say, wondering if she knows how close I got to him. I've always wanted to keep it a secret, those visits to the flat while they were away, and the fact that my trip to Rome was specially to see him. Even now, though it's Michel I long to be with, could I be tempted to leave everything behind and just go with Juan? It would be so much simpler, a pure, spiritual thing, like St Teresa's relationship with God. No Jeanne and Charlotte.

'He's been such a comfort to me,' says Monique. 'It's so good to talk to him.'

'You mean …?' I say.

'Well, you know, at the beginning of May, the evening I discovered Claude was having an affair, and I realised then that it was not the first, that all these years when he said he was away on business trips he was with his …his mistress …' Her eyes are filling with tears and it's a moment before she can go on. 'Well, I just took the car that evening and drove and drove. I just wanted to be alone. You remember?'

I'm feeling guilty. She's been so unhappy and I've hardly noticed. I remember her going away for a few days suddenly and Nounou coming and looking after the children, and feeling hurt because she never told me she was going.

'I found myself in this hotel in the Italian Alps and then I realised that the person I needed to talk to, the only person, was Juan. So the next day I went on driving till I got to Rome. He was wonderful, we just talked.'

'Yes, he's very understanding,' I say. I'm pouring myself a second glass of wine.

'Yes. Do you know *Le Petit Prince*? It's a lovely story, I read it as a child. But I don't think I understood it properly then. It's about …'

'Yes, I know the story,' I interrupt.

'Well, I was so angry with Claude and so hurt, I had been making up my mind to leave him. But Juan talked about the rose that was so precious to the little boy. A woman is like a precious rose, and a man needs that. More than anything else in life, a man needs to feel that somewhere a rose exists that is his rose.'

'And you are Claude's rose?' I ask.

Yes, according to Juan, she explains, Claude gets involved with other women because men are weak but deep down she's the only one who really counts, the mother of his children. And one day he'll realise this and come back to her. Meanwhile she has to accept her cross, offer it up. Juan's beginning to sound like the priest at home.

'That's what they all say, all the priests,' I burst out. 'Men are weak, women are the strong ones, it's up to them to look after the children and keep the home going.'

'Well, they should send the men packing,' is what I want to add. But Monique's not like me. And then, what else can she do anyway? The children are happy enough with the way things are and she has no money of her own, supposing she did decide to leave Claude. But she doesn't want to leave him, does she? She loves him.

'That's right,' says Monique, nodding sadly. 'And I still love him, I can't help it. And it helps knowing that Juan is there somewhere, supporting me, almost as if I was his rose too.' Her face has brightened.

'Have another glass of wine,' she says. 'I'll open another bottle.'

We don't go to *Chez Gilbert* on Saturdays. Marie Claire and I usually go to the café round the corner for a sandwich. Marie Claire's in a very good mood today. She's in a new black linen two piece that looks really cool on her and Bertrand did her hair this morning. There tend not to be many clients late Saturday morning. Most of them have houses in the country and they like to get away from Paris as soon as the kids come out of school at one o'clock. She tells me she's cooking a meal for Bertrand this evening. She's doing him a *coq au vin* followed by *crème caramel*. I could just about manage to make shepherd's pie and rice pudding, which is what we learnt to do at school. I'm wondering whether she and Bertrand are actually living together but that's not the sort of thing you can ask someone. They looked intimate enough this morning as he told her to bend her head a little, while he did the nape of her neck, and then I saw him stroking the back of her head and their eyes meeting in the mirror.

One Saturday she does the cooking and the next week it's his turn. Apparently he's a very good cook.

'We've been doing it like this for more than five years now,' she says.

'That's a long time,' I say.

'Yes.' I think for a second she's going to cry. She bends down and gets her powder compact out of her handbag and starts squinting at her face in the mirror. She went to see a make up specialist during the week, who calls himself a *visagiste.*

'He told me I was smiling too much. I'm developing crow's feet.' She grimaces at herself in the mirror.

'Can you see them?' she asks me. What am I supposed to say? I take a cigarette out of my bag.

Marie Claire gave up smoking because Bertrand didn't like the smell of it on her breath.

Surely there are other men around that Marie Claire can fall in love with, I think, as I walk slowly towards the Trocadéro Gardens, a couple of hours later. I feel sorry for her, so completely devoted to Bertrand. But maybe I should be envying her, her loyalty and devotion, and the simplicity of her life. She's like a story book heroine. They're always like that in stories, there's just one man they're in love with. They don't get mixed up with a whole lot of men like me - Andrew, Alberto, Juan, Michel. Even Jack maybe - I got a postcard from him the other day from somewhere in South America, saying he hoped to see me in Paris on his way home in September.

Actually, Alberto shouldn't be on the list any more. He's phoned once since that night but I told him I was busy. He said he'd ring again. I'd like to have said 'No, I'll give you a ring when I'm free' - just to give him a taste of what it's like to be waiting for a phone call - but it isn't done for girls to say that. I sometimes think it would be much better being a man, being in control - *maybe I'll ring her, maybe I won't*. On the other hand, it must be quite humiliating, ringing a girl and her saying No all the time. At least when the phone doesn't ring, nobody but you needs to know you're waiting for it to ring. Though some of the girls at work don't seem to mind publicising the fact that some feller's not getting in touch with them when they promised they would. *Ah, les hommes, vous savez, on ne peut jamais compter sur eux*, they're always saying to each other.

And they're right, of course, you never can count on men. I'm still angry with Juan, giving me the impression that I'm the only woman in his life and then discovering he's been saying the same sort of things to Monique. Maybe I should just not turn up. I'm so busy thinking about all this, I very nearly get knocked down by a huge black DS coming round the corner like a tank as I try to cross the road to reach the Trocadéro Gardens.

Looking down from the terrace I can see him sitting there in front of the fountains, his dark head perfectly still. He must be hot in that black *soutane*. All around him there are people passing - men in short-sleeved cotton shirts, women in floral dresses and floppy sun hats. I walk slowly down the steps.

'Lucy!' He has jumped to his feet and is gazing at me with those intense liquid eyes. He's just being very nice to Monique, it's normal, he's an old friend of the family. But with me it's different. I'm special. There's a lock of hair that's fallen across his forehead and it's shiny with his sweat and I can't help myself. I reach across and push it back and my hand lingers there. I want to run it down over his face and across his lips. He draws me down beside him on the bench. A group of children are roller skating up and down in front of us and I'm aware of them looking at us and at Juan's breviary which he has open now on his lap.

'Lucy,' he says again, 'this is the last time we will meet. I am flying back to Mexico immediately after my ordination next week.'

I'm remembering what I nearly said to him once – 'I'll come with you. I'll get a job wherever it is you are so that we never need to part. We won't be able to live together but we'll be happy, knowing that we are close to each other, seeing each other every day.'

'Lucy, you will be like my rose,' he says softly, looking down at his breviary. 'I will never forget you. We will never see each other ever again but it will make me happy knowing that you are somewhere in the world.'

'But …' I begin, but I don't know what to say next.

'Lucy, you must marry, you must become someone's wife, someone else's rose too. You are meant for marriage, Lucy. I see you sharing your life with a man who cherishes you and with children, lots of children.'

So he wants me to be like Monique, creating a home, keeping the family together, being a support to my husband, this is the life he sees for me. I jump to my feet. I find myself shouting at him in English. The children have stopped skating and are staring at us.

'I don't want to be anybody's stupid rose,' I shout. 'You just want to keep women in their place, where it suits you, don't you? You're not interested in me, you think I'm silly wanting to be a top hairdresser, you don't take me seriously, you just want me to be the way *you* want me to be, the way the whole of the Catholic church wants women to be, you just want us to be your servants.'

I'm walking up the steps by this time, screaming back down at him and he goes on sitting there like this is his first taste of martyrdom. For a moment I think he's going to get up and come after me but he doesn't and I'm glad. I stride home feeling exhilarated and at the same time upset.

Chapter 14

Madame Chenier is sitting in the chair, her hair shampooed, and I'm looking at her in the mirror. I'm holding the scissors above her head.

'So, je coupe? I cut?' I ask her, giving her a last chance. She gives me a smile - I think it's the first time I've seen her smile - and tells me to go ahead. I'm always happy cutting. I feel confident. Snip, snip, the permed curls float to the floor. Berthe, the new apprentice, is standing, watching. She keeps glancing across at Bertrand as I work round the head, but he's busy putting a young woman's long blonde hair into a chignon and doesn't notice what's happening.

When I've finished I can tell from the expression on Madame Chenier's face that she doesn't recognises herself.

'You look great,' I say.

'And now I'll put a little colour on the tips, just to soften the effect. If that's all right,' I add, but I'm already mixing the dyes - a sort of bronze colour and a darker amber.

I set to, with Berthe handing me the clips. It's a bit tricky as I only want to dye the ends but there's not much more than ends left of her hair. When she emerges from the dryer a short while later, Berthe removes the hair net and the cotton wool pads over her ears and I comb through what little there is left of her hair. I think she looks majestic, like a warrior about to do battle. As I take her over to the desk for her to pay Marie Claire, she presses a *billet* into my hand as a tip and it feels more like a *billet doux*, as if we were conspirators in something.

I have lunch with Marie Claire and Jean François. Marie Claire has been back to see Brigitte Bardot in *And God Created Woman,* which is on again in her local cinema. They're talking about BB's stupendous figure - the only thing worth going to see the film for, in Jean François's opinion. My mind is still on Madame Chenier, it's not God but me this time who's created a woman. This must be how the man who painted those portraits that I saw at Vinny's feels when he's finished one.

It's a bright sunny day and I'm feeling light hearted and cheerful as we make our way back to the salon. I suddenly remember it's the day of Juan's ordination, I must remember to say a prayer for him. After my outburst last Sunday I'm feeling quite benign towards him.

Bertrand's standing at the entrance to the salon talking to a stocky, middle aged man in a grey suit, with a thick moustache. I assume it's a friend he's just had lunch with but as we approach I hear Bertrand saying 'Ah, here she is!' and the next moment I'm staring into the furious eyes of this man who's shouting at me and I realise that it's Madame Chenier's husband and he's not happy with the way I've done his wife's hair.

With all the stream of language that's pouring out of his mouth, the only words I make out are *dégoutant* and *ma femme* this and *ma femme* that. I don't get a chance to open my mouth, not that I'd know what to say. I'm not going to say *excusez-moi* or *je suis desolée* or *je regrette*, I don't see why I should say I'm sorry. I just stand there and wait for him to finish and go off, which he does eventually, still shouting abuse at me over his shoulder.

Bertrand is obviously very shaken and tells me I should know better than to be experimenting with people like Madame Chenier but I keep telling him she'd said she *wanted* me to do her hair like that. Though it's true she'd never have had the idea if I hadn't suggested it. Jean François told me later that Monsieur Chenier said that his wife looked like one of those women who had their heads shaved after the war for collaborating with the Germans. He said he wasn't going to let her out of the house till her hair grew back, and that was the last time she'd ever come to *Bertrand*'s.

I feel like crying as I put the duchess's hair into the usual little curls. I wish with all my heart that Michel was there. I want to phone him but I can't from the salon, they'd all prick up their ears. As soon as I've settled the duchess under the dryer I grab my handbag and rush out and make my way to the nearest café with a telephone.

'Lucy!' Just the sound of his voice is like ointment on a burn.

'He's a *con*. He's a fool. They're all *cons*,' he keeps saying, when I tell him what's happened. 'These spoilt *bourgoises* coming every week to have their hair done, they live in their selfish little world, all they think of is themselves and their money and what they look like.'

'I love you, Michel, I miss you.' Outside a big white car has run into a 2CV and the drivers are on the pavement shouting and waving their fists at each other.

'Me too,' he shouts down the phone.

I make my way to the kitchen when I get in that evening. Monique is there with Daniel and Catherine eating their soup, and I find myself a plate and join them - carrot soup with a blob of cream in the middle of it. I ask the children what they did at school today but they had the day off to go to Juan's ordination. Monique thought it was the occasion of a lifetime they shouldn't miss.

'All those young men prostrate before the altar. It was *beau, tres beau.*'

Monique's stroking Daniel's head as she speaks. Maybe she's thinking that one day he too might become a priest. I didn't realised she was so devout. It must be the influence of Juan, casting a spell over her as he'd done once over me.

'We will miss Juan very much,' she says. 'He is leaving for Mexico on Sunday morning. I said I would drive him to the airport.'

'Can we come too?' Catherine asks. 'And Lucy?'

'No, it is much too early for you, you will still be fast asleep.'

She wants him to herself. She wants to be the only person to see him off. I could say 'No, it's not too early, I'll come too, I'd like to.' We'd stand there together side by side, waving him goodbye.

'Goodbye, Juan, and good luck,' I'd call out cheerily as I watched him disappear out of my life for ever. But I don't say anything.

'Have you had a busy day, Lucy? You look tired,' Monique says.

So I tell them about Madame Chenier and the hairstyle and Monsieur Chenier turning up in a fury and Daniel and Catherine are staring at me with saucer eyes.

'You mean you cut her hair short like this?' Daniel measures a centimetre on the end of his spoon.

'And you dyed it orange?'

They're screaming with laughter and then Monique and myself are joining in and I'm beginning to feel like a giddy schoolgirl again. Daniel starts imitating Monsieur Chenier. He catches hold of Catherine's hair and shouts at her

'You naughty girrel, naughty naughty. *Méchant! Méchant!* Go straight to your room and do not come out until your hair has grown again - 10 centimetres!'

I don't feel so cheerful the next morning, though, as I go down the stairs on my way to work. The thought of facing Bertrand with that reproachful bok still on his face and Berthe and Agnès sniggering to themselves. And the dreariness of the clients. This morning I'm seeing Madame Duclos who'll no doubt arrive with a picture of a member of the English royal family in her handbag - last time it was Princess Margaret - and she'll want me to do her hair in the same style.

I'm pushing the door open onto the street when I notice a man sitting on the step. He's got his back to me but I recognise him immediately, only I can't believe it. It's Michel. He's supposed to be 400 miles away. I'm laughing and we're kissing, and I'm running my hands up and down his jacket, just to make sure that he's really there. After I phoned him yesterday afternoon he decided to cancel his appointments for today and take the sleeper up to Paris.

'I'm starving,' he says, 'I haven't had any breakfast.' So we make our way across the road to the café where we order *grands crèmes* and croissants. I daren't ask him how long we have before he goes away again, I'm frightened he's going to say he'll have to go soon, he's got to go and meet Jeanne and Charlotte. I'm sure part of him wants to be with them.

'Can you take the day off?' he says. 'Can you phone them to say you're not coming in?'

There's a phone in the corner. I go over to it and put a *jeton* in and it's Marie Claire who answers.

'Oh, Marie Claire, I don't feel at all well, I think it's better if I don't come in today. I think I must be catching flu and I don't want to pass it on to Madame Duclos.'

The *patron* of the café suddenly starts shouting at the waiter who's talking to a friend in the corner

'Et dis donc, Hubert, do you think you're on holiday?' And then to some customers just arriving 'Bonjour, Messieurs Dames.'

I try to cover up the phone so Marie Claire won't hear but she immediately asks what's going on in the background. So then I have to say the phone where I live is out of order so I had to struggle out to phone from the café. She tells me to look after myself, she sounds quite sympathetic. Only she's probably thinking it's because of yesterday, I can't face going in to work today and she's feeling sorry for me. If only she knew, I'm the last person in the world she should be feeling sorry for.

We finish our croissants and order two more *grands crèmes* and then we say goodbye to the *patron*, who knows me quite well because I always wave as I'm passing on my way to the shops. I feel so happy imagining him thinking to himself, as we walk out of the café with my arm around Michel 'What a nice couple.'

We don't need to talk about what we're going to do next. We just start walking back to the *rue Galilée* and then past Madame Pie and the main stairs and the lift, and up the narrow stairs at the back that lead to the sixth floor. I haven't been in the room since Michel left at the end of April and it's our first time being there in the morning. The sun is coming in through the little window and it's June, so for once it's warm. It's nearly ten o'clock and Madame Duclos is arriving Chez Bernard. I start undoing the buttons of Michel's shirt.

'This is where I grew up.' We've just come out of the lift at the *Buttes Chaumont M*étro station. It's the first time I've been anywhere with Michel, apart from the salon reeking of shampoo and lacquer or the *Belle Ferronnière* or my little attic room where you can just about see chimney tops out of the window. I'm in my pink and white gingham dress with the nipped in waist and full skirt, and I feel like pirouetting all the way down the hill from the Métro.

'We used to live just there,' he said, pointing to an enormous building site across the road, with a deafening noise coming from it. On the hoarding around it there are lots of *Paix en Algérie* - Peace in Algeria - posters. Michel did his military service in Algeria but he's never wanted to talk about it. I think he was really shocked by what he saw there, and maybe what he had to do, I don't know.

We walk down the *rue Simon Bolivar* to the *tabac* on the corner, holding hands. Simon Bolivar was the great liberator of South America from the Spanish colonialists, Michel explains as we go. It's like being in a completely different city. It's reminding me of where I grew up in Manchester - tired old men walking their mangy dogs, women with frizzy over-dyed hair trudging along weighed down with shopping bags, kids in clapped out push chairs. Michel keeps meeting people he knows, who give him big smacks of kisses and hugs. I'm worried they're going to say 'And how is Jeanne?' 'How is Charlotte?' glancing across at me with a *What's she doing here?* sort of look. But Michel puts his arm round me and says 'This is Lucy' and they give me big smiles and shake my hand. They're all smelling of garlic and *saucisson*, like in the Metro. One old man, when he realises I'm English, comes out with *Geezness is good for you*. He keeps laughing and shouting back at us *Geezness is good for you* as he goes up the street and we have to keep turning round and waving and laughing.

We sit down at a table in the window of the *tabac* and the waiter comes and lays a white paper cloth and we're just about to order when he says *Excusez-moi, un instant* and disappears. A moment later we see him outside on the pavement. He's carrying two large shopping bags for an old woman with flowing white hair and horn rimmed glasses. She's tottering along beside him.

'It must be his grandmother,' says Michel. Behind them, shuffling along, there's a man of at least sixty wearing a wig of ginger hair, and a matching ginger cat walking just in front of him on a sort of lead.

The waiter comes back a bit out of breath and gets us something called *croque monsieur,* which is toast with cheese and ham in the middle, and two glasses of red wine. Michel starts telling me a complicated joke about a maid who was working in a house where the master died. She'd been told that it was polite to refer to any man who came to the house as *monsieur* so when the undertaker arrived, instead of announcing the *croque mort* - which is the French for undertaker, apparently - she announces him as the *croque monsieur*. I splutter with laughter over this and catch the eye of the woman in the corner sitting by herself, drinking a tiny cup of coffee, and she smiles back. She's a little hunch back woman in pink with a fuzz of dyed red hair, and cavernous eyes with lots of dark eye shadow on the lids. I'd love to have eyes like that - no matter how old you got, you'd always look dramatic.

'Salut, Michel.' Suddenly there's this man standing there who looks a bit like Meriche. Michel has stopped laughing.

'Mohamed!'

Michel has got to his feet and they're embracing, but it's not the carefree sort of greeting like with the others. Mohamed's asking Michel if he'll be at the meeting tomorrow evening, but Michel's telling him he's only up for the day, he's going back down to Nice this evening. But they're not wasting their time down there, he tells him, they're not wasting their time. They talk for a few minutes and I don't understand a thing and Michel doesn't introduce me, not like with the others, and then Mohamed goes away.

'Let's go to the park,' says Michel. So we walk back up the *rue Simon Bolivar*

I've never seen a park like it in my life. The park I played in as a kid had a lot of grass you couldn't walk on, flower beds with rows of pale yellow antirrhinums in them, a bowling green, tennis courts and a bandstand where a brass band played boring music on a Sunday. This park is enormous, with huge trees everywhere I don't know the names of. Michel says it used to be a hill with a whole lot of disused quarries and rubbish dumps on it but then they turned it into this park, with wide paths and steep slopes of grass. There's a waterfall, and a lake with an island in the middle of it. The island is really a mountain of rocks from the old quarry with a bridge across to it that they call the suicides' bridge, because in the old days when the walls were lower people used to throw themselves off it.

There's nobody else around, apart from a few couples lying on the grass, and four old men sitting on a park bench, gesticulating a bit like the three men in *Chez Gilbert*. And crows and pigeons, and orange ducks swimming in the lake. We walk across the bridge and climb up the steep mountain of rocks. It's like walking up a cliff face. It's quite scary, and I'm clutching hold of Michel as we look out over the grey roofs of Paris. No sign of the *Sacré Coeur* or the *Eiffel Tower*, just grey roofs.

'That's the *Gare du Nord* down there.' Michel starts pointing out different places. He's been sort of preoccupied, since he saw Mohamed.

We walk along to the waterfall and stand there for ages watching the water thundering down the knobbly rock. We can hardly hear each other talking, the noise is deafening. Michel shouts that it's reminding him of the time he went to the mountains once on a *colonie de vacances* - a sort of school camp.

Seeing the courting couples lying on the grassy slopes is making us want to make love again. There are bits of the park with quite a lot of undergrowth and I'm looking and wondering and I sense Michel is too. I've never made love in the open air before. Love in the woods is like picking wild flowers that don't last and that you have to throw away before you get home, I read some place, but I don't think it's like that at all. Our love is not like that.

But now we're at the exit to the park and we haven't stopped walking and there isn't time to go back to the room. We take the Metro, which is packed. We're crushed up against each other. And now we're saying goodbye at the *Gare de Lyon* and I'm telling him I'm coming down. I don't care about anything else. I just want to be with him.

Chapter 15

Dear Mum and Dad,
I'm writing this lying on the beach in my new red swim suit. I've put lots of suncream on so I don't get burnt. My legs and arms are getting really brown.
I went to early Mass at eight. It's in a little church in a back street just five minutes walk from the flat where I'm living. There were only a few people there and the priest was a little old man who reminded me of Father Kelly. Anyway, there was no sermon, which is just as well as it would have been in French and I'd have understood hardly anything.

I can hear the thud of the waves hitting the sand. It reminds me of the sound the packets of laundered sheets made when they were slapped down onto the counter of the *Dyers and Cleaners* where my Mum used to work. I used to call in on my way home from school. She'd come out from the back of the shop in her fawn twin set, the pearl necklace I bought her from *Woolworths* round her neck. She'd tug at my skirt to straighten it. She was always tugging at my skirt. There was this customer, a Mr Gannon, who sometimes came in while I was there. He had sandy coloured hair, and he was always getting his trousers and shirts cleaned – he was a bachelor. We knew him because he was a Catholic; he went to the same church as us.

'Are you still dyeing, Mrs Duffy?' he used to ask her and then he'd roar with laughter and my mum would laugh too. He made the same joke every time he came in. Was there something between them? The thought has never occurred to me before and I find it a bit shocking. But I'm certain there wasn't. My mother wasn't like that at all.

A man is coming past. He installs himself near me. Out of the corner of my eye I can see his hairy legs. I chose this spot because, when I arrived, there was a family here so I was safe, close to them. But they've just gone back to the hotel for the midday meal. Everybody's going back for the midday meal; the midday meal is sacred in France. Soon there won't be anybody here except for me and this man. The hairy legs have moved closer. I look down at my letter pad and start writing again.

It gets so hot in my flat. I have the fan on all the time and the window open but I still have sweat rolling down my face. It's very noisy too because the flat looks out onto the street. It's a narrow street and all the windows are open and people are always shouting across to each other. And there's the clatter of pans and the smell of olive oil, and babies crying as well. Actually, though, I don't mind the noise.

It's true, it doesn't bother me. It's much better than Sunday afternoons at home with nothing happening except for the brass band playing in the park and people going for boring walks, and nothing on the radio except *Down Your Way*.

The voice is asking me if I want to go into the sea with him. I pretend I haven't heard. He has a strange accent, quite different from Michel's. Michel explained to me that it was *l'accent du Midi*. The Midi is where I am now, apparently, though I thought *midi* meant *midday*.

I'm feeling a faint sensation on the sole of my foot. At first I think it's a fly and then I realise it's the man's finger tickling me. The beach is almost empty now and I'm suddenly nervous. I jump up, pull my sun frock on over my swim suit, slip my feet into my espadrilles, grab my towel and stuff my writing pad and pen into my beach bag. I can feel him watching me. I try not to run as I make my way up to the promenade and the café along the front. Out of the corner of my eye, I can see his hairy legs keeping pace. In the café I find a table with just one chair at it and order a lemonade.

The salon is very busy but it's quite relaxed, not like in Paris, as they're all on holiday. There are a lot of English women here, you can recognise them immediately because their faces are always bright pink from too much sun. Their hair's usually a complete mess too from the sun and the sea water. And they pay all this money for me to put their hair in rollers and they know it's going to be completely ruined when they go into the water.

'You should never go into the sea without a bathing cap,' I say to them, sounding like Miss Quigley at school. But I'd never wear one of those horrible things myself so I don't blame them if they don't.

Hairy legs has disappeared. The café's full of people having aperitifs before their huge Sunday lunch. Michel and I are having chicken, and salad and peaches. We did the market this morning after I'd been to Mass and before he went off on what I call his paper round.

It was lovely doing the market together, smelling the melons, feeling the furry skin of the peaches, trying to decide which *pâté* to choose from the row of *pâtés* spread out on the counter. The nearest I'd come to *pâté* before I came to France were those little pots of brawn in the windows of the UCP shops, next to the plates of tripe. I wanted to tell Michel about these this morning and to explain that UCP stood for *United*

Cow Products but I decided it would be too complicated.

But it didn't matter. I didn't need to talk about that, or about anything. I was brimming over with happiness. All the stall holders were smiling at us. They kept shouting questions at me that I didn't understand and Michel had to answer for me.

'Elle est anglaise,' he told the man selling meat and he put his arm around me. But then, at the fish stall, the fish woman was giving a little girl a tiny crab to take home in her bucket and I noticed Michel looking at her. She must have been the same age as Charlotte. Then she shouted something at Michel and he shook his head. I made out the word *enfant*. Was she asking him if we had children? Or maybe she was asking him where Jeanne and Charlotte were. Maybe he'd come here other Sundays with them. Suddenly it was like being on the down bit of the switch back, at the end of the ride.

Well, I'd better finish here. I'll post this on my way back to the flat so that you get it on Thursday. Love to you both and to Jim, Helen, Jonnie and Teresa,
Love, Lucy.

I hate writing letters like this to my parents. I hate not being able to tell them about Michel. My Mum thinks it must be very lonely for me here and it would be if it weren't for Michel, I wouldn't be here at all if it weren't for him. But I have to tell them it's a good career move, which is a lie because it isn't really. Most of the time all I'm doing is setting hair and taking 'a little bit off'. Not many clients want a re-style over the summer and at first it was always Michel or George who nabbed them until I protested that wasn't fair.

153

In any case, my Mum isn't interested in a good career move. All she wants to know about is whether I've met somebody. Well, I have and I never ever want to meet anybody else. Only I know we can never marry because he's married already so deep inside I feel really sad.

I must get back to the flat. Michel will have finished his paper round. That's another thing I wouldn't be able to put in my letters, even if he wasn't married. Every Sunday he goes round distributing *L'Humanité Dimanche*, which is the Communist Sunday newspaper. Michel has always been a Communist because his parents are Communist like my parents are Catholic. He's tried explaining to me what it's all about. He was actually quite excited when he found out I came from Manchester. That's where Karl Marx's great friend, Engels, lived, he said. Karl Marx was the man who invented Communism. Engels was German, like Marx, and his father owned all these factories in Manchester so he was very rich. So Engels used to send Marx money, so he could sit in the British Museum all day, writing political articles and things.

I liked the sound of Engels. He had an Irish girl friend called Kitty Burns who worked in the mills and he wrote a book about the condition of the working classes at the time, saying how terrible life was for them.

We've finished the chicken and we've almost got to the end of the bottle of wine and Michel has got round to talking about Engels again. The window's open and the fan is going like mad but I can still feel sweat running down my legs. Michel took off his shirt as soon as he came in so all he's got on are his shorts and his espadrilles. I've pulled my sun dress up so my bare leg's pressing against his and I'm looking at the curve of the muscles in his arms which is reminding me of those statues I saw in Rome.

'You know the railway bridge in the centre of Manchester?' Michel sometimes talks about Manchester as if he knows it better than me. 'Well, people used to live under it, whole families, with no sewers, no proper drinking water and never money to buy enough food, even after working sixteen hours a day in one of Engels' father's factories.'

'Carmel's Gran used to work in the mills,' I say, 'and I suppose her Gran's Mum and her Gran's Gran probably worked there too, so they must have been the sort of people Engels was writing about.

We've moved to the bed and we're lying there with nothing on. I'm thinking back to us in my attic room in February, huddled under the blankets. It was always too cold to lie with all our clothes off like this. We'd rub each other's hands, like mothers rubbing their children's hands - 'What happened to your gloves? What have you done with your gloves?'

'Maybe Carmel's great grandmother was Kitty Burns, maybe her great grandfather was Engels,' I say, and Michel laughs.

Last week Michel found an old iron basin in some junk shop. We fill this now with cold water and take it in turns to sit in it. Then we spread our beach towels out on the floor and lie there with our skin and hair all damp and shiny.

'Wouldn't it be great if one day we could use one of the bathrooms in the hotel? The baths are enormous, we could easily sit in one together,' says

Michel. 'I must start courting Delphine. She'd give us a key.'

Delphine is one of the receptionists at the hotel. I don't like this idea at all. She might think it's her he wants to share the bath with. She doesn't know about me and Michel, nobody does in the salon, so this means they all think he's 'free'. She's always looking at him like a sick cow. And George is the same. George is the other stylist and he's English and he's queer, like Francis and Etienne at *Gilbert's,* but maybe he's hoping Michel likes men as well as women. It doesn't seem to matter that Michel's a married man with a child. A lot of people in France, apparently, think that a man isn't a man if he doesn't have *'une petite amie'.* So I'm Michel's *petite amie,* his 'little friend', 'his little bit on the side'. It's not like that at all, what we've got between us is the most important thing in our lives if they only knew.

'I much prefer our basin. The bathrooms in the hotel sound too *bourgeois,*' I say. I'm quite pleased with myself, using that word back at Michel.

'Tu as raison, you're right,' he says, catching hold of a towel and putting it over my head so I feel a bit like a nun in a veil. He squeezes the water out of the ends of my hair ever so gently as our lips move closer.

Later we go out to meet these two men in a café up near where Michel's flat is. He has to call in on the flat on the way. I've never been to Michel's flat. I couldn't bear it. There's sure to be signs of Jeanne and Charlotte there - photos, and things left behind from their visits - toys, a dressing gown hanging behind the bedroom door, a jar of face cream in the bathroom. Michel needs to call in to get a book, but I wait down below in the street. A woman comes out of the building, gives me a funny look as if she knows Jeanne and wonders what I'm doing there, waiting for Michel.

The two men are Communists like Michel. He delivers *L'Humanité Dimanche* with them every Sunday. One of them's about the same age as me and Michel. He's called Gérard. His hair's all sleeked back with Brylcreem. The other man's much older.

'This is Antonio. Antonio's Spanish - he fought in the Civil War,' says Michel as he introduces him.

'Like Juan's father,' I think.

'I knew someone in Paris whose father was in the Civil War,' I say. 'He went to Mexico. His son was at the seminary in Paris.'

'Studying to be a priest?' asks Gérard. I haven't told Michel much about Juan. He doesn't have any time for the Church and for priests. He makes a face now at the mention of Juan.

'No, no, there were also priests on our side. Some good men, some very good men,' says Antonio.

I'm waiting for him to tell us about some of them but he doesn't say anything else, just goes on nodding his head and looking depressed - like he's opened a drawer with lots of old photos and letters in it he wished he hadn't opened.

But this has got Michel and Gérard started on about the Catholic Church and the Pope during the war and I can't follow what they're saying, and, in any case, I've started thinking about Juan and wishing I hadn't been so hard on him. Except that the other day I passed a book shop and, in the window, there was a whole row of that book - *Le Petit Prince* - on display, and that reminded me of how angry I'd got at the thought of a woman being somebody's precious rose, sitting there, hoping some man wouldn't forget to water her.

'What was the Mexican son of a Spanish Republican doing at a seminary in Paris, anyway?' Gérard asks me. He has to repeat the question twice and then Michel explains in English.

'Juan - why Paris? Why not Mexico?'

'I don't know,' I say and then Michel laughs and says it's probably because they can't fill the seminary with Frenchmen because nobody in France wants to be a priest nowadays.

I'm feeling uncomfortable about all the anti-Catholic talk. Where I come from in Lancashire they used to make fun of us being Catholic, going to Catholic schools, which we were always fighting to keep. In the past, we'd had to suffer for our faith, been persecuted for it. My favourite hymn at school had been *Faith of our Fathers living still in spite of dungeon, fire and sword.* It ended with *We will be true to Thee till death.* I love that hymn, particularly the *dungeon, fire and sword* bit, I still hum it to myself sometimes.

I'm glad when this other man turns up. He's Algerian, like Vinny's friend, Meriche, and Mohamed that we met last month in Paris, but he looks much older and very thin, with a small black moustache and receding hair. He's called Abbas.

Anyway, Abbas is upset about something. He's telling them that this French couple - Pierre and Jacqueline - have been arrested and they're in prison. Last night, apparently, the police stopped the van they were driving, with money inside that had been collected for the war. Michel's already explained how the Algerians living in France give money - even those working on building sites, earning very little, have to give a big part of their wages - to support the war back in Algeria. But the problem is how to get the money out of France, to a bank in Switzerland, or across to Algeria. The police are always stopping and arresting Algerians so it's mostly French people who act as couriers, transferring it. Three suitcases full of dirty franc notes they'd had in the van.

We're all drinking that stuff that tastes like cough medicine but Abbas sits down and says he'll have a glass of milk. He doesn't smoke either. He sits there staring straight ahead of him, tapping the table with his fist. Two girls walking past in tight skirts and high heels suddenly recognise Gérard and they're kissing him on the cheeks and telling him they're off to a place where you can dance on a Sunday afternoon. They want us to come along too. Gérard goes off but Michel just sits there.

'So what do we do now?' he keeps saying, as he pulls on his cigarette. It suddenly occurs to me that maybe he's been involved in transferring money, too, and it could easily be him in prison instead of Pierre and Jacqueline.

Abbas was held for a month by the French Army in Algiers, Michel told me as we walked back along the promenade. The sea was an amazing sapphire blue and there were little white sails out on the water, bending ever so slightly this way and that, and on the beach a boy and a girl with streaming blonde hair were flying a bright green and red kite.

'They used torture on him - electrodes inside his mouth and on his penis, day after day, and when they weren't torturing him he was in his cell listening to the screams of others being tortured, like animals being put to death. A lot of them died under torture - they used to collect them all up and drop them into the sea from a helicopter. But Abbas survived and he managed to get here.'

'But, in a way he died too,' said Michel, as we arrived back at the flat. 'There's something about him, as if he's empty inside. He thinks he should have stayed in Algeria, stayed fighting.'

Chapter 16

It's Sunday again and I'm having to write home and I don't know what to say. I try to fill the letter up with what's happening at work. I tell them about the other people working there but I know my mother's not very interested. Unless I can think of some unhappy things that have happened to them, like that Francesca's boy friend has gone off with her best friend, or Nicole's husband has left her - that sort of thing. That'll make her feel better about me and she'll write back *Poor girl* or *What a shame!*

She's interested in George though, because he's English. I don't tell her he's queer, of course. I say things like 'I went with George and a few of the others to the pictures the other evening, to see this funny film which was really good' - just to make her feel that I'm happy, which I am. I've never been happier in my whole life but I can't tell my Mum and Dad why.

The only thing I'm not happy about is the others not knowing about me and Michel. They keep asking him about Jeanne and Charlotte. And Delphine's always calling him over on some excuse when he arrives in the morning. We come in separately so they don't know we spend the nights together in my flat.

'Oh, Michel,' she trills, 'I want to show you something.' It gets on my nerves. And then George is always making eyes at him too. Michel thinks this is a joke but I think he shouldn't be leading him on, making him think he's available, when he very definitely isn't.

'We often go for a swim at the end of the day,' I write. *'Most of the crowds have gone back to their hotels for their evening meal, so we have the place to ourselves. The water's lovely and warm. The big*

problem, though, is getting to it because it's a pebble beach and it's murder walking on it. The other thing is that I miss not having a tide, the water's always more or less at the same place on the beach and it's incredibly salty. I think the sea at Blackpool's much better, tell Helen.' Helen comes from near Blackpool.

Michel can't swim; he just does a dog paddle. I'd like to teach him but he's not really interested. I think he's a bit nervous of the sea. He comes in till the water's up to his knees and then he goes back out again. Except the other day I pulled him suddenly and we both sat down and we stayed there for ages with the waves sloshing over us.

My Mum's real hope, of course, is that I'll come home and marry Andrew. She never writes a letter without mentioning him in it. 'I saw Andrew at Mass last Sunday.' 'I saw Andrew's Mum in the town yesterday.' 'Why don't you invite Andrew down to Nice?'

I know they're upset about me coming down to Nice instead of going back to see them. Andrew's upset too, I can tell by his letters. Though it's much easier, in a way, writing to Andrew, than to my parents. There's more to write about. I can talk about singers he's heard of like Johnny Hallyday, and the latest films. We both like going to the pictures. That's how we started - in the back row of the *Odeon*, watching *Passport to Pimlico*. We saw all those films. So I can talk about the films I've seen.

Though I know I should have written to him and made it clear I wasn't going to marry him. It isn't fair keeping him on a string like this. But I seem to need to have him there. It's a bit like having a big brother to shelter behind. My Mum's less worried about me as long as Andrew's around. One day I'll see sense, she thinks, and come home and marry Andrew. My friend, Carmen, thinks I should, she thinks I'm mad not to jump at the chance of marrying someone like Andrew.

Close to me on the beach is this family. The man looks a bit like Andrew, his hair's the same tawny colour and he has the same muscular calf muscles, he must be a cyclist too. The mother doesn't look much older than me. They have two small children, about three and five and they're all the time fussing around them, putting sun cream on them, straightening their sun hats, telling them not to do this, not to do that. I'm only sitting here so I don't get pestered by some hairy legs or other plonking himself down beside me.

I've finished my letter to my Mum and Dad. It's not very comfortable sitting here. I've bought a mat but you can still feel the pebbles underneath. But I owe Andrew a letter. I could tell him about Antonio and Abbas and the march I went on last Sunday.

Dear Andrew,

It was good to get your letter. It's funny to think of you working in a canning factory, tipping green stuff into grey peas. I hope you find a proper job soon. The one in Leeds sounds promising. Have you applied for it?

I'm sorry I haven't written for so long but we've been very busy at the salon. I feel shattered when I get home in the evenings and all I want to do is go to bed. The heat doesn't help, it's always in the 80s from the middle of the morning till late in the afternoon.

I'm too tired and too hot to do any cooking either. I usually buy something on my way back. There are these stalls selling a sort of open sandwich - onions and olives and tomatoes on bread soaked in olive oil.

It's really funny, how we've always thought of olive oil as just something you put in your ears when you had earache, but here they use it all the time in their cooking.

Nice is a really boring place. It's full of rich retired people who spend their days sitting in deck chairs on the beach with panama hats on their heads, reading their newspapers. Delphine at work - the one I told you about who got all her clothes pinched when she was in the sea and had to go to the police station in her bikini - is always getting involved with some old man or other. At the moment it's one who keeps inviting her up to his room to drink champagne with him.

I've managed to fill two sides. My handwriting's quite big. I fold the page over and put it in the envelope. I'm almost at the end of my writing pad and this is my last envelope. I write:

Mr Andrew Moore,
677 Dickinson Rd.,
Manchester 12,
Angleterre

I'll get stamps in the *tabac* on my way back to the flat.

Why didn't I tell him about the march? I should tell him about the war in Algeria and people trying to stop it. I don't need to say I was with this group of people I've met who are Communists and I don't need to mention Michel. I take the writing pad out of my bag and start writing again. The family next to me are preparing to leave.

I forgot to tell you about something quite exciting that happened last Sunday. You know about the Algerian War? Algeria is a French colony and they're fighting for their independence from France.

It's very peculiar to be writing to Andrew about politics. He'll wonder what's happening to me. Politics is something I've always thought of as dead boring, I've never been the slightest bit interested in politics, I just about know whether the government is Labour or Conservative.

Anyway, last Sunday I went on a march with a few people I sort of know - one of them's called Abbas and he's Algerian. There were thousands on the march carrying banners with things like **Paix en Algérie** *on them and* **Into the Junk Shop with Charlie** *- that's General de Gaulle. The police broke it up, it was very frightening, they carry guns in France and they have these batons they lash out with. There were people with blood running down their faces and there was one man on the ground and three policemen kicking him like he was a football. We tried to rush into a café but the café owner had bolted the door because the café down the road had been completely wrecked a few weeks before.*

How much more can I tell Andrew about it? I was really scared but, at the same time, it was very moving, being in a crowd of people like that, all there for the same reason. I lost a shoe as we ran from the police and Michel had to almost carry me all the way to the bus stop. On the bus this woman started shouting at us about how we were traitors to France because she saw the placard Michel was still carrying with *Algérie Indépendante* written on it.

Michel will have finished his round and be back in the flat by now. Later this afternoon we're going to go dancing with Gérard and those two girls that we saw the other Sunday. As I get up to go, I notice the little girl's white cardigan lying there. I can just see the family way ahead in the distance, so I run after them with it. *Merci, Mademoiselle*. The man has the same sort of crooked smile as Andrew has. With Andrew you think he's got this boring ordinary sort of face and then he smiles and it's like a pebble's just been thrown into a pool of still water.

The Sunday I wrote that letter, that was the Sunday I actually saw the inside of Michel's place.
    'I've got to call at the flat first,' Michel said as we set off from my flat in the middle of the afternoon to meet Antonio and Gérard and the others. 'I've got to try to find this pamphlet I promised Antonio. It may take me some time so it would be better if you came up.'
    So I went up with him. It was a funny feeling, standing there while he put the key in the lock, knowing that he must have stood here so often with Jeanne and Charlotte by his side.
    I hadn't expected there to be so much of them around the place. The first thing I saw was a wooden hair brush on the floor by the window with matted brown hair in it that was obviously Jeanne's. And there was a big children's book beside it, open at a page with a picture of a girl that looked like Little Red Riding Hood on it. And there were stacks of empty yoghurt pots in the kitchen. Michel never eats yoghurt.
    'This is Charlotte,' said Michel, handing me a photo. 'I took it one Saturday afternoon in the *Jardin des Tuileries*.' He maybe thought I'd be pleased to see a picture of his little girl but it was the last thing I wanted to be looking at. She was on the roundabout they have there, on one of the wooden horses, looking at the camera and laughing. Her head was a mass of

blonde curls. Jeanne had her back to the camera. She was wearing a neat fitting flowery dress and her hair was loose on her shoulders.

'Charlotte looks very pretty,' I managed to say and handed it back like it was a hot coal. The door was open into the bedroom and I could see a double bed with a green chenille bedspread on it and Jeanne's slippers poking out from under it - blue slippers with broken down backs.

'Michel,' I said 'I think I'm going to go back to the flat. I've got a headache, I need to lie down.' I was already at the door. I thought he was going to rush after me and put his arms around me but he was busy looking for the pamphlet.

'Okay, that's probably a good idea if you've got a headache. I'll see you this evening. Or maybe it will be better if I just sleep here this evening and see you tomorrow at work.'

'I don't know,' I said. It would be the first night we hadn't spent together since I'd arrived in Nice.

I went down into the street. It was very hot and there was nobody about. It had been stupid to walk out like that, we could be walking together now, hand in hand, to the café where Antonio and the others were sitting, and then afterwards we'd go to that place to dance. And then we'd go back to my flat together.

What if I turned up at the café, even now, said I'd changed my mind, and that my headache had cleared? They'd all be so pleased to see me, after the march the other week we'd got quite close. And Michel would light me a cigarette, place it between my lips.

But what would be the point? It wouldn't change anything. Michel was married to Jeanne, his real life was with her and Charlotte. There was no one, no one in the world I cared about more than Michel but it was not the same for him. He had Jeanne and Charlotte.

If I were with Andrew now, there wouldn't be any of this torment. I was at the centre of Andrew's world, the most important person. Forget Michel, go back to England, marry Andrew, put an end to this torment.

And end up giving Mrs Cartwright and Mrs McGrail and Mrs Entwistle shampoos and sets for the rest of my life, with a perm thrown in every six months? I was passing a church. I went in, pulling my chiffon scarf over my head. It was cool inside, and completely empty. Except for God, of course - the little red light was burning there at the altar, meaning that the bread which had been turned into the body of Christ was in the tabernacle.

I sat down opposite a statue of the Virgin - Our Lady of Lourdes. Her hands were joined in prayer and her head was bowed in submission as befitted the handmaid of the Lord. I thought of Juan again, and the little prince and the rose, and my spirits began to lift. At least I wasn't like her. As I sat there in the silence I started thinking of the competition in Paris in the autumn. I would create a hairstyle that would astonish. I walked home, buying bread and a bottle of wine on the way.

I spent the evening looking through the recent hair magazines. The hair's getting longer again. *Short hair? There's no place like Paris for completely snubbing what isn't the latest. Fashion says grow it longer. And that's it!* The *Audacity Line* of the spring had alarmed a lot of hairdressers because the hair was too short for perming. *Last spring's slick chick hairdos are being replaced by hair à la Marilyn, Grace and 'Jackie' – the fluffy, the smoothy and the wavy.*

I even succeeded in not thinking about Michel, and Jeanne's blue down-at-heel slippers poking out from under the bed in their flat. Then, just as I was about to go to bed the doorbell rang and there was Michel, like a long lost traveller returned from a foreign country.

It's now the beginning of August and today I had my first real piece of work since I arrived in Nice. It was on this fashion model who wanted a really short cut. It took ages but I walked away from the salon feeling pleased with myself. Michel's already there when I get back to the flat.

He's bought a whole roast chicken from the shop round the corner. They cook it on a spit. Usually we play a game as we sit there eating it, holding pieces in our hands and looking at each other as we bite into the flesh, and run our tongues along the drumsticks. Today though, there's something up, I realise immediately as we sit down opposite each other. Just as I'm biting into a juicy bit of breast, he tells me.

'I phoned Jeanne from the *tabac* on the way home,' he begins. I suppose if I'd thought about it I'd have known that he must phone her a lot, at every opportunity even. 'Charlotte is really missing me. It's weeks since I saw them. I said I'd try to get up to see them one week end. But ...'

I've stopped eating, waiting for him to finish. He's speared a piece of chicken with his fork and is putting it into his mouth.

'She says it would be much easier if they came down here.' He swallows. 'So they're arriving at the beginning of the week.'

'Oh,' I just about manage to say. How long will they be there for? There wouldn't be any reason for them not to stay for a few weeks, would there? There's the empty flat and the beach for Charlotte to play on.

'They won't stay all that long,' he says, 'Jeanne thinks Nice is much too hot for Charlotte in August. She's better in the country. And, anyway, the grandparents will be disappointed if they're away for too long. They'll probably go back before the week end.'

'Well, it will be nice for you to see them,' I say, hoping that he'll contradict this, but I know he won't. I can sense his happiness at the prospect of them being here.

'Won't it?' I persist, trying to force him to admit that it will be nice. But he says nothing. He just looks across at me with a slight twitch of his shoulders.

Chapter 17

'Have you met Michel's wife?' Delphine asks me. I'm sure she knows there's something between me and Michel and she's asking me this on purpose. She's as bad as Marie Claire. You have to pass the hotel reception desk on the way into the salon so there's no avoiding her.

'Just once,' I say. 'She came into the salon in Paris.'

I'm looking at Delphine's hair. It's light brown and it's been what you call de-permed to make it straight, because it's naturally frizzy. It's quite long and I can imagine it done in what they call a Dutch *coif* that I was reading about in one of the journals. You wind it at the back of the head like a twisty loaf from nape to crown. It would give her a staid look which would be a disturbing contrast with the rest of her.

'Would you like me to do your hair some time?' I ask her, as if the subject of Michel and his wife's not very interesting. 'I'd like to try out a new style on you.'

'Michel always does my hair, he might be offended,' she says. She's probably thinking I'm jealous of seeing Michel bending over her, flirting with her. 'No, I was going to say,' she continues, leaning forward so that her blouse falls away and you can see her breasts blossoming inside her bra. She's wearing one of those pointed ones that makes her jut out like a window sill. 'His wife's hair looks as if it could do with having something done to it. It's just pulled back in a pony tail. A little surprising for the wife of a hair stylist. You'd think she'd have something more elaborate.'

Madame Bizet's waiting for me when I go through the door into the salon. Nicole has just finished washing her hair and she's coming towards me with a pale lilac towel around her head. She's a woman of about seventy who spends most of the year in hotels on the *Côte d'Azur*. Pots of money. She's always got this sour expression on her face, as if she's just lost all of it in Monte Carlo, which I'm sure she hasn't.

Madame Bizet's all I'm needing this morning. I didn't sleep much last night, the first night I've spent alone in Nice without Michel. I lay there listening to some boys playing football in the street below with what sounded like a sardine tin until after midnight, and then all the cats in the neighbourhood started fighting amongst themselves.

I give her a smile in the mirror and start putting rollers in. She's going bald so I haven't got much hair to work with and I have to arrange it carefully to cover the gaps. She comes into the salon about twice a week for this treatment so I've got quite good at it. I wish I'd made similar progress with the conversation but this remains non-existent. I gave up trying after the first few weeks. Instead I start imagining things about her as I stick pins in and arrange the hair net over her, ready for the dryer.

My favourite is that she's a retired brothel Madame. I look down at her jewelled fingers, at all the diamonds, rubies and sapphires sparkling there like raindrops on the washing line, and I think of heavy velvet curtains and pouting girls in flimsy skirts and riding boots, and Madame Bizet giving them pep talks like Miss Quigley at school. Nicole, on the other hand, just thinks she's someone who had a very rich husband in pharmaceuticals.

George is fussing around. Michel hasn't come in yet.

'I don't know where he can be. He's always in at nine,' he keeps saying to Francesca. He must know very well why he's late. He knows Michel's wife and daughter arrived on the train yesterday evening. They're probably still having breakfast in that tiny kitchen. I try not to think of this as I lead Madame Bizet over to the dryer. She opens *Le Figaro* at the page that has the easy crossword and spreads it out on her fat lap. Her legs are very short and Nicole brings her a footstool for her plump little feet which are bulging out of her black court shoes like squashed bananas

I need a cigarette. I go through to the back and nearly bump into Michel who's just arrived. He looks a bit embarrassed, says *Bonjour* as if I could be anybody and then starts trying to make up for that, as if he's suddenly remembered who I am, by putting his arm around me, but I shake him off.

'George has been wondering where you were,' I say.

Later in the morning George says to Michel how it would be nice to meet Jeanne and Charlotte while they're here, and maybe we could all have a drink in the café down the road one evening after work. Nicole and Francesca think this is a great idea. They all know Jeanne and Charlotte, of course, because they were here most weekends during May and June.

Charlotte is sitting between George and Delphine drinking *Orangina*. The rest of us are drinking Martinis. George is making a mouse out of his handkerchief and Charlotte is screaming with laughter.

Delphine is caressing Charlotte's hair. 'Quels jolies boucles!' she keep exclaiming. What pretty curls! Funny to be woo-ing Michel via his little girl, I'm thinking. It seems to be working. Michel is looking on, smiling.

I'm not much good with kids. I never know what to say to them, even Jonnie and Teresa. But it's worse with Charlotte. She looks up at me and she has the same eyes as Michel. George is remarking on this now.

'You have the same eyes as your Daddy,' he is telling her in English. I hadn't wanted to come for this drink at all but I couldn't think of any excuse not to. Jeanne is sitting just a few yards away from me but I've hardly dared to look at her. I'm afraid to catch her eye. This is the woman Michel shares his life with, the woman that, until a few months ago, he went back to every evening. She's more casually dressed than the rest of us. She's wearing a black sleeveless top and a flared yellow skirt and black pumps and I can just imagine her on the dance floor.

They met when she started her first job as a primary school teacher. It was in a school near where he lived in *Belleville* and he met her for the first time in the café round the corner. She was sitting there crying into her coffee because she felt so lonely. She came from the country and she knew nobody in Paris.

He's very fond of her but he was never in love with her, he told me once as we lay in the little attic room, looking up at the paint peeling off the ceiling.

'It's just that we started sleeping together and then she got pregnant with Charlotte so we had to get married.'

That's all he's ever said about him and Jeanne. That he was never in love with her, that I'm the first girl he's really been in love with. That's what they all say, they tell you in the magazines, but I think it's true in Michel's case. It's the first time for both of us.

But it's not true for Jeanne; I'm sure, she did fall in love with him. And she's still in love with him, I feel, as I sit here. She isn't like me, she isn't the sort of woman who can spend a night or two with an Italian colonel, or who can be in love with one man and, at the same time, imagine going off to Mexico with another, with a newly ordained priest, at that. And with yet another boyfriend at home. She's neat, she's all of a piece, she knows what she wants, she's clear about her life. And her life is Michel and Charlotte. I feel terrible.

She's looking across at me. Up to now she's been talking to Nicole whose daughter is ten, the same age as the children Jeanne teaches. She seems a really nice sort of person, genuine as my Mum would say. She asks me how I'm enjoying Nice. Everybody's gone silent as if they're all waiting for my reply.

'Oh,' says Delphine before I can open my mouth, 'Lucy loves it here, don't you, Lucy? What a change in her since she arrived! She was all pale and sad and thin, coming from Paris. But look at her now!'

They all look at me, presumably to admire how healthy and cheerful I look, and I don't know what to do or say. I'm furious with Delphine. She's so patronising, though she's younger than me. I have a good mind to tell Jeanne what Delphine thinks of her hairstyle but, before I can say anything, George is telling them that we English all love Nice. Why else do so many of us come here? Why, the boulevard we're on is actually called the *Promenade des Anglais*. George can be a right pain.

'I quite like Nice,' I say 'but I think I prefer Paris. There's a lot more to do there. And there are too many women coming into the salon here, just wanting shampoos and sets - it's not very good from the point of view of my career. I'll probably go back to Paris next month.'

I avoid looking at Michel, though I feel him getting tense. I'm glad I managed to get that bit out in French about my career. A lot of the women who come in talk about their sons and their *carrière*s and what would be good for them and what wouldn't, so I'm used to hearing the word.

'I think it's time we were going,' says Francesca to me. We've fixed up to go to the pictures together. I look at my watch. The film starts at seven thirty. I jump to my feet.

'It was very nice meeting you and Charlotte.' I say to Jeanne. I can hardly believe that I'm managing to seem so relaxed. I even look straight at her and then, as we leave, I give Charlotte a little wave.

'Dis au revoir à Lucy et Francesca,' I hear Michel saying to Charlotte as we start walking away. There is a slight breeze blowing and the sea is sparkling and I breathe in great gulps of air as we walk along. The film we're going to see is the latest Marilyn Monroe - *The Misfits.*

The film was good. I love Marilyn Monroe.

'I think this is her best film,' I was saying to Francesca as we left the cinema, when we heard this voice behind saying 'Ah, no, I don't agree. *Some Like it Hot* is her best film' and there were these two fellers in cotton shirts and with untidy hair. So we got talking to them and we all ended up in a café having a drink. We've fixed up to see them again this evening.

Francesca's younger than me, she's only nineteen, but I think she could make a really good hairdresser, she's got flair. Only she's a bit like the girls I trained with in Manchester. They used to sit in the tea break with these Bridal magazines open on their laps, dreaming about walking down the aisle. That's all they ever thought about - men and getting married. Working in a hairdresser's was just a way of filling in time and earning a bit of money until they became Mrs Somebody or other. They were all dead scared of being *left on the shelf*, as my Mum puts it, as if they were flower pots or something.

Well, Francesca's a bit like that, she's not that interested in making a career out of hairdressing, she really just wants to find *someone to keep her*, to use another of my Mum's phrases. And she's already beginning to think that Didier might be a possibility. He's one of the fellers we met at the cinema yesterday evening. The other one's called Alain. They're both medical students from Bordeaux, here doing holiday jobs, renting deck chairs on the beach. But one day they'll be doctors.

'I like the idea of being a doctor's wife,' Francesca was saying on our way to meet them. She was only half-joking. She was already seeing herself in a smart flat in Bordeaux, giving cocktail parties. Francesca has dark hair and dark skin. She's wearing a white sleeveless dress and I think she's looking smashing. I'm in my new black linen dress, straight up and down, but I can see it's getting badly creased.

Anyway we're in the same café with them as yesterday evening, wondering what to do and where to go. I'm feeling a bit out of it. They're talking away and it's quite difficult to understand what they're saying. When I talk to Monique or Michel in French they talk quite slowly and clearly so I can follow them, but these three are just talking fast, the way I'd talk with my chums back home, with lots of slang. And they keep laughing and expecting me to join in. I start looking down at my dress, trying to smooth out the creases, wishing I was back in Manchester. Or that Andrew was here. Suddenly I'm thinking how nice it would be if Andrew was here.

Alain asks me in English where I come from in England. His English is quite good but Francesca doesn't speak English so I'd prefer to speak in French. I don't want to start having a private conversation with Alain. I can see he's keen to start up a relationship by the way he's looking at me. He's probably all set for a holiday romance like you read about on the problem pages of women's magazines.

Dear Evelyn,

I met this boy at Butlin's in July and we fell in love but since I've been back home in Birmingham I haven't heard from him. He promised to write so I can't understand what's happened. I don't have his address, otherwise I'd write to him. I'm feeling so worried in case he's fallen under a bus or something. I can't stop thinking about him. Please write and tell me what I should do,
Julie

Dear Julie,

I'm afraid you are the victim of yet another holiday romance ....

We're all quite hungry and they do food in the café, so we're in the middle of ordering hot dogs and chips and more beer when I see Michel. Alain is just asking me how you say 'heut dueg' in English. Very funny. I'm on the point of smiling politely when I see him coming through the door of the café. Alain turns round to see what I'm looking at because of the expression on my face. I think he's expecting to see half a dozen police. Instead there's just this man with the dark hair with a woman with mousy hair and a pony tail and a little girl in a pink dress. Francesca, who's also seen him, cries out
'Michel!'
He just waves and then Jeanne and Charlotte wave as well and they go and sit over the other side. Not before Michel has seen Alain, but where he's sitting now he's out of sight, so I don't need to smile and look as if I'm enjoying myself. Just as well.
When we leave some time later I don't turn to look at them but I can feel Michel's eyes staring at me as I walk out of the café. Alain is putting his arm around me, which I think is a bit of a cheek, but maybe it's no bad thing for Michel to see me with another man's arm around me.
Only I feel cheap. I don't want to be with these people I hardly know. I want to rush back into the café and scream at Jeanne and Charlotte that Michel doesn't want to be with them, he wants to be with me because

I'm the person he's in love with. Life with them is boring, it's stifling and he wants to escape.

'It's true, isn't it?' I'd turn to him and he'd look at me and he wouldn't know what to say.

'I've got a bit of a headache, I think I'll go home,' I say once we're out on the pavement and, without waiting for anyone to say anything, I walk quickly off. I'm starting to cry and the sun, which is shining straight at me, is turning my tears into tiny pieces of glass.

I run into Antonio and Abbas as I turn into my street. They're working on a building site just round the corner. They both look at me as if they're noticing the tears in my eyes, but surely I can't expect much sympathy from them if I tell them why I'm upset. They know Michel has a wife and child and that he's no business getting involved with me, and I should know better anyway.

'We're on our way to try to see Pierre in prison,' says Antonio. They think I'm more involved with politics than I am. I feel awkward. I remember what Michel said about Abbas, about how he'd been tortured, about how thousands of Algerians were being tortured and killed because they didn't want to go on being a French colony.

'Come with us if you like. Maybe they'd let you visit Jacqueline,' says Abbas. He's looking straight at me but I can hardly bear to look back, to look into those eyes. When we met him in the café I thought he was a man of about fifty but Michel told me he was only thirty one. He looks even thinner and more hunched up than when I've seen him before, like a frail old man.

'I'm afraid I can't,' I say in a panic. 'I've things I must do.'

I spend the evening looking through the same hair magazines, but I keep seeing Michel with Jeanne and Charlotte. And Abbas's eyes.

Chapter 18

A man's voice is calling out the names of the stations over the loudspeaker: *Cannes, St Raphael, Toulon, Marseille, Lyon* ... It's like a litany - *Mother most pure... Mother conceived without original sin... Star of David... Help of the Sick...*

The compartment's crowded and it smells of sweat and garlic. The man opposite is already cutting himself slices of *saucisson* and spreading them onto a baguette. There's a litre bottle of wine sticking out of the bag at his feet. Beside him is an elderly couple. The man's braces are stretched tight over an enormous stomach. What must it be like to make love with someone as big as that? She's fat too but she's neat and tidy with dyed black hair that she carefully washed and set last night before the journey. They're staring straight ahead, not talking, as if they don't need to, they know what each other's thinking. Or do they? His mind is maybe on that girl he saw walking ahead of him along the street the other evening. And she? Maybe she's dreaming of a life she never had, working in a bank, sitting behind the counter counting all that paper money, with a rubber thimble on her finger to make it easy to pick up the notes. Beside me is a long-legged youth, his head's buried in a comic and sitting beside him is his mum telling him to do up the buttons on his shirt. She's trying to straighten his parting with her fingers and he keeps pushing her away.

I'm staring, without realising, at the man cutting the *saucisson* and suddenly he's smiling at me and offering me a piece. I'm a bit taken aback, shake my head, 'Non merci'. I try to manage a smile. I don't feel like eating. I feel as if I'll never feel like eating ever again. It's been like this for two weeks now. I've never experienced anything like it before. All my life I've had to struggle not to eat too much. I never have biscuits in the cupboard because I know I could eat a whole packet of them just like that. But the last two weeks I have to force myself all the time, and after two mouthfuls I stop.

Nicole noticed I wasn't eating and she told me I should go to the doctor to get some medicine that would bring my appetite back. I'd never been to a French doctor before. It was a Saturday afternoon and there was nobody else in the surgery. He made me lie down and then he started feeling up and down around my stomach. He was an oldish man and I began to think it was a bit funny, him feeling me like that. Nothing else happened, but I still don't like thinking about his hands on me. He gave me a prescription for a large bottle of some pinkish liquid. I have to take two tablespoonfuls of the stuff an hour before every meal. Except that I'm not having any meals.

I don't know why I suddenly lost my appetite. Or rather, I do. It was after Michel stopped wanting to make love with me - or stopped being able to make love with me. He didn't have any desire any more, he said, he couldn't explain why.

'It'll come back, I'm sure it will,' he kept saying, standing there not touching me, not putting his arms around me. We still went on spending the nights together, I couldn't bear the idea of him not being there, even though he didn't want me.

The trouble started the day he put Jeanne and Charlotte on the train back to her parents. He came up to me as I was leaving the salon after work.

'Let's meet in the *Café du Commerce*,' he said. This is the café at the end of my street. I thought it was strange saying to meet there and not at the flat. And when he came into the café he looked really upset and agitated. He sat down opposite me and just announced it.

'Lucy, Jeanne and I have been talking. I think we're going to separate.' He stopped to light a cigarette. 'That means that eventually you and I can get married.'

I was stunned. The thought that was running through my mind was 'But it's not possible. We can't get married because you're married already. I could never ever break the news to my parents that I was going to marry a divorced man.'

I was wondering how I could start saying this but I didn't get a chance, he was going on talking. Jeanne hadn't liked being in Paris, and she likes Nice even less. She hates cities, she said she never again wanted to live in a city, she's happiest in the country. She says she wants to get a job in a school in a village near her parents, and it would be better for Charlotte, to be close to her grandparents. And I could go and see them at week ends. But I think she knows that's not a very satisfactory way of being together and that sooner or later …

'Oh, Lucy,' he said, putting his hand on mine. But I was sitting there, still not knowing how I could say what was on my mind. We could never get married; I couldn't marry a divorced man; it would be the death of my parents.

A few days later I decided I'd go and see the priest. Not the funny little old one that said Mass in the church I still went to every Sunday, but one in a big church in the centre of Nice. They had a priest there who spoke English, it said on the notice outside. I was just hoping that maybe there was some way Michel and Jeanne could get an annulment. Someone in our parish at home, someone called John Byrne, had had his marriage annulled because they said the marriage hadn't been consummated.. His parents never got over the shame. It was a great slur on poor John and his family when it all came out. People said terrible things about the wife, not to have kept quiet about it, John not being able to be a proper husband to her. There were other women who'd gone before her whose husbands had been like that so that they could never have children, but they'd offered it up. Obviously Michel's marriage had been consummated but maybe there were other reasons for getting an annulment.

'Were they married in a church?' the priest asked me. He was called Father André and he was about forty, coarse-featured with a big heavy nose and small intense eyes but with a kind expression.

'Yes, I think so,' I said. Jeanne's parents were not very devout and Jeanne herself didn't go to church, and Michel was an atheist, but they'd followed the custom in the village to have a church wedding and then a big meal in a tent afterwards.

So if they were married in a Catholic church, this Father André didn't see any way round it at all. He looked very sorrowful as he told me. I would never be able to marry with the blessing of the Church.

'You will have to give up this man,' he said. 'You know, my child, we are in this world for a very short time and what does it profit a man if he gains the whole world and suffers the loss of his eternal soul? Is it worth damning yourself for all eternity just for the sake of this man who belongs to another?' He was looking at me with his little eyes.

I wanted to tell him that I wasn't interested in my soul; I just didn't want to upset my parents. But I said nothing. I just went away saying I'd have to think about it.

This was the first time in my life that I was up against what looked like a brick wall, with only a locked door through to the other side and they wouldn't give me the key. At work I couldn't stop thinking about it. One day, I noticed Francesca giving me a funny look and I realised I'd been combing this client's hair for ages and the poor woman was just sitting there. But I couldn't bring myself to talk about it to Michel. It didn't occur to him that I had a problem. It was he who had to make the big decision and he'd made it.

But then he started not being able to make love with me and that was terrible. It was completely unexpected. It put my parents and not being able to marry a married man right out of my mind. Instead, now in the salon I'd be there hoping to catch his eye they way I used to. I tried to coincide with him in the cloakroom, just the two of us, giving him a chance to put his arms around me and whisper something that would make me laugh. But he'd just brush past me with a quick smile, back to a waiting client.

Marseille, Marseille - 2 minutes d'arrêt. The old couple are getting out, reaching down their battered suitcase and brown imitation leather holdall from the rack. 'Au revoir messieurs dames,' they say as they leave ,and the old geezer suddenly flashes me a smile which makes me think he must have been quite a guy when he was young. A man's walking up and down the platform calling out *Glaces, Limonade, Evian,* and the boy's mum is fishing in her purse. The boy leans out of the window and buys two cornets and they sit there licking them frantically before all the ice cream's melted. I light another cigarette. The man opposite has been smoking *Gauloises* non-stop since he finished his *saucisson*. There's quite a fug in the compartment.

A man of about thirty has got in with great patches of sweat showing under his arms. He has a shiny face and his hair's plastered with hair cream that's trickling down his forehead, mixed up with sweat. I turn my head to look out of the window and pull on my cigarette to get less of the smell and think it would be a good idea if there was an advertisement for men like the one for women of a girl holding up her arm and stroking *Odorono* into her arm pit. My armpits are sore because I used *Veet* on them yesterday evening and when you put deodorant on the skin afterwards it really stings. I should do like a lot of these French women and not bother about removing the hair from under my arms, but I think they look a bit coarse with all that fuzz showing whenever they move their arms. Though Marie Claire said once that some men find hairy women sexy.

There are fields and fields with rows and rows of plants with long yellow leaves drooping down their stalks. It's not like any plant I ever saw and if I weren't feeling so depressed I might ask the man opposite what it is but I don't feel like talking. It was only three days ago I made up my mind to leave. I couldn't stand it any longer, Michel not having any desire for me. We'd lie there at night on our backs, not able to sleep much, our sides just touching, talking. But all the time I'd be hoping that he'd turn towards me. But we just talked.

Not about us - we'd stopped talking about us and the future. And we kept off the subject of hair. What we talked about mostly was politics. I still went with him to meet up with Antonio and Gérard and Abbas, and some evenings I even helped them deliver leaflets. I was actually getting more and more involved in the Algerian war, it took my mind off my own problems. For three hours, delivering leaflets telling people about what was going on, I completely forgot about myself, about being unhappy and not able to eat and Michel not wanting me.

Not that I knew much about what was going on; all I could manage was that I thought Algeria should be independent. It was a bit frightening as well, at times. One evening, I got separated from the others and this man suddenly opened his door and came at me with his fists, shouting and swearing. There was a dog behind him, an Alsatian, that was growling and I was scared he was going to set him on me. I went rushing down the stairs terrified, dropping half the leaflets and twisting my ankle. I felt quite good after that, limping round the salon feeling like a soldier wounded in battle. Madame Bizet for once opened her mouth to say something. She noticed the ankle was a bit swollen and she said I should bathe it in the sea.

I was actually going into the sea for a quick dip most evenings after work with George and Francesca. Francesca was still going out with Didier. She said they were madly in love. She'd go off to meet him after we came out of the sea and I'd have a drink with George. Queers are usually very nice to talk to. You can chat to them about clothes and gossip like you can with women, but they're not catty like women. When they say they like the way you do your hair you know they really mean it.

But I couldn't talk to him about Michel, of course. He said once 'Isn't Michel's little girl lovely?' and I'm sure he said that because he wanted to give me a chance to talk, but I just said 'Yes, she is, but I'm not actually that interested in children, I never know what to say to them.' I started telling him about Jonnie and Teresa and how I felt guilty that I wasn't a better aunt to them.

That's another reason why I like talking to George, I suppose. He isn't into the domestic scene either. Though that might be a bit sad for him, not being like other men, not able to look forward to settling down with a nice wife and starting a family. We sit there in the café with our glasses of Pernod and I can see his eye roving around. You can pick up men quite easily here, he says. That's maybe why he decided to spend the summer in Nice. It can't be much use to him otherwise, from the point of view of his career. Though he thinks it will sound quite good back in England, saying he's worked in a French salon on the Riviera.

Dijon, Dijon - 2 minutes d'arrêt. The man with the sweaty armpits is getting out, thank goodness. The *Gauloise* smoker opposite looks across at me now and again as if he'd like to start a conversation and I feel a bit mean, not giving him any encouragement. I'm hoping I'm giving the impression that I don't speak any French, which isn't far from the truth anyway. But he probably notices how sad I'm looking and he maybe thinks he'd be able to cheer me up. He'd shrug his shoulders and tell me *C'est la vie'*.

A young couple have got in who can't stop feeling each other and kissing and laughing. Michel and me wouldn't behave like that. What I like about Michel is the way we just hold each other's eyes for a second or two, or I catch hold of his little finger and curl it round mine, just briefly, or I slide my foot up the side of his leg under the table. I feel all knotted up inside as I think of this.

I haven't eaten anything all day, apart from a bit of bread at breakfast. I remember the apple Michel gave me at the station. I get it out from the bottom of my handbag. There's also the bottle of pink stuff there that I'm supposed to take before meals. And Andrew's letter that I haven't opened yet. He's supposed to be arriving in Paris some time in September.

The next time I'm on a station platform again, I think, as I get off the train at last in the *Gare de Lyon*, 'it'll be up at the *Gare du Nord*. I'll be waiting for Andrew to step off the train.

As I walk into the flat I'm remembering the last time I was there all alone without Monique and the children, that afternoon in February, when Juan knocked on the door. I wonder if Monique has heard from him.

My room is just as I left it with the poster of the girl saying *Some day I'll get organised* still on the wall. Monique hasn't been in. She didn't need the room, she said, and I might be back. So I left a lot of my stuff behind, all my winter clothes and my records and turntable. I just have the two suitcases to unpack.

I put on a record of Harry Belafonte that Monique gave me as a present for my birthday at the end of May. His voice fills the room, sounding like he has honey running down his throat. *Oh Island in the*

Sun … My room is almost as hot as in the flat in Nice. I open the window but the din from the traffic outside means I can't hear the record so I shut it again. I start to cry, only it's more like a few strangled sobs, with Harry Belafonte still singing.

I go down the corridor and into the kitchen, hoping there might be a bottle of wine I could pinch. There's usually a stock of plonk in the cupboard under the sink. On the shelf by the door there's an envelope with a Mexican stamp on it. I hesitate and then pick it up. Juan's tiny handwriting. Monique won't mind if I read it. If she didn't want people to read it, she wouldn't leave it lying around like that.

Ma chère Monique... It's a nice friendly letter telling her about his parish in Mexico City and how poor the people are and what a great consolation the Church is in helping them to bear their hard life. But he misses Paris, he misses his friends, he wishes he could get on a plane every few weeks and arrive in the flat to spend an afternoon with them like he used to. *And how is dear Lucy? I hope one day she will find happiness*, he writes. The check. *Dear Lucy* indeed. He ends the letter with a paragraph about Monique, saying he understands how she feels but she is working for her reward in the next life, and meanwhile her children have a devoted mother who will be a wonderful example to them throughout their lives. And then at the bottom of the page a P.S. *I often remember the few days we spent together last year in the Alps.*

A few months ago I would have been jealous to read that, I think, as I go back to my room with a litre bottle of *Nicholas* and the end of a packet of *biscottes*. But now I feel glad for Monique that she can dream about Juan when she's feeling depressed.

Harry Belafonte's still singing but I'm tired of his voice which is just going on being cheerful. There's a record Michel gave me before he left for Nice of a French singer, George Brassens. I've never even taken it out of its sleeve because I knew I wouldn't understand the French. But Michel played it a lot down in Nice and I got to like it, even though I don't understand half of it. I put it on now. He's got a voice like I imagine the voice of the man opposite me on the train would have, if he'd started singing. It sounds rough from a lifetime of smoking Gauloises. In the first song he's saying that the only thing he cares about is that he's going to meet up with this woman. *J'ai rendez-vous avec vous.* I've a rendez-vous with you and nothing else matters. It's got a light-hearted rhythm to it and we used to dance to it. But the one I want to listen to now is the song at the end. *Il n'y a pas d'amour heureux* -There's no such thing as happy love. I play it over and over as I work my way through the bottle of wine.

In the night I have a dream. I'm being attacked by Michel. He's there with a sword and he's pressing it into me and it's hurting but I'm wanting him to go on, I want to die so that I can become part of him and be with him for ever. I'm filled with joy when I see my clothes are becoming soaked in blood. When I wake up I realise it was the picture of St Teresa that Juan sent me that made me have that dream. I take it out of the drawer where I'd put it, face down, and look at it now, at the sculpture of her prostrate, with the angel holding a spear over her. *The ecstasy of St Teresa* is printed underneath. Juan said that she described how she felt in the ecstasy. It was like a mixture of pain and pleasure that she wanted to go on and on feeling, she didn't want it to stop. Just like me in the dream. Only with her it was God she wanted to be with, and with me it's Michel. Why did I leave Nice like that, saying goodbye for ever? I should have stayed. Maybe he'll ring this evening saying he can't live without me and I'll take the first train back and it will be like it was in July again.

Chapter 19

Marie Claire is filing her nails, moving the emery board vigorously up and down. I've read in a magazine that that's the wrong way to do it. You're supposed to file them just in the one direction. I'm wondering whether I should tell her this. But she's talking about Bertrand's wife, who's in Paris at the moment. This savage attack on her nails is probably meant for Bertrand's wife.

'You mean she's staying with Bertrand?' I ask. We're in the little cloakroom and I'm making an effort to be interested in what Marie Claire's saying. I wish there was more work for me to do but there's hardly anybody coming into the salon at this time of year. Marie Claire looks at me as if I'm daft. Not Bertrand's wife, she's staying in the *George V,* some posh hotel in the eighth district. So I don't know why Marie Claire's so worked up.

'But he's fussing about her so much. She's not happy with the room they've given her, and yesterday she ate fish in their restaurant and it didn't agree with her, and also she's got this pain in her back he thinks she should see a specialist about. *Mince!*' She's broken a nail.

'Marie Claire - Madame Leconte is ready to leave.' Bertrand has put his head round the door. She jumps up, and strides out of the room, glaring at Bertrand as she goes. He gives me a gentle smile. The trouble with Bertrand is that he doesn't want to hurt anybody, he's trying his best to please both Marie Claire and his wife, Antonia.

'Lucy, *ma chère*, how are you?' I've told him I came back from Nice suddenly like that because I was worried about my health as I'd stopped eating.

'I'm feeling much better,' I say. I'm not, of course, and he can see that. It doesn't help to have so little work to occupy me.

'That woman who came in this morning to make an appointment,' I say. 'Do you think I could take her on?' I'm thinking of the competition. The woman had jet black hair, very straight, that she was wearing in a conventional page boy style. I could imagine cutting it in a sort of wedge shape, coming down over her left eye, and cropped at the back.

'But she asked specially for me,' said Bertrand. 'I don't think...' Of course not. Imagine how outraged the woman would be if she turned up and found she'd been palmed off with Lucy. Bertrand went back into the salon, his next client had arrived. The only person I'm seeing today is the duchess this afternoon.

In a week's time Andrew would be here.

Dear Lucy, I read, when I finally got round to opening his letter. *I hope this catches you before you leave for Paris. I'm arriving Saturday week. The train gets in at 6 o'clock at the Gare du Nord. I hope that's okay and that you'll be able to meet me.*

I've booked a hotel near the English Church in the Avenue Hoche. Somebody at church gave me the address. It's called the Hotel de l'Univers and it's not too expensive.

Looking forward to seeing you, love, Andrew

I'd been a bit surprised by the letter. Andrew's usually chattier than that and more loving. And why has he gone ahead and booked a hotel? I hadn't actually said he couldn't stay at the flat. It's empty, except for me. Claude might be there from time to time, Monique said, but she and the children won't be back before the end of next week. I'd assumed Andrew would want to stay with me.

'Lucy!' It's Marie Claire again. 'There's a girl just turned up. She wants a cut in a hurry. An American.'

She's very tall and thin and she has hunched shoulders and longish mousy hair in no particular style, and a serious look about her, and she's wearing a sack dress you know didn't come from *Monoprix*.

'Just give me the same style again, I just want a bit off,' she says.

She's delighted she's fallen on an English girl. She starts talking about the wonderful art galleries there are here in Paris. She's just discovered this Museum of Modern Art which is up the road and which is fantastic - full of pictures by people I've never heard of. 'Lots of cubists', she says. I'm worried she's going to ask me what I think about cubists and all I can think of are oxo cubes and she can't mean them. I start talking to her about her hair.

'How about me cutting it a lot shorter?' I say. 'You have a nice shaped head. And pretty ears,' I add as I lift up her lank locks. 'And your hair's a good texture. You could have it clipped back behind your ears and then curling round.'

She looks at me as if this is the first time anybody has said anything nice to her. She hesitates and then takes a deep breath like someone's asked her to come to bed with them and says 'Why not?'

'Thanks a lot, Lucy,' she smiles at me an hour later as she presses a huge tip into my hand. 'And don't forget to go and see the cubists!' Well, maybe I should. I've talked her into having an auburn rinse as well, and she walks out of the salon looking almost chic, with her shoulders straight back.

'One day when I'm famous,' (I'm thinking) 'that girl will say: 'But I know that name. That's the young woman who cut my hair in Paris that summer.'

'Well done, Lucy,' says Bertrand as he watches her disappear. He's imagining her going back to her swanky hotel and loads of other Americans descending on us, wanting the same treatment. I must say, I feel more cheerful too. I decide I'll go and see Vinny after work today.

Before I got that letter from Andrew I'd been struggling with my conscience about what I should do about him. I was worried that I was being dishonest, leading him on when I wasn't serious about him while he *was* serious, wanting us to get married and all. I should never have invited him to Paris, to give him fresh hope. He'd arrive all excited that we were going to have a dream week together, just the two of us, no hole in the corner fumblings any more, completely free. Maybe I should telephone him to tell him not to come, I was thinking. I should pluck up courage and be blunt.

'I'm very sorry but I really don't think there's a future for us. I'm very fond of you but I just don't want to marry you.'

Or should I let him come and we'd have a nice week together and then at the end of it a sad parting? But it wouldn't be a nice week, I'd be missing Michel, I wouldn't have any desire to make love with another man. It would be a terrible week, I should phone him straight away to put him off.

But now his letter, sounding so distant and saying he's fixed up to stay in a hotel. Why am I not relieved and glad? The problem's solved. We'll have a relaxed week together, I may even confide in him about Michel, we may even make love, for old times' sake, and then we'll say goodbye. Both of us will know, without saying anything, that this is the last time. Gradually, my mum will have to come to terms with the fact that Andrew and I will never marry.

But now I'm disturbed at the idea of him not finding me attractive any more. I'm beginning to want him, like in the old days when we started going out together. I'm in the back row of the stalls again and he's feeling my breast under my blue woollen jumper, and I'm embarrassed and moved, all at the same time. Nobody has ever touched me there before.

So maybe it isn't the end. Maybe it isn't dishonest of me to have invited him. Maybe there's still hope for him. Next week I might even find myself saying 'Let's get married.' He'd be overjoyed, so would my parents and I'd be out of this mess I've got myself into. Everything would be simple. My mother would rush out and buy herself a smart rig out from Kendall's and we'd have a lovely Catholic wedding with Teresa and Cathy, Andrew's little sister, as bridesmaids and Jonnie as a page. And now that Andrew's going to be settled in Leeds with a proper job as a quantity surveyor, I could get a job there too, and eventually have my own business. It would be goodbye to this misery of missing Michel.

The bus has just gone past the Boulevard St Michel. Mine's the next stop. I catch a glimpse of Notre Dame through the trees. I don't feel like going there today, I've had enough of religion for the time being, especially if I'm going to marry Andrew and return to the fold. It's starting to rain and I'll get drenched walking up the hill to Vinny's flat. I didn't bring a mac with me and I never carry an umbrella.

'Mademoiselle will permit?' A man with a strong accent who looks like Alberto is bowing in front of me with his black umbrella.

'No thanks,' I shout as I race up the hill away from him.

Vinny's there with this small, intense-looking man. It's the artist who did the portraits of the women that were propped up round the walls watching us while we were dancing. He's called Marc and he's from Belgium. I'm quite excited to meet him.

'I noticed your paintings last time I was here,' I tell him. 'I loved them. I think you've made the women look like themselves, the way they want to be, not like the women you see in magazines, I think they're super.'

I want to go on to say how they've inspired me as a hairdresser but he's shrugging his shoulders as if he's not very interested in what I'm saying. Vinny's handing me a glass of wine. She's wearing a sleeveless sack dress in emerald green which shows off her slender arms and delicate wrists and her creamy skin. She gives me a knowing smile and I suddenly remember the pass she made at me the last time I saw her and feel uncomfortable.

'Oh those portraits - I've sold them all. This guy came in and bought the lot,' says Marc. 'I don't paint like that any more. That is the past.' Vinny flashes him a smile and puts her arm around him. Are they lovers? Where's Steve?

'I'm sorry,' I say, 'I really liked them.' I'm feeling a bit the way I felt when they knocked down the old pub at the end of our street.

'If I had known I would have made you a present of one. But they were old-fashioned. Now I paint with my soul. Let me show you.'

Against the wall, instead of the portraits of the women, there are two large pictures, all bright colours mixed up together - purples, yellows, greens, blues, reds, oranges.

'I like the colours,' I say. I feel I have to say something, but I don't actually like the colours at all. I like things to match or, at least, I like colours that go together. I'm not as bad as my mother who thinks you should always have matching gloves, handbag, shoes and hat, I like a bit of contrast. But I'm finding these pictures much too harsh and garish.

I'm trying to figure out what they're of, too, but I can't make sense of them. I'm relieved when Marc starts talking about them, explaining.

'You see, these are examples of what is known as Free Art, *l'art libre*. In Art School they tell you, 'Draw this, paint that.' So the result is boring, boring, because it does not come from you, from inside yourself, from your soul.' He's beating his chest as he talks in the place where I suppose he imagines his soul to be. 'You paint a vase of flowers - very pretty - or a boat on the sea - very nice. With stormy clouds up above, maybe, to add a touch of emotion ...'

Vinny's lighting up a cigarette. By the smell of it, it's pot. She passes it to Marc to have a pull on it. What will I do when it's my turn? I'll try it, yes I will. But she takes it back and puts it between her lips. I get one of my *Raleighs* out of my handbag, as Marc goes on about how you have to free yourself before you can paint.

'You have to empty your mind,' he keeps saying, 'and then you can create. All this thinking, this planning of what you are going to do, all the time saying to yourself : *I must be careful to do this, I must be careful not to do that*. All these restrictions, this is not freedom. We are bound in by so much convention. We have to free ourselves. N'est-ce pas, Vinny? Isn't that right?' He turns to her and takes the cigarette out of her mouth and has a deep puff. 'We have to empty our minds and then we can create.' He looks admiringly at his two pictures.

'How was Nice?' Vinny asks me, installing herself on the big floor cushion. I hesitate and then sit down beside her. I'm in my mid-calf lilac cotton dress with the wide skirt, which I spread out either side of me. It's still damp from the rain; I got soaked running up the road. Vinny lent me a raspberry coloured towel for my hair when I arrived and it's draped around my shoulders.

I sent her a card from Nice - back in July when I was so happy. I make a face now.

'I'm glad to be back in Paris,' I say. I almost start telling them about Michel but I've never talked to anyone about Michel - except for that priest. So I just stay silent. But they can sense I'm depressed, though they don't ask me any questions. I feel easy with them, I feel they understand suffering, that sort of suffering, the sort that comes from an unhappy love affair. *Il n'y a pas d'amour heureux.* I ask them if they've heard of George Brassens and at the mention of music Vinny immediately says I must listen to the record Steve's made. She puts it on and lights up another cigarette and this time I take it from her and inhale as deeply as I can. I suddenly feel the need to empty my mind too.

Meriche comes in as we're sitting there, listening to all these funny sounds swooping up and down, with Vinny's voice whispering eerily in the background. I'd been floating off into a dream world, starting to think that Marc's paintings were the most beautiful paintings I'd ever seen in all my life, but at the sight of Meriche I'm back in Nice. Is Meriche involved in the struggle for independence? Michel said all the Algerians working in France were. Did Meriche go on marches too? I think of telling him about the march I went on in Nice, I want to talk to him about Algeria, to tell him I'm on his side but he's installed himself on the mattress in the corner with a Moroccan blanket on it and he's closed his eyes and he's moving his head slightly from side to side. I'm just wondering if I won't go across and sit down beside him when Steve walks in.

Vinny's got up and she's over the other side of the room with her arm around Marc. Steve is towering over me, looking down at me and I'm staring up at him.

'Hi,' I say and the next moment he's beside me on the cushion, kissing me and pushing me back down so that I'm lying there, feeling really stupid and uncomfortable, wondering how all those glamorous Hollywood stars managed to look so relaxed, reclining on sofas with men leaning over them. Then he's got his hand under my skirt and he's pulling at my knickers and now he's touching me down there and I can see Vinny standing behind him, looking. I struggle to get onto my feet, pushing him away as hard as I can.

'Whoa,' he says, 'not so rough.' He's laughing as if he thinks I'm a silly girl to be so embarrassed. I want to leave but I'd feel even sillier just walking away like that so I ask Vinny if I can have a cup of coffee. Steve has strolled over to talk to Marc. I follow her into the kitchen and for a few minutes I stand there watching her, trying to recover from Steve going at me like that.

'I've a friend coming over from Manchester next week,' I tell her at last, finding a bit of wall to lean against. 'He's called Andrew, I've known him a long time. It's a bit of a bore. He's very square. I don't know what I'm going to do with him.' I feel really mean as I say this.

'You could bring him round here,' says Vinny, handing me a cracked cup with lipstick on the side. I try to find a clean bit of the rim and take a sip.

'He's just qualified as a quantity surveyor,' I say, pulling a face and feeling even more disloyal. Vinny gives a shudder. I know she's thinking semi-detached houses and lace curtains and a ding-dong door bell and a nine to five job with the little wife standing on the doorstep waving hubbie goodbye.

'My Mum'd love me to marry Andrew and settle down,' I say in a rush. Vinny says nothing to this as if it's not even worth considering. 'What about *your* parents?' I ask her.

'I've no idea what they want. I don't have much to do with them. They know nothing about me.'

Lucky her. Only it must be strange to be so out of touch as that with your parents. I wouldn't like that, all the same.

'Anyway, bring him round,' she says as we go back into the room. There's a look in her eye. I remember at her party two men in suits over in one corner, sticking out like sore thumbs. Maybe she gets a kick out of leading men like that astray, seducing them, weaving spells around them as she blows smoke into their eyes and then floats off mysteriously, with them stumbling after.

'Okay,' I say, 'I'll come round with him one evening.' I start to see Vinny in a floaty dress popping a cigarette between Andrew's lips and then raising her arms and dancing in front of him, her head thrown back so that her blonde hair is almost touching her waist, her hips swaying. And Andrew not knowing what to do, especially with me there looking on.

But I could be somewhere else with Steve. I'd look over my shoulder at Andrew as I disappeared with Steve into some inner room, flashing him a this-is-Paris-not-the-North-of-England smile as I went.

'See you next week then,' I say to Vinny as I leave, looking briefly across at Steve. I'd been avoiding catching his eye because I didn't want him to think that I liked men to be fresh like that, but I didn't want to give the impression that I was a prude either. Though, if I'd been a prude, I'd certainly have slapped his face. There was this girl, Betty, back in Manchester, who was always slapping men's faces. She should have been flattered, I always thought, when they made passes at her, because she has a face like the back of a bus and no figure. But, according to her, she spent her time shouting 'Who do you think I am?' at them.

I'm thinking this as I wait at the bus stop, when this car stops. It's full of people of about the same age as me. Two of them put their heads out of the window and ask me if I want a lift so I hesitate for a moment and then I get in. The men are laughing and talking all at once and their girl friends are smiling and looking at me. They're really pleased when they discover I'm English. They're going to a party somewhere and they want me to come with them but I tell them I have to go home. So they drop me at the end of my street and hoot at me all the way as far as the Marcels' door. When I tell Bertrand next day he thinks it was very foolish of me, I could have got kidnapped, they could have been part of the white slave traffic. But I thought they were just really nice and friendly, probably students.

Back at the flat it's early still so I get out the *Hairdressers' Journal.*

Chapter 20

Nounou arrives as usual just as I'm about to leave for *Bertrand's*. 'I haven't slept a wink all night,' she tells me every time, as she wraps her blue pinafore around herself and ties it in a tight knot at the front. She's a liverish looking woman in her fifties with sad eyes and enormous circles under them. She lives in the same district as where Michel was brought up and has the same accent. Maybe she knows Michel's mother.

When I arrive in the salon, Marie Claire's standing behind the mahogany desk in her cream blouse with the big bow. She's looking tense. I know there's something she wants to tell me and, at the first opportunity, she whispers it in my ear.

'C'est un cancer,' she breathes. I don't know what she's talking about and then I remember she'd told me Bertrand was worried about his wife having trouble with her back, and him wanting her to see a doctor about it.

'You mean … ?' I start off and she says, 'Eh oui,' and nods her head up and down and pulls a face and says Eh oui again. Over lunch she can talk more freely. His wife's in hospital with cancer of the spine as far as I can make out, and she's being operated on tomorrow.

'It's terrible, terrible. La pauvre... The poor woman,' she keeps repeating. 'And she's only forty nine. That's young, you know.'

Then she jabs at a tomato and bursts out 'But I don't know why Bertrand's in such a state about it. He's always called her a pain in the neck. He has only stayed married to her out of duty and because the Catholic Church forbids divorce. But the way he's behaving you would think that she is the great love of his life. 'This is tragic, this is tragic,' he keeps on. I told him he should get a room in a hotel close to the hospital so he could be by her side all his free time. I expected him to say that No, no, that was completely unnecessary. But he thought it was a very good idea and how kind and generous of me to suggest it.'

'Ma chère, que tu es bonne. You are a very good woman, you are so kind, so generous. I don't deserve you.'

Marie Claire stretches out her hand and puts it over mine and looks at me earnestly as she does an imitation of Bertrand. I can't help smiling, after a second, Marie Claire smiles back, shaking her head.

In the afternoon Bertrand comes up to me.

'Lucy, can you take my next client, it's Madame Cousin? I'm not feeling very well,' he says, 'I must go home.' He's not in the next day, the day of the operation, nor the next when Marie Claire comes up to me as I'm taking off my jacket in the little cloakroom.

'There's no hope,' she whispers. 'C'est sans espoir. They opened her up but it was no good, they just stitched her up again. They can do nothing. Bertrand broke the news to her this morning.'

Bertrand appears the next day, looking drawn and wild-eyed, and we all say how sorry we are about his wife. Marie Claire is standing there straight and tight-lipped, looking as if she's trying to be on her best behaviour.

'I'm very worried about him. He hasn't eaten for three days,' she tells me over lunch. I'm wondering if she's going to start on about why she doesn't see why he should be so upset, but she just goes on eating her *salade niçoise* in silence.

When we get back to the salon who's there at the reception counter but Madame Bizet, in a beige costume and a matching hat and looking quite different from in Nice. I've got a free slot so I'm able to take her straight away. She wants the same as usual, just a little bit off. If I were feeling brighter in myself I'd be dreaming up something more adventurous for her. But the memory of what happened about Madame Chenier sitting in this same seat also put me off. Besides, I wouldn't have enough hair to work on, though I could make a feature of that, ending up with something like my father's attempt at growing grass in the garden out the back : fresh green blades with the light shining through them. Instead I'm there with the scissors worrying she's going to ask me for news of the people in the salon in Nice. 'What about that nice man with the dark hair, Michel I think he was called?' He still hasn't rung though I've been back 10 days.

The phone's ringing as I come through the door that evening. I rush to answer it. It's Alberto. *'Ma chérie.'* He's heard from Bertrand that I'm back in Paris. He sounds tender, like a dear friend, promising reassurance and comfort. When are we going to see each other? It has been so long. Am I free on Saturday evening? I'm doing nothing. We fix up to meet - in *Fouquet's* again.

I've hardly put down the phone when Claude comes through the front door with his brief case, looking, as always, impeccably groomed. 'Like a tailor's dummy,' my Mum would say, only he's too short and stout to be a tailor's dummy. His hair is smoothed back to cover the bald patch and he's dressed in a beautifully cut light grey suit, a colour that shows off his tan. We shake hands and he asks me if I've had a good summer in Nice and would I like a drink. He strides across to the cocktail cabinet. Although he's a short man he moves with great authority. Monique's told me that his hero is Napoleon who wasn't very tall either.

He opens the door of the cocktail cabinet with a flourish. A light comes on and it's like Aladdin's cave with all the glass bottles filled with amber and ruby and emerald liquid. I can see the Green and Yellow Chartreuse Juan and I helped ourselves to - just tiny glasses so that it wouldn't be missed, though by the end we must have made quite an inroad into the two bottles that afternoon. Claude turns round to ask me what I'd like, so I go over to see what there is. As if I didn't know.

He's putting on a record - just like Juan used to do - only instead of Mozart's Clarinet concerto, it's music from some Opera or other. He seems surprised when I say I've never heard of it. I'm just in from work and I'm still in my short straight skirt which barely covers my knees, which is okay in the salon where I hardly ever sit down. But in this deep armchair I'm having to be careful to sit with my legs close together.

He's looking at me, making me feel nervous. I'm glad I don't work for him, I'm thinking. 'Miss Smart, take a letter. Miss Smart get me the file on Sales for 1955. Miss Smart undo your blouse so I can see that pointy little bra you're wearing underneath.'

'So, Lucy,' he keeps saying as he fondles his cut glass tumbler. He's poured himself a large whisky and soda. I've already drunk most of my dry Martini, trying to think of something to say. On the shelf behind him there are these huge books with titles like *Les Cathédrales de France* or *L'Histoire de France*

Volumes I à X or *La Renaissance.* I notice a big dictionary among them and remember there's something that I want to find out about. Michel and his friends spent a whole evening once talking about something called *le matérialisme dialectique.* I asked one of them what it meant and he said it was the same in English - dialectical materialism. 'But what's that?' I asked him but he wasn't very good at explaining, not in English anyway.

But Claude is very learned - he must be, with all those big books - so I ask him now what dialectical materialism is. He seems a bit surprised by the question, but then he jumps to his feet and says it's easy, all we have to do is look it up in the dictionary. He gets down this massive book and lays it on the desk and reads out what it says. But it's in French so I tell him I don't understand, so then he looks at me and the next minute he's come round the side of the desk and he's throwing himself upon me as I'm sitting there. They're huge armchairs so there's plenty of room for me and him on top of me but this is the last thing I want.

'No, no, please, no,' I say as he starts undoing my blouse. I manage to wriggle and push at him with my free hand so that, after a moment, to my relief he understands and returns to his armchair. But I can't very well go on asking him about dialectical materialism after that. I'm still holding my glass, so I drain it and put it on the desk and get up, trying to act as if nothing has happened.

'I'd better be going,' I say, trying to sound relaxed and friendly. 'I've got a rendezvous - I have to get ready.' This isn't true but, after what's happened, I don't want to be under the same roof for a while.

'Sans rancune?' he says as he stands up.

'Oui,' I say, wondering what *rancune* means. Without *what*? When I get back to my room I look up *rancune* and it says *rancour*. So I look up *rancour* and it says *a feeling of bitter unforgiving hatred.* That seems a bit strong. I certainly don't feel that. In a way I feel a little flattered that he finds me attractive, him being so full of himself, but I also think it's going to be awkward now, living under the same roof, imagining him there, desiring me all the time.

I hear the bang of the front door. That's good, he's gone out, so I don't need to go out after all. I plug in the little electric stove, empty a packet of *Maggi* soup into a saucepan, add water and stand there stirring it with the door ajar, listening for the phone. It's getting on for eight o'clock. Michel will soon be on his way home, or having a drink with Antonio and Gérard, or at a political meeting about Algeria. In a few minutes it will be too late for him to ring.

Bertrand was supposed to be doing my hair today in preparation for my date with Alberto this evening but he's not there so I get Xavier to do it instead. Xavier is the man who replaced Michel and he fancies himself as a second Antoine who's the most famous hairstylist in France. He's sure it would suit me to have my hair swept up on top and tied with a bow but first of all he gets one of the girls to give it a copper rinse so that it's the colour of a forest in autumn, then he sweeps it up and sticks lots of pins in it. I walk home feeling like an African woman carrying the week's wash to the river on her head. This evening I'll snap out of it, I'll get dressed up to the nines. I'll wear my spiky heels and my dangling earrings and the tight black dress Monique passed on to me that she got too fat for and I'll feel like a completely different woman.

I have the flat to myself so I open up the cocktail cabinet and pour a large dry Martini and then go along to the bathroom with it. It's crazy to be having a bath, just after having my hair done, but Xavier's put so much lacquer on it, it's as stiff as a board. There's some swish Swiss bath stuff in the cabinet that's supposed to invigorate you so I pour a whole lot of this into the bath and just lie there propped up so as not to get my hair too wet, with *Radio Luxembourg* on my tranny and my glass of Martini beside me.

It's a very posh bathroom with tiles on the walls and floor and the whole of one wall is a mirror. When I get out of the bath I stand there, inspecting my fading tan and checking to see if I'm developing what the French call *cellulite*. I've known about flabby arms and hairy legs and spots and dandruff and bad breath and underarm odour ever since I was a teenager, but I'd never heard of this affliction till I came to France. But you can't pick up a French magazine without finding advertisements for *produits contre la cellulite*. It sounds worse than TB.

I decide I'll trim the hair down there. I'd never thought of doing that before but in a French film I saw last week this girl who'd just come out of the bath was taking the scissors and bending her head. That's all you saw but you knew what she was doing. Funny how it's so much curlier down there than anywhere else. Even Michel, who's got very straight hair.

Here I go again thinking of Michel. I heard this little boy in the bus the other day going on to his mum about something. 'Tu peux pas changer de disc?' she snapped at him. 'Can't you change the record?' I'm as bad as the little boy, I keep playing the same record, I can't help it. Why doesn't he phone me to say he can't live without me? The radio's playing *I wonder who's kissing her now*. I'm suddenly thinking of the words. It's never occurred to me before. Has Michel got friendly with someone else since I left?

I totter down the *Champs Elysées*, feeling like a million dollars. Or a tart. There's a group of men who've just passed who were nudging each other and ogling me and giving me wolf whistles. And there's one behind me now, an American, trying to talk to me in French 'Voolez voos venir avec moy?' I stick my chin in the air and try to imagine I'm the Duchess of Kent. My mum's a great admirer of the Duchess of Kent, she thinks she's very elegant.

As I get near to *Fouquet's* I see Alberto already there, sitting outside under the red awning with his glass of something, reading his Italian newspaper. I stand on the pavement watching him for a second. There's a man and woman sitting at a table close to where I'm standing. He's big and fat with an untidy moustache. She's much younger, with long straight black hair and a pale skin and large liquid brown eyes. She reminds me of Francesca. She dresses like her too – she's in a neat-fitting brown linen dress. The American who's been following me is still just behind me. I must move forward to join Alberto, bent over his newspaper. But at this moment he looks up and I see his face and it's the face of a stranger. I have nothing in common with this man, I don't want to be with him, spending the evening having silly talk that doesn't mean anything. And then we'll go back to his flat and for an hour it will be all excitement, after which I'll want to go home. And then I'll be back in my room in the grey dawn between my cold sheets and nothing will have changed.

There's a taxi rank on the other side of the road and the traffic lights are red. I rush across. *Rue Galilée*, I say to the taxi driver as I get in. I sit there looking out at the traffic. I lean back, trying to give the impression to any passer by who may happen to glance in that I'm on my way to a fashionable dinner party. What was I thinking of, fixing up to meet Alberto? As if my life isn't complicated enough. Next Saturday Andrew will be arriving.

Chapter 21

I get out of the Metro opposite the entrance to the *Gare du Nord*. I haven't been up in this district since I arrived last January, emerging out onto this street in my new sage green coat with the imitation fur collar and matching hat. I hadn't given the porter a big enough tip and I was still recovering from his curses as I stood waiting for a taxi. I've got plenty of small change now in my purse to give to Andrew's porter when he gets off the train. I'm only just in time.

The first feeling I have when I catch sight of him jumping onto the platform is embarrassment. He looks so English in his blazer and grey flannels, and that tie I bought him at Christmas. And his short back and sides and the dead straight parting. I want to run my hands over his head and ruffle it all up.

Because that's the second feeling that comes over me as I see him - tenderness. All the good times we've had together seem to have arrived with him. I walk quickly towards him, wrap my arms round him and we stand there for a moment, hugging each other. All around us are people struggling with cases, calling for porters.

'Is your case heavy?' I'm surprised he hasn't got it out of the compartment himself. 'Do you need a porter? We'd better find one.'

'No, I don't need a porter, I've only got this,' he says, holding up a small brown case. Is he going to spend the week in the clothes he's got on? There can't be room in that little case for anything much except pyjamas and a toothbrush. How long is he staying? 'I'll explain,' he adds. What is there to explain? What is he going to tell me?

'Let's find a café where we can sit and have a drink,' I say.

It's Saturday evening and the pavement cafés are crowded with people having aperitifs. There's no room outside so we have to go inside to a table next to where three young fellers in black leather jackets are playing *ping-foot* at the pinball machine - pulling knobs and shaking the sides of the table and making a terrible noise. The juke box is playing a Johnny Hallyday song.

'It's this new job,' he says. 'They want me to start next week. I said I couldn't possibly start before Tuesday, but this means I'll have to leave here Monday morning.'

'I'm going to have a *Dubonnet*,' I say, getting out my cigarettes. 'You can put water in it to make it into a long drink.' Andrew says he'll have the same.

'Deux Dubonnets à l'eau,' I say to the waiter, relieved when he doesn't screw up his face and say *quoi?* and I have to repeat the order. I light my cigarette, while Andrew looks on. He's given up, he told me in a letter

'So we've only got tomorrow really. I pick up my *Dubonnet* and take a pull on my cigarette. I contemplate trying to blow him a smoke ring but the look on his face stops me.

'You look brown,' he says. 'You must have got a lot of sun in Nice.'

'It was too hot down there, you'd have hated it,' I say. He'd have loved it, lying in the water with me, with the waves washing over us.

'Lucy,' he says - he hasn't touched his drink - 'Lucy, we must have a talk. That's mostly what I've come over for, you know. I need to know whether there's a future for us.' He's looking me straight in the eyes and I don't know what to say. This is the moment I've been dreading ever since I left Manchester.

'Yes, but not just now, you've only just arrived,' I say, 'let's not think about it for a little while. Let's just enjoy Paris. It's really nice having you here.'

'But I need to know. Now that I've got a job and I'm moving to Leeds I need to know where I stand.' He's looking so tense and earnest.

'I realise that,' I say. I smile at him but inside I'm in a panic. If only I could say, 'Yes I'll marry you, and we'll settle down in a semi detached in Leeds, with a ding-dong bell,' then everything would be wonderful. We'd be able to walk along the Seine together in the sunshine and stand on the bridges holding hands and kissing, like all the other young couples here in Paris.

The tune on the juke box had changed and some man is singing *You belong to me.* I stub out my cigarette and reach for the packet to light another one. Andrew stretches out his hand as if to stop me but then thinks better of it.

'Let's go to the hotel, so you can check in,' I say as we finish our drinks.

We take the bus, instead of the Metro, so we can go past the *Opéra* and up the *Champs Elysées* and I can point to the avenue where the salon is.

'You'd easily find a job in Leeds, you know, Lucy. And one day you'd be able to open your own salon with *Lucy of Paris* over the door.' We laugh, and he reaches for my hand and I fit it into his, just like in the old days at the cinema. He has big comfortable hands, surprisingly soft for a man's.

'*Lucy of Paris*!' he repeats. 'I'm sure there'd be some rich businessman who'd be ready to put up the money for you to have your own salon.'

But, at the end of the day, I'd still be coming back to Andrew and the ding-dong bell. And if we had children I wouldn't be coming back at all because I wouldn't be going out. It would be Andrew coming back and me at home waiting for him, asking him if he's had a good day at the office.

Outside the hotel I tell him I'll wait in the café down below. I know if I go up with him he'll want to start kissing me and then we'll make love but I need time to get used to him again. Besides, we'd be no further on after it, I'd still not know what I'm going to say to him before he goes away on Monday morning.

Two men at the next table keep looking across at me. I'm feeling good in my new beige terrylene shirtwaister and the matching slip-on court shoes with the high heels, higher than I normally wear. I'll stop worrying about what I'm going to say to Andrew before he leaves. I'll know when the time comes. Between now and then, let's enjoy ourselves.

When he reappears, he's put Brylcreem on his hair and his hands smell of soap. I ask him if he's hungry.

'We could have frankfurters and chips here,' I say, pointing to the sign which says *frankforts frites*. 'Or you could come back to the flat and I'll make us a meal. All the shops in the little street round the corner will still be open. We could buy a baguette and some wine and cheese and some funny sausage and eat in the Marcel's big kitchen. They're away, they don't come back till tomorrow evening.'

As we get up I can feel the two men's eyes upon us. I put my arm round Andrew's waist. I bet they think we're two typical English lovers, here on our honeymoon.

It's raining. I lie there watching the silvery drops running down the windowpane. It's beginning to get light. Andrew is still asleep beside me, one hand between his thighs, the other resting on my shoulder. He has the same colour of skin as the cherubs floating around in those paintings I saw in Rome and, in sleep, the same soft angelic face. His hair is ruffled, going in all directions. I imagine it longer, curlier. I feel sad, I feel he really loves me.

I slip carefully out of bed not to disturb him and put on the scratchy pink nylon wrap I bought in the *Galeries Lafayette* sale in June that I've hardly ever worn. The room looks strangely empty - I pushed all my junk under the bed before I went out yesterday evening. The table, which is usually strewn with hairbrushes, combs, hairpins, scarves, lipsticks, scrumpled up bits of paper, is bare except for a glass vase I borrowed from the kitchen and filled with the bunch of deep red carnations I took home from the salon. It's usually Marie Claire who, on Saturday evenings, takes home the flowers adorning the reception desk but yesterday she said 'Lucy, these are for your room. You have your friend, Andrew, coming, haven't you?' She's as bad as my mother, she thinks Andrew sounds like a good catch. When I go in on Tuesday, she'll be there expecting me to make an announcement.

'Et alors?' she'll say, hanging over the desk with her eyes all lit up, a bit like Maureen in Manchester who was always greeting other girls with 'So, how did it go?'

'Above all, he is free to marry,' she said the other day when I told her he was coming over, thinking, of course, of herself and Bertrand, and thinking of Michel too, no doubt.

I trip over one of Andrew's shoes and he stirs in his sleep. His clothes are all over the floor, mixed up with mine. I get dressed and put my raincoat on and go out to buy croissants in the *Boulangerie/Pâtisserie* on the corner. There's already a queue of French women there, though it's only just nine o'clock. They must be on their way home from early Mass with those silly transparent rain covers protecting their expensive hats. They take ages because they're all buying tarts or cakes for the Sunday lunch and the assistant has to put these in a box and do it up nicely with ribbon saying: 'Et avec ça, Madame?' and 'Je vous remercie, Madame'. The woman in front of me's choosing small, individual cakes - chocolate é*clairs*, and little blueberry tarts, and something called *mille feuilles,* which means *a thousand leaves.*

'Oh no, I think after all I'd better take ten. Give me two more *éclairs*,' she says.

So the assistant has to find a bigger box. My purchase takes all of thirty seconds. I get four croissants *au beurre* - rather than the cheaper ones made with margarine or something.

There's a faint noise coming from the kitchen when I get back. That must be Claude. He must have arrived late last night. Monique and the children are not due back till later today. He'll have found our dirty plates and knives and glasses all scattered around, and the wine stains on the Formica top that Monique's always careful to wipe up immediately. We were going to clear up this morning.

I don't feel like meeting him so I open the door of my room as quietly as possible and nip inside, scaring the life out of Andrew. He'd been standing there stark naked by the washbasin and, as the door opened, he'd grabbed hold of a towel and was holding it in front of him. I laugh and put my arms around him, but then I move away quickly and start plugging in the little electric stove.

'I bought us some croissants,' I say, avoiding looking at him still standing by the washbasin. I want to fill the saucepan with water but I'm waiting for him to move away and start getting dressed, which at last he does. At which point I feel a tiny pang of regret.

I spoon some instant coffee into the two blue bowls I bought in *Prisunic* the week after I arrived. I couldn't find any big cups anywhere, in any of the shops. All those snooty shop assistants wrinkling up their noses as I tried to describe what I was looking for and saying 'Ça n'existe pas, mademoiselle' and turning away as if they'd something better to do with their time than listen to a stupid English girl asking for a thing they'd never heard of and which therefore didn't exist.

I don't want to go into the kitchen to get the milk in case I meet Claude so we drink it black with sugar, which seems more continental anyway, and I ask Andrew what he'd like to do with the day. It's still raining.

'We could go and see a film,' he says. 'What time is Mass, by the way?'

'Eleven, we've plenty of time. So, we could go to the cinema this afternoon, and then this evening we could go and see this friend of mine, Vinny. She lives the other side of Paris but we can get a bus most of the way.'

We hardly talk on the bus. The film was a stupid American one but it was the only one we could find that was in English with subtitles. I keep thinking of questions I could ask him about his job and where he's going to live in Leeds, but this is a topic I'd rather steer clear of just now. Instead, I say things like 'That's the Louvre' or 'Look, you can just see the Eiffel Tower over there.'

'Would you like to see *Notre Dame*?' I ask him as we get off the bus. 'It's just down the road.'

Seeing the towers through the trees is suddenly making me want to go back there. Evening Mass is just coming to an end as we go through the door. I realise I don't have anything to put over my head. Andrew produces a handkerchief – a big white nicely-ironed one with 'A' in blue in one corner.

'You walk around, I'll just stay here,' I whisper to him. I kneel where I can see the statue of Our Lady with the Infant Jesus in her arms that I really like. She's not at all like in those *Annunciation* paintings, where she's just kneeling there when this great big angel comes flying in through the window and tells her she's preggers. I feel really sorry for her. But here she looks as if she's pleased with the turn her life has taken.

I start thinking about me and Andrew. I know he cares about me and he knows that I want to have a career, but, deep down, I feel he can't really understand why any woman would want to go out and work if they had a man to keep them who thought the world of them. But I love my job, I'm not just doing it till I find a man. And I know I've a good chance of winning that competition next month. I'm just as talented as either Michel or George anyway.

Andrew has finished looking round and he's come to kneel down beside me. He gives me a smile, the crooked smile that breaks up his face. I'm sure he thinks I've been praying for guidance.

'Shall we go?' he whispers, so I get off my knees and we set off.

'Vinny, Steve, Bill, Marc, Han, Tan ...' I stand introducing Andrew, though you can hardly see any of them as the curtains are drawn and the only lights are naked purple and green bulbs stuck into bottles converted into lamps. They're all sitting on the floor and Steve is doing things with the tape recorder. He's got his guitar by his side and he picks it up now and starts playing. I'm expecting Vinny to stand up and start swaying round the room wailing, but instead she turns to Andrew and asks him what he does. He tells her he's a newly qualified quantity surveyor so she asks him what's that exactly and he's explaining about cement and reinforced concrete and she's looking up at him as if she's never had such an interesting conversation in all her life.

I sit down next to Han and Tan. They seem really pleased to see me. It's nice talking to them in French because their French doesn't sound that much better than mine. But then I start asking them about Vietnam and Indochina. I ask them how they like having the Americans interfering in their country. Michel and his friends in the café on Sunday afternoons were always saying it was going to be worse having the Americans there than the French. But they just smile back at me as if they don't want to talk about it. So I try to think of something else to say, I ask them what's the difference between Vietnam and Indochina, and they get all relaxed again and explain that Indochina was the name the French gave to the whole peninsula, not just Vietnam but also Laos and Cambodia.

And then Steve's joining us. Andrew's totally absorbed in his conversation with Vinny. I'm trying to hear if he's still telling her about reinforced concrete, only Steve's asking me about the duchess and her little pin curls. So I get talking about hairdressing, and I tell him about the competition I'm going in for. I want to tell him how inspiring it was talking to him that time, and looking at those portraits propped up against the wall, but he interrupts.

'Let's get some more wine,' he says, catching me by the hand and drawing me towards the kitchen. In the kitchen he closes the door and leans up against it and pulls me towards him. He starts kissing me and the door, which is painted a dirty blue, starts turning incredibly bright, when someone suddenly gives it a push from the other side and we're thrown onto the floor practically. It's Marc. He gives us a funny look. Steve goes across and pours himself a large glass of wine and strides back into the other room and I'm left there talking to Marc.

When we go back in, Steve has joined Vinny and Andrew. Andrew has got his arm round Vinny and Steve's asking him if he's going to spend the rest of his life in a suit doing a nine to five job. They've lit up, Andrew included. I lean over and take the cigarette out of his mouth and put it between my lips. Vinny looks at me and flutters her eyelashes. Marc's standing there with a bottle of wine and I hold out my empty glass. Steve's saying how people take life much too seriously. They should remember what they were like when they were children, when what they did was play all day. Life should be fun.

'Search out what you love!' cries Vinny, turning to Andrew. I expect him to look across at me but he goes on looking at Vinny.

'You have to transform reality, Andrew, be adventurous,' says Steve, playing a dramatic chord on his guitar. 'Grow a beard and dye it purple.'

I'm wondering if he's making fun of Andrew. Bill, who all this time has been sitting in a corner with his wooden leg propped up against the wall beside him and his nose in a book, looks up at this and raises his arm: 'We must unscrew the locks from the doors!' he shouts. 'We must unscrew the doors themselves!' He picks up Andrew's blazer which is lying beside him on the floor and starts putting it on. I think Andrew's going to object but he seems to find it funny, the sight of Bill putting on his smart blazer on top of his dirty grey shirt with half the buttons missing.

The talk has stopped and we're all sitting there in a sort of trance, smoking and drinking and listening to the music that's unwinding on the tape. It doesn't have much tune to it and I can't make out the words except for one word that sounds like *reblochon* that they keep repeating. I suddenly feel incredibly tired. I put my lips against Andrew's ear.

'Let's go,' I whisper. Han and Tan get up too.

Half way home in the taxi Andrew remembers he's forgotten to get his blazer off Bill. We have to ask the taxi driver to turn round and go back. I sit there while he goes in. I don't feel like moving. Maybe, when he comes back, we could stay in the back of the taxi until it's light, snoozing to the soothing noise of the meter ticking over.

He's being a long time. I open the door of the taxi to get out. The driver, whose head has been completely immobile up to now, suddenly springs to life, swings round and tells me I owe him I can't make out how much - it sounds like a lot of money. I push a note at him and stumble out worried that he's going to jump out after me and pull me back and tell me it's not enough.

Vinny, Steve and Marc are drifting round the room looking grotesque in the purple light. Vinny's hand is between Steve's thighs and he's reaching out to fondle her breasts which seem to be on the outside of her blouse, while Marc's wriggling his hips in quite an alarming way and reaching out to touch Steve's bottom from time to time. Bill's slumped against the wall, fast asleep. Andrew's busy trying to get his arm out of the sleeve of his blazer but Bill keeps falling forward. The pocket's torn and there's a wine stain down the front and three of the brass buttons are scattered over the floor. Andrew gives up and subsides onto the floor beside him. Then he sees me and he holds out his hand.

'Come here, Lucy,' Steve calls to me softly across the room but I go towards Andrew. I lie down beside him and together we fall into a sleep.

We're woken by the sound of Bill banging around in the kitchen. There's no sign of Vinny or Steve or Marc. There's a nasty taste in my mouth and I have a splitting headache.

'It's nearly ten o'clock,' Andrew hisses in my ear, jumping up. The only way he's going to catch the boat train is by taking taxis - back to the hotel to grab his bag and pay and then to the *Gare du Nord*. His blazer is lying in the middle of the floor mixed up with a loaded ashtray and a broken wine glass. He picks it up and shakes it out and then bends down to collect up the buttons scattered around on the floor. He's missed one. I crush my swollen feet into my shoes and hobble across the room to get it. I'm badly in need of a cup of tea but there's no time.

We arrive at the station with two minutes to spare. We've hardly said a word to each other all the way, we feel too ill. He leans out of the compartment, and catches hold of my hand.

'Are you going to grow a beard and dye it purple?' I ask him but he doesn't laugh. He's back in the real world.

'Lucy,' he says 'you were going to tell me …'

The train is starting to move.

'I'll write to you, I will, I promise,' I call after him as the train gathers speed.

Chapter 22

I can hear music coming from the library when I open the door of the flat. When Claude's there he always puts a record on, turns it up loud so it fills the whole flat and then usually goes out of the room. I recognise it. It's the record Juan always played as we sat there in the leather armchairs gazing across at each other. Mozart's clarinet concerto. I stand for a second, listening. The music hasn't changed, it's still sad and beautiful, and my head still feels bad so it should be soothing. But above it I can hear Juan's voice – 'Lucy, in two years time you will be twenty five.'

Claude emerges from the library just as I'm about to open the door into my room. I'm worried he's going to make another pass at me but he's on his way out - he's turned the music off. As he opens the front door to go out, I give him a brief smile and close my door.

I'm still in the dress that I put on yesterday morning to go out and buy the croissants. There's a wine stain down the front of it and a cigarette burn near the hem in the front. I take everything off and wash myself all over in the washbasin. Then I put on the cherry red Italian jumper I bought in the little shop down the road the other day to cheer myself up. I haven't bothered to put any lipstick on since I said goodbye to Andrew and, in the mirror, my face looks a fright against the bright colour of the jumper. I exchange it for my old dark green jumper. With it I'm wearing the black corduroy skirt I made last spring. The skirt's loose on me now.

I straighten the bed and finish the bit of croissant still left on my plate and wash up the blue bowls. Pouring the remains of Andrew's coffee down the sink is like I'm saying goodbye to him. I slow down as I think of this and let the last drops trickle slowly out of the bowl and then I hesitate before turning on the tap to see them disappear completely.

I've decided to go to the Museum of Modern Art the American girl was talking about since it's just down the road. So I put on some pale peach lipstick - *First Blush* - and set out. I'm trying to work out a hairstyle for the competition. I'm pretty sure I know what I want but I may get ideas from looking at some of the paintings there. Bertrand was saying how that really eccentric French hairdresser, Antoine, used to go to the *Louvre* to look at paintings by well-known artists in order to get inspiration.

'You mean pictures like the *Mona Lisa*?' I asked him. I don't think she'd be much inspiration, with those long dull brown locks falling onto her shoulders.

There are three boys roller skating on the concrete outside the museum. One of them asks me the time. He's got smooth brown skin and nice cheekbones, like Michel, and I think of Michel at that age. Only Michel wouldn't have been roller skating here, in this posh district, he probably never ever possessed a pair of roller skates in his life. 'Pampered brat' I think as I look at the boy. I tell him I've no idea what the time is.

The museum is full of pictures by people I've never heard of. There's one by someone called Braque that's a muddle of faded browns and greys, and there are big pictures by someone else of what look like bits and pieces of machinery all jumbled up together - gear wheels and screws and things. There's a small picture by Picasso - it's of a harlequin, only he's all straight lines and squares of colour - nice blues and pinks but he looks sinister and threatening, he looks more like a soldier than a harlequin.

Then I see a picture I really like. It's not of anyone or anything, it's just bright red and green and yellow and black half circles and zigzag lines - it looks brazen and energetic and full of life. It's by a woman called Sonia Delauney. That's just like the way I want to cut hair, that's like my geometric cut with definite lines, some straight, some curved, and with lots of movement. No pin curls or rollers or even lacquer, just hair that looks as if it's full of life. I get my writing pad out of my handbag and, on a page at the back, I start drawing the sort of style I'm looking for.

There's hardly anyone else in the gallery except for a few intense-looking women in lace-ups and glasses. I wander outside. It's a huge white building with high columns, which makes you feel like an insect crawling around underneath. I walk towards the great big terrace with wide steps leading down to the river Seine. You can see the *Eiffel Tower* the other side. There's a small café in one corner with chairs and tables outside and there's a man sitting at one of the tables, reading. He looks like an intellectual, he's wearing dark corduroys and a black sweater and he has a beard. Then a woman arrives in a rather stylish jacket and she leans across the table, kisses him on the lips and sits down opposite him and I turn my eyes away. I didn't think of Michel all the time I was in the museum.

I decide to go and have a sandwich at the café on the *Place de l'Alma* and go on sketching. It's the café where the waiter ran after me, telling me I hadn't paid but there are no other cafés around and my feet are hurting. I ease them out of my shoes as I sit there with my baguette with a slice of gruyère cheese down the middle and a glass of fizzy water with a slice of lemon floating on it. Monique and the children are arriving back this afternoon at last. It will be really nice to see her, especially since what happened the other evening with Claude. I don't like being in the flat alone with him now.

The waiter's standing in front of me with his tray by his side, wanting me to pay. Maybe he remembers me as the girl who tried to make off without paying. I nearly give him a big tip just to show him, but then I don't, why should I? I'd really like to be the sort of person who leaves large tips, I hate it in the salon when you see them dithering and then counting out some meagre sum to press into your hand, instead of flourishing a note like the duchess. But I feel like one of the stingy ones today as I count out 10% exactly, to the nearest centime. My head's still hurting and I didn't have enough sleep last night on the floor at Vinny's and I'm upset about Andrew.

Back in the flat Daniel and Catherine are running up and down the corridor. They're glad to be home. But Monique looks funny. I can tell straight away when I see her there's something wrong. I expected her to be happy and relaxed after her holiday and glad to see me since I haven't seen her all summer. But she's rushing around, unpacking and bossing the kids around and hardly stopping to say hello to me as if there's something on her mind she doesn't want to think about. It must be to do with Claude. He's probably just told her he's off for a week on business - again - and she knows this means he's having a week away with his mistress. It's all very well for Juan to tell her to offer it up, that she's earning her place in heaven, she can't help but feel hurt. If it's anything like what I feel when I imagine Michel being with another woman, like maybe Francesca. But then I'd be making scenes, I couldn't be dignified like Monique. Monique's so ladylike. If Michel phones I know it'll be a struggle not to scream down the phone at him 'I know you're having an affair with Francesca.'

She doesn't tell me till after the children are in bed. We're in the kitchen and she's opened a bottle of wine.

'It's Juan,' she says. I know immediately what she's going to tell me: he's decided to leave the priesthood, he's written to Monique to say he's in love with her and he can't live without her. He wants her to leave Claude and come away with him, and she's in a state, she doesn't know what to do.

'He's dead. He was killed while he was saying Mass in his church two Saturdays ago. Some madman …' She bends her head, she can't go on. I get up to put my arms around her and she stands up. The questions are coming at me but I don't like to ask. Who killed him and why and how? And how did Monique find out? She's shaking her head.

'He was too good for this world,' she keeps repeating. 'Poor Juan, he was so pious, so full of goodness. I haven't told the children yet.' She goes across to her handbag and gets out the letter she's received from a priest that Juan was friendly with, a Father Pedro. The letter tells how some madman attacked Juan with a knife, stabbing him in the back, just as he was reciting the *Agnus Dei qui tollis pecata mundi, ora pro nobis*: Lamb of God who takest away the sins of the world, pray for us. He died a few hours later in hospital, forgiving his attacker and asking Father Pedro to get in touch with his friends in Paris.

'That means you, too, Lucy. He was fond of you,' says Monique, blowing into her handkerchief and pouring us both another glass of wine. 'But why? How could anyone do such a thing? His parishioners all loved him, Father Pedro says in his letter. He gave them hope, he talked to them about the immense love God had, particularly for the poor, and how, one day, they would have their reward in heaven.'

I can hear Michel and Antonio talking in the café and the scorn they had for that sort of priest, the sort who told their parishioners to put up with their lives as they were. Priests shouldn't be telling them just to accept, as if they were farm animals. Maybe the 'madman' was someone who thought Juan was doing harm not good, telling them not to protest but to accept.

'And he was happy there, happy to be back among his people, doing good. You remember how he used to say that, in Mexico, because of the sun, people were full of laughter and gaiety, they danced and sang and made music in spite of being poor. And they helped each other, not like here in Paris. The knife went deep into him, Father Pedro said. There was no hope of saving him. There was nothing to be done.' She gets up from the table. She hasn't eaten anything.

'I must write to Father Pedro,' she says and then, as she stands at the door, 'Juan was too good for this world. He's up in heaven now, looking down on us. Tomorrow I must tell the children.'

As I lie in bed that night, I'm remembering Juan's story about the little prince and the rose that he cherishes - *As long as you remember that, somewhere in the world, there is someone who loves you.* But now he's no longer in the world. Was it one of the poor people he was always talking about who killed him? The poor had such a sense of fun, he always said. Was it one of them who stabbed him? Like the painting I saw today, of the harlequin. A harlequin's meant to be full of fun but Picasso has made him look sinister.

I can't sleep. I keep seeing Juan's face looking at me as I went up the steps at *Trocadéro*, shouting abuse down at him. I'd give the world now to be able to go back down the steps and put my arms round him and say… But what would I say? I don't know. I still don't think he should have been telling me that the best thing for me was to get married. He shouldn't have been telling the poor people of Mexico City, that they should willingly accept the dreadful conditions they were living in. But he didn't deserve this shocking end.

Chapter 23

This morning, when I arrived at the salon, I was expecting Marie Claire to want to know how things were going with Andrew. She'd look up from her appointments' book and greet me with 'Eh alors?' But she just said hello and then went on writing things down. Even when I told her that Andrew had gone back, he only stayed two days, she didn't scent a drama or anything.

    I asked her about Bertrand - he's not in again today and I have to take his client, the one I had last week, the day Antonia had her operation. He's practically living at the hospital, she told me. But Antonia comes out today - that's why he's not in - and goes to a nursing home just outside Paris. I asked her how long they think she's got, but she just said that's not the sort of question one asks. Marie Claire has lips that turn down at the sides like an upside down U and today they're almost touching her chin. But the pillar box red lipstick is still in place. I asked her if she felt like going for a drink after work.

    Bertrand's client – the actress from the *Comédie Française* – is quite well known, Jean François told me, after she'd left last time. Anyway, this morning I'm not sure what she wants me to do with her hair. I did the roots last week - the dark hair shows against the blonde as soon as there's a centimetre of growth.

    I unpin the chignon and her hair flops down around her face and she grins at me and says she looks like '*a cloon.*' 'A clown,' I say, so she repeats *clown*. She wants to practise her English in case she's asked to do a film in English or something. I suppose a harlequin is a sort of clown. Was the person who stabbed him one of the altar boys? It might have been difficult for anyone else to have got onto the altar. It might have been an altar boy that Juan had got close to, that he talked to like he talked to me and Monique. Or maybe he was someone Juan didn't know at all, who disguised himself as an altar boy. It would be easy to conceal the knife in the white vestment with the deep lace border that altar boys wear.

She's having lunch with some important director who might choose her for a part in a play he's putting on, so she wants me to make her look spectacular. 'Would I do 'er a bee -'ive 'airdo?'

I used to quite enjoy doing the bee-hive hairdo in Manchester but it takes ages and I don't think it would suit her. If I felt in the mood, I'd probably suggest putting her hair into plaits coiled tightly round the head. They'd go with the serious look she has, that changes completely when she smiles. But I feel too sad this morning. I end up giving her the bee-hive she's asked for.

It's well past midday before it's finished, with Berthe standing there patiently handing me the enormous rollers you need for the style. And then all the backcombing and lacquer. She'll have to wash it all out before this evening's performance, because she'll be wearing a wig. The play's set in the eighteenth century, she tells me, when they had some funny hairdos then too.

I feel guilty as she thanks me, saying she's very pleased with her hair, the way I've done it. I think she's just being polite. It makes her look like the sort of doll you win at the fair, and it's my fault. All the time I was doing her hair I was having an idea. She's got the sort of lively face with good bone structure that would look stunning with the hair done in the style I'm creating. And she has the right sort of hair for the style too – dead straight and with body.

'There's a competition next month I'm going in for and I'm creating a new style for it. Only I need a model to work on and you've got just the sort of face and hair. Only I suppose you're much too busy ...'

'You want to do me another bee-'ive?' she asks.

'No, no, I'm thinking of something short, something very modern. If you could wait a moment.' I disappear into the back to get my sketch pad.

She looks at the sketches I've been doing. I'm worried she's going to say that there's no question of cutting her hair short like that but she seems interested. She takes a card out of her handbag and gives it to me:

Mademoiselle Mathilde Boussaroque
Comédie Française.

'Give me a call,' she says.

Jean François asks me if I'm coming to *Chez Gilbert* for lunch but I tell him I don't feel like it. I haven't been there since I came back, it reminds me too much of going there with Michel. I don't go to the *Belle Ferronnière* either for the same reason. I go to the little café round the corner for a sandwich. Even this reminds me a little of the café in Belleville where we had lunch the day we went to the *Buttes Chaumont*. Though there's no old man with tortoiseshell hair going past, walking his tortoiseshell cat. Today I'd just like to go and sit on that bench in the *Trocadéro* gardens where I met Juan but Marie Claire wants to join me in the café as she can't come for a drink after work. Bertrand will be coming for dinner, maybe, after settling Antonia in the nursing home.

Marie Claire's been getting sick of hearing him going on about HER and how she's suffering and she only has him in the whole world. 'I know I'm awful but I'm sick of it,' she kept repeating the other day.

'But then yesterday he arrived with this beautiful bunch of orchids. I was just thinking they're to take to HER when he was holding them out to me. He'd bought them specially for me.' Marie Claire's eyes fill with tears.

'But let's not talk about all that. Tell me about Andrew,' she says. I don't feel like talking about Andrew - my mind's full of Juan. But I can't tell her about Juan. She didn't know him so for her it would be like reading something in *France Soir*.

'I don't think I can marry him,' I say. 'He's nice, but I don't think I'm in love with him. Besides, what would become of my career, living in Leeds?'

'Marry him, Lucy. Don't find yourself in the situation I'm in.' Marie Claire was living with her parents till a few years ago when she got a little flat she could never have afforded, only Bertrand helped her to buy it, Jean François whispered to me once. But what she wants is to share a proper home with Bertrand.

'Well, maybe I will marry him, you never know,' I say. 'I'll get him to grow his hair long and have a purple beard and we'll have a garden full of marijuana and magic turnips and I'll have a hairdresser's of my own where there'll be a ban on permanent waving. I'll send all the old women away looking wild like witches.'

I start mussing up my hair and pulling a crazy face and the man at the next table looks at me as if he thinks I'm barmy. Marie Claire shakes her head and says 'Oh, Lucy.'

There's no one in the flat when I get back that evening so it's me answers the phone when it rings. I let it ring long enough to go on enjoying the hope that it'll be Michel. I'm still hoping, right up to the few seconds between picking it up and saying hello.

'Je veux parler avec Lucy Duffy,' says a voice that isn't Michel's.

'Speaking,' I say and then he says 'Oh, hello, it's Jack here.' He's passing through Paris on his way home and would I be free to have dinner with him?

I'd forgotten completely about the Scotsman who was going round the world that me and Marie Claire met that evening in the café in the Champs Elysées. He's passing through Paris on his way back to England. We fix up to meet at a place called *Denfert Rochereau*.

Chapter 24

Monique's in the hall when I come in from work. She looks sad but her face brightens up when she sees me. I tell her I wish I didn't have to go out. It's true in a way. Part of me would much rather spend the evening with her than with this man I hardly know.

    I change into the very Parisian-looking outfit I bought with the money I saved up in Nice. I was going to wear it to impress Andrew but didn't get a chance. It's a little box jacket in navy blue wool, with a matching straight, pencil-slim, sleeveless dress which comes to just below the knee. I tie my hair back with a black velvet ribbon and rummage in the drawer for the off-white ruched kid gloves.

    I've plenty of time. I walk across to get the Metro at *Kléber* that'll take me all the way to *Denfert Rochereau*. I can hear a train coming in as I trip my way down the corridor so I start to run. The woman at the barrier punching the tickets doesn't want to let me through and I have to push past her. 'C'est comme ça qu'on arrive à l'hôpital,' she screams at I jump into the train. That's how you end up in hospital. I sit there imagining it. Instead of meeting Jack I'd be lying on a trolley somewhere and they'd be going through my handbag to find out who I was and who they could get in touch with. At least I'm wearing decent underwear.

    I'm a bit taken aback to see how many stops before *Denfert Rochereau*. Stops with names I've never heard of - *Bir-Hakeim* ... *Sèvres Lecourbe* ...... *Edgar Quinet.* I'm going to be late. Maybe I should just go back home, I've only met this man once and for not even half an hour. Or I could keep going, past stations with more strange names - *Glacière* ...

Dugommier ... Bel-Air .... I could spend the whole evening in the Metro, changing trains, finding myself at *Bobigny* or *Villejuif* or *Pré-Saint-Gervais*.

Opposite me there's a young couple holding hands and staring straight ahead, not talking, except that, now and again, they look at each other and smile, like they've come to the best bit of their favourite tune or they've hit the jam in the doughnut. The girl looks like she's come off the front of a knitting pattern, her hair's dyed black and it's rigid with mousse. He's spent hours on his, sleeking it down with sugar water. They look as if they know where they're going.

I recognise Jack straight away, though he's leaner and browner than when I saw him in the spring. And how come I hadn't noticed the blinding blue of his eyes? The eyes keep saying hello to me as we sit opposite each other, and I'm wondering if I'm going to manage to eat.

It's a cheap restaurant and I feel a bit out of place in my smart outfit. We've both ordered *pot au feu*, which is a sort of boiled beef and carrots dish with lots of potatoes. And a big jug of red wine. And it's very noisy in a jolly sort of way. You eat at a long table so you get a bit elbowed by the person on either side of you.

I don't know if it's the effect of the wine but, now I've got used to the eyes, I'm finding him very easy to talk to. I've even started telling him about how I spent the summer in Nice because of this French feller called Michel.

'But then it wasn't working out,' I say, 'so I came back to Paris.' Should I mention Andrew? He might think I'm fast, too available. Or just boasting.

'Then there's this feller I know from Manchester who came over to see me.'

He laughs and says it's not surprising I have so many men after me, because I'm very attractive. His laugh makes me feel good, it makes me feel I'm silly to be getting so depressed about not knowing what to do. I shouldn't be so serious about it all.

'He wants to marry me,' I tell him.

'Who? The one in Nice or the one in Manchester?' I could say Both but I don't want to say any more about Michel.

'The one in Manchester. He's just got a job and he's going to be living in Leeds.'

'But what would you do in Leeds? What about your hairdressing? You said you wanted to be - I dunno - *someone*.'

There are tears coming into my eyes that I'm completely unprepared for.

'You're right,' I say. I want to continue with *But it isn't easy,* but I can't because there's a lump in my throat. I wait for a moment and then I tell him about the competition and about this woman I want to use as a model and how she's an actress with the *Comédie Française* and she's in a play at the moment that's set in the eighteenth century. He's really interested because he says he's studying history and the period he's specialising in is eighteenth century France, just before the Revolution.

'They had the most amazing hairstyles, the women, in those days,' he's starting off when the man by his side asks him in English if he can pass him over the ashtray. He offers Jack and me a cigarette and then starts asking Jack about whether he actually lives in Paris. I'm fed up because we were in the middle of a conversation, but this man and his friend opposite - they're both American - seem to assume that all we want to do is talk with them about what we're doing in Paris and how we like it. Jack's actually launching into an account of his travels round the world and the other feller keeps saying 'Gee'. His friend, who's next to me, asks me if I went round the world too. I just say *No*. I'm not going to tell him I'm a hairdresser, which would provoke more 'Gees'. He asks me what I think of the French, drops his voice.

'Actually, I don't dig them myself. I dunno, they're too sure of themselves, and they're darned rude here in Paris.' I have to agree with him, they *are* rude but I quite like it. At home people are always too nice, I've sort of got used to people here complaining all the time and being aggressive and I'd miss it, I *will* miss it, if I go back to England.

'Pete's wondering if we want to go to this jazz club in the Latin Quarter,' Jack says to me.

'I think I have to go home. I have to get up early in the morning,' I say, feeling prim. I'm afraid they're going to ask me why I have to get up early, but they don't. We say goodbye to them and leave. Jack, all the same, makes a note of where the night club is, saying he might join them there later.

I feel this as a sort of betrayal. I was sort of assuming he'd be going back to his room in the hall of residence, still thinking of me, not sitting in some smoky night club, drinking whisky with two Americans.

He accompanies me all the way back in the Metro. *Edward Quinet ... Sèvres Lecourbe .... Bir-Hakeim* ... and I'm feeling happier than I've felt in a long time. It's as if I'd dumped all my worries in a Left

Luggage and I'm free. I'm sitting beside someone who takes me seriously and who's nice to be with and who has the most amazing blue eyes and who's not married – as far as I know – and doesn't look as if he'd ever want to live in a bungalow in the suburbs with a ding-dong bell.

The Eiffel Tower is all lit up and there's moonlight on the river and I'm wanting to reach forward to touch his hand which is on his knee. I reach out, pretending I want to look at the map of Paris he's holding, but he straight away gives it to me, so I have to unfold it and show him the street where I live.

Outside my door he gives me a kiss on the cheek.

'We could meet for lunch tomorrow, if you like,' I say, trying to sound casual. He's going back to England tomorrow evening. 'There's a restaurant just round from where I work that you'd really like.'

He's already standing outside *Chez Gilbert* when I arrive at one o'clock with Jean François and Marie Claire. I feel proud of him, propped up against the wall in his battered jacket, with his old rucksack over his shoulder. As we sit down Marie Claire whispers to me that he reminds her of James Dean.

I haven't been inside the restaurant since before I left for Nice but it's all exactly the same, as if time hadn't moved on at all. There's still the same menu written up - *carrottes rapées…, entrecôte…, pommes de terre vapeur…, haricots verts…, tarte maison… .*

'Ah, la belle anglaise,' Etienne exclaims as we sit down at the usual table. I introduce Jack to him, and to Francis, who's also come over to greet us.

'And you are an 'airdresser, too?' Francis asks Jack, and we all laugh.

'Jack knows all about hair in the eighteenth century,' I tell Jean François and Marie Claire as we start on an *hors d'oeuvre* of different sorts of sliced sausage with gherkins and olives. He was starting to talk about this yesterday evening when those two Americans butted in. Did he go to that night club? Anyway, he's here now. I realise I don't even know his second name but he's across the table from me, and we're exchanging smiles.

'Did you know that Marie Antoinette …' he starts off, but Marie Claire interrupts him to ask him how long he's staying in Paris. She's trying out her English and my heart sinks.

'You arrre 'eere for 'ow long time?'

My French isn't very good but I hope it's better than that. And Jack seems to speak it very well. So I go back into French to tell them this joke that a client was telling me yesterday about an English man staying in a hotel. In the morning he complains to the receptionist that his *maîtresse* is too hard. He thinks that *maîtresse* is the French for *mattress* but it's the French for *mistress.* They've all heard the joke before.

'Zee Frensh for *mattress* eez *matelas*,' Marie Claire tells me, quite unnecessarily.

Jean François has started asking Jack if all the men in London wear bowler hats like Major Thomson and carry a copy of *The Times* along with their rolled umbrella and brief case. Major Thomson's this character in the *Figaro* that they're always laughing about when they come into the salon - 'e *eez so Eengleesh!* Michel says the *Figaro* is a very bourgeois paper.

Jack is being very polite with Jean François but he keeps grinning at me across the table and I'm wishing Marie Claire and Jean François would leave and go back to the salon. I'll stay on, and we can sit here telling each other the story of our lives. We seem to have finished the jug of wine. Etienne has noticed and he's come over to ask us if we want more.

'Will you 'ave a leetle more wine?'

To my joy, Marie Claire and Jean François both say No with a little flourish of the hand. They have to work this afternoon. The French are quite disciplined in that way.

'I don't have anyone till three o'clock,' I say to them, and to Jack 'I wouldn't mind sharing another jug with you.' Marie Claire draws in a breath and looks at me, like when Jean François told her the girl from the Number 63 bus wanted him to cut her hairs. But then I notice how Jack's looking up at Etienne and laughing and how Etienne is looking down at him.

'Why not?' says Jack picking up the jug. I'm staring at their hands - their fingers are almost touching. I think Etienne's never going to take the jug, it's as if they're waiting for someone to take a photo of them. And now Etienne's striding off and I'm expecting Jack to turn and look across at me, but his eyes are still on Etienne, following him until he disappears through the door into the kitchen.

I can see that Jean François has noticed too. I try to give him a knowing smile, to make him think that I knew already, it's not a shock to me. He and Marie Claire are getting up to go, and now I want to go with them.

It's like being with a different person. I'm feeling self-conscious about the way I'm looking at him

- it's changed, but I don't want him to notice. I go back to telling him about Michel. I tell him about how he's married and he has a little girl but he and his wife are thinking of separating. But it would be the death of my parents if I were to marry a divorced man, so I don't know what to do, I say.

Jack doesn't see why I'm so bothered about upsetting my parents.

'You're not a Catholic so you don't understand,' I say.

'But what about his child?' he asks. He seems much more bothered about her. So I say how I think his wife's a bit fed up of being married to a hairdresser. But he still goes on looking serious.

'He's very ambitious is Michel,' I tell him. I feel really funny mentioning his name like that.

'So you'll be competing with him in the competition, will you?'

'That won't be a problem,' I say. 'We love each other' I add, keeping my voice low. It's the first time I've ever said that out loud. And I'm wondering if it's true, even. Why doesn't he phone me?

'More wine? Or a little dessert? *Crème caramel*? *Tarte maison*?' Etienne is coming forward, smiling at Jack.

'I have to get back to work,' I say.

'I think we'll have the bill,' says Jack, returning his smile.

'EEt eez a pity you are leaving for England where it eez always raining cats and dogs.'

'But I'll be back,' says Jack, tilting his head and laughing up at him.

I offer to pay my share, now that he's a sort of mate, and then we walk slowly back to the salon.

He asks me to write and let him know how I get on in the competition. I tell him I've already thought of a style - close to the head and curving round the cheeks and over one eye - inspired by a picture I saw.

'It's a really colourful painting's that's got a sort of rhythm to it.'

'I've got rhythm, I've got music ,' Jack starts singing and we very nearly break into a dance on the pavement.

We say goodbye. I watch him till he's out of sight, striding along jauntily under the leaves of the plane trees that are a burnt gold in the sunlight.

It's two o'clock, a good time to phone Mademoiselle Boussaroque from the public phone box I phoned Michel from in May. She doesn't know who's talking at first. 'C'est Mademoiselle Lucy from Chez Bertrand' I have to repeat, but then she's quite friendly. I ask her if she still wants to be my model and she says Yes. We fix up for her to come into the salon so we can talk about the style and I can make quite sure she's happy about how I'm going to cut her hair. I don't want her in the middle of the competition getting up out of her seat and screaming 'What are you doing to my hair? I never agreed to this' and running off, leaving me with my scissors in my hand and no hair to cut. I also want to change her hair back to her own colour if I can persuade her.

There's a letter from my mother when I get back from work. I glance through it and then put it back in its envelope. She's asking me how my week with Andrew went. I can't put it off any longer. I'm twenty three. I'm old enough to know my own mind. I don't want to hurt my parents and I don't want to hurt Andrew but I have to decide. Marrying Andrew would mean turning into a little supportive suburban housewife and that's the last thing I want. My parents will just have to accept that. I take out my writing pad. *Dear Andrew*, I begin.

Chapter 25

I can hear the phone ringing and Monique answering it and then she's knocking on my door and saying it's for me.

'Lucy.' It's Michel. I open my mouth but I can't find any words.

'Lucy,' he repeats, 'are you there? How are you?' I tell him I'm fine.

'And you? How are you?' I ask, as if I'm talking to a stranger. Why has it taken him so long to get round to phoning me?

'Oh, Lucy. You've no idea how much I've been missing you but I've never dared phone you before.' It's like a door has opened and the room's ablaze with sunlight. He starts to tell me about the salon.

'How's Abbas?' I ask. He's gone back to Algeria.

'Come back down to Nice, come down tomorrow,' he says and I laugh and look at my watch and wonder it I'd be in time for the night train. But there's the competition to think of. I'm seeing Mademoiselle Boussaroque tomorrow evening.

'But you'll be up here at the end of next week for the competition,' I say. Can we wait that long - a whole ten days?

'If you can't come down I'll come up early,' he says. 'I'll come on the Friday morning.'

I put the phone down and open the door of the library, ready to throw up my arms and dance, but Monique's waiting outside.

'Would you like a drink?' she asks me. We go into the kitchen and she tells me she talked to the priest in the church down the road about Juan and he was very sympathetic. He thought it might help if she talked to Father Pedro on the phone, the priest who'd phoned her about Juan. So she did and Father Pedro told her that Juan has joined the ranks of those who've died for their faith, that he has become a martyr.

'So I think I'm going to go,' Monique says.

'Go?' I ask.

'To Mexico. I'll be too late for the funeral but Father Pedro said he thought Juan's mother would like it very much if I came. It would mean a lot to her, to meet someone from his life in France. They were so cut off from him all those years. The children can stay with my friends in *Neuilly*. Claude can't afford the time to come with me, but he's glad I'm going. He said straight away how he'd willingly pay the air fare and all the expenses.'

She wants an early night so I go back to my room. I'm very sad about Juan but inside myself I can't help singing. It reminds me of playing ball once in the hall at home and my father telling me to play quietly, but the ball was very bouncy and almost impossible to control. It's like this now. He still loves me, he still loves me, and in just over a week's time... And between now and then I can throw myself completely into preparing for the competition. I want to do at least as well as Michel.

He's just come off the night train and we're climbing up the narrow winding stairs to the little attic room. I went up yesterday evening to check that it was still there, I hadn't been up to the sixth floor since that morning in June. It looked exactly the same - the little bed in the corner with the faded cover, and the small table under the window. I'd forgotten to empty the ashtray so the room reeked of stale tobacco, as well as of paraffin from the stove in the corner. I opened the window and threw out the fag-ends. Some of them were quite long, perhaps they'd land at the feet of a passing tramp, like manna out of the sky.

There was still some wine left in one of the glasses on the table. It had a thick skin of fungus over it. I took the two glasses to wash them in the basin at the end of the corridor. There's only cold water so my fingers were freezing cold by the time I got them clean. It must be awful living here all the time, having to go down the corridor for a wash or a pee, not able to heat water in the room.

'I told them in the salon I'd be late in.' Michel is undoing my blouse and I'm unbuttoning his shirt and then we're on the bed and I'm wishing I had a dozen hands and a dozen tongues to be feeling him with.

The duchess is waiting when I arrive in the salon. I'm ten minutes late and my hair's a mess. 'You can always tell when a woman's been making love,' Alberto says. 'You only have to look at her hair.' I push it back and give her a smile. I always think the duchess understands me and approves, there's this roguish look in her eye. I wonder sometimes about suggesting something other than the little pin curls for her, but they actually suit her. I have a feeling that long ago she decided that that was the way she wanted to have her hair and she has stuck with it.

I caught Bertrand's eye as I came in. He looked reproachfully at me for keeping the duchess waiting, but the duchess herself didn't seem to mind. As she leaves she presses the usual *billet* into my hand and this time I think I really will go away and spend it on a pair of saucy knickers in my lunch hour, instead of the usual cotton ones from *Prisunic*. As I put it in my handbag I notice the letter from Andrew that came yesterday still unopened. I don't want to read it just now. I'll wait till after the competition.

Michel's coming into the salon at the end of the day. He promised them all he'd call in when he was up for the competition. They're all keyed up because they think he has a good chance of coming first and that will be marvellous for the reputation of the salon.

They know I'm going in for the competition too, but it's obvious they don't think I've much chance at all, though I feel Berthe thinks I'm good - I've practised the cut on two of her friends. Anyway, Mademoiselle Boussaroque - Mathilde - came in last week and I discussed the style I was planning for her. I said I wanted to get rid of the blonde and get back to her own colour which is a rich dark brown, so she said okay. For the competition, I want to cut it so that it swings round her face and down over her left eye, but at the back it'll be very sleek into the head. She's got a nice shaped head. Marie Claire and Françoise stood there looking as if they'd got humbugs stuck in their throats as I explained this to them, after she'd gone. Bernard was listening too and he shook his head and looked sad at what I was going to be doing to her 'crowning glory'. He looks sad all the time these days, because of Antonia, so I was sorry to depress him even more. He's probably thinking he should never have let me take Mathilde over.

'Oh, Michel, how nice to see you. And how are Jeanne and Charlotte?' they're all asking, and I have to pretend it's my first time seeing him, too, since Nice. They want to know about the style he's chosen for the competition but he tells them to wait and see. And then they ask him what he's doing this evening, it would be lovely if we could all eat out together in a restaurant. Even Bertrand seems to be thinking he might join us. Michel and I have fixed up to meet at eight o'clock in a café the other side of Paris, to be sure not to bump into any of them. I'm worried he's going to look across at me with a *Sorry, I can't very well get out of this, but it'll finish early, and we'll have the long night together* look on his face. I know very well that it won't just be a meal, they'll want to go on to a night club and Françoise will get drunker and drunker and drool over him and it'll be three o'clock before we get back to the room and by then we'll be too tired and ill from drinking too much to do anything except fall into a stupor.

But he's telling them that this evening he has to go to see his mother who's just moved out to one of the new suburbs. Actually he went to see her when I set out for work this morning. But it's a good excuse, they're all looking at him approvingly now. What about tomorrow evening, though? Oh, he has to meet his model off the train from Nice. Francesca, I think immediately. But it's Delphine.

'She's the receptionist down in Nice,' I explain. Delphine must be over the moon. 'I thought you'd have chosen Francesca.' I'm surprised I have the courage to come out with this.

'Oh, she's too busy, she's off to Bordeaux every weekend to see her boyfriend,' he says. They're engaged, she's getting married.'

'Jean François's getting married too,' Marie Claire buts in.

'Everybody's getting married!' I exclaim foolishly, without thinking. I'm so relieved that Francesca's getting married. Marie Claire and Michel both give me a look.

'Ahaa,' says Marie Claire, poking me in the ribs. 'Is there something Lucy isn't telling us about?' And now everybody's looking at me.

It's on Michel's mind still when I eventually meet up with him, half way across Paris.

'What did Marie Claire mean?' he asks me, so I tell him that she's thinking of Andrew. Michel knows about Andrew, at least he knows that he exists and that he wants to marry me.

'He was over in Paris for a couple of days the other week so Marie Claire immediately began to hear wedding bells,' I say, raising my eyes to heaven, trying to make Marie Claire sound totally ridiculous. But Michel's looking serious. 'I love you, Lucy,' he says so I tell him I love him too. Then he says why don't we go to the fair, it's just near by.

I love fairs and this fair's bigger and better than any I've gone to in Manchester or Blackpool. What I like best are the bumping cars where you can whack other cars as much as you like. We won't be going on those this evening though. It would be awful if you so much as tweaked a finger before a competition so you couldn't hold the scissors properly.

Just after the entrance I suddenly feel a great whoosh of warm air and the next moment my skirt's flying up round my neck. I'm wearing the knickers I bought with the duchess's tip - what they call French knickers with wide legs, in flame red - and I think they're going to fly up round my neck too. There are a whole lot of Teddy boys roaming around in their drainpipe trousers and winkle picker shoes and funny haircuts and they give a great roar when they see this.

We come to a place where you can look down and there's this huge drum and there are people pressed up against its side. And then the drum starts to turn round and as it goes faster and faster the people leave the ground and they're suspended in the air against the side of the drum. We decide to have a go. We pay our money and lean up against the side and, s the drum starts to move, I tighten my hold on Michel's hand. But actually it doesn't feel at all as if you're off the ground. It was much more fun watching.

There are quite a few Algerian-looking men wandering around. A policeman has stopped one of them and he's bawling something at him, right into his face. Policemen in Paris aren't at all like the fatherly bobbies at home. They're always shouting at you to show them your papers. This one's pushing the Algerian with his elbow and the Algerian's trying to back away. Suddenly Michel has caught me by the arm and he's leading me towards them.

'He's with us,' Michel interrupts, but the policeman just gives Michel a nasty look and tells us to …….. off. So then I start saying to the policeman in English 'What do you want? What's wrong?' I nearly say 'I'm British. Please direct me to the nearest consulate' like it tells you how to say in the phrase book Andrew gave me when he knew I was coming to Paris. And Michel's turning to the Algerian and saying 'Where did you go, Abdel? We've been looking everywhere for you.' So, in the end, the policeman walks off, swearing.

Once he's out of sight the Algerian shakes our hands and thanks us and tells us his name is actually Ali and insists on buying us pink candy floss, what they call *barbe à Papa* - Dad's beard. We stand there together eating it. The music's blaring out and there are lots of other people round about but, for a moment, it's as if there were just the three of us there.

The concierge, Madame Pie, is standing behind her glass door as we creep in about midnight.

'Ah, c'est vous,' she barks at me, looking Michel up and down. She's in her curlers and an old fawn dressing gown and probably, like Nounou, she has trouble getting to sleep. We don't have any trouble at ll. By the time the church clock down the road strikes one we're already asleep, curled up close together in the narrow bed.

It occurs to me, on waking, that the flat downstairs is probably empty. Monique's in Mexico and the children are staying with a friend and Claude will, by this time, have left for his office. I slip my clothes on, run down the back stairs, open the door into the flat and find myself face to face with Claude. There's a young redheaded girl by his side and they're both carrying leather holdalls. He gives me a long steady look with those small questioning eyes of his and says Bonjour Lucy, this is Giselle. Giselle, this is Lucy. He sounds really businesslike, as if we're at some meeting or other, so I shake her hand in quite a formal way and then he tells me he'll be away for the next few days and they go out.

I run back up to the sixth floor and get Michel. We decide to have a shower. We stand there, running our hands all slithery with soap up and down each other, with the water rushing over us and dancing off us. Tomorrow's the big day when we'll be showing them what a brilliant pair of hairstylists we are.

Chapter 26

The place where the competition is taking place is in an enormous hall not far from where Michel was brought up. We spent most of yesterday there setting things up, practising on mannequins. The place was full of representatives from all the big manufacturers of hair products. They're setting out their stalls with samples of setting lotions, shampoos, lacquers, hair dyes, wigs, toupés, the latest in scissors and barber's chairs. It's very commercial, the hairdressing world, it's mostly about making money out of people, you've got to be quite strong to turn your back on all that when you're developing a hairstyle.

We're both keen to get to the Hall early. I'm wearing comfortable black court shoes with just a bit of a heel, and a black top and black flared skirt. It's not important what I wear as long as it's comfortable. What matters is what the model's wearing as it's not just the hairstyle they judge but how it goes with the rest of her.

Delphine's already there, simpering in a heavy white crepe thing with drapery round the neck. Michel told me he was doing a style inspired by the French Revolution, like the statues on the *Arc de Triomphe* he pointed out to me once, that have these frightful expressions on their faces and their hair going in all directions. I've asked Mathilde to wear a black blouson and a long tight black skirt and lots of eye shadow to make her eyes look even more enormous. She turns up looking sensational, I think, and I can see Delphine eyeing her.

There are about thirty of us competing and only three women - me and a very tall older woman with orange hair and horn rimmed glasses, and a petite woman with short jet black hair, who looks very chic but very tense. She's standing there moving from one foot to the other, banging her hairbrush with the palm of her hand and then frantically brushing her model's hair. I'm wishing I could have a cigarette but we're just a few minutes away from the count down and they're telling us to wet our model's hair ready for the cut. And then it's five four three two one and we're off.

I know exactly how I want to cut Mathilde's hair. I'm good at cutting, it's what I'm best at, knowing how to snip at an angle, work from underneath, watch the line of the head, the way the hair grows. I feel confident and Mathilde gives me a smile now and again as I work.

All the others have finished cutting before me and they're busy with the rollers. I can see Delphine with her lap full of different sized ones. She keeps handing Michel the wrong sort and she's almost in tears. I've decided all I need is one or two pins for the lock that curves onto the right cheek, so I'm taking my time.

Mathilde's the last to go under the dryer but she's the first to come out. Her hair's so short now it dries very quickly and it's mostly loose anyway under the hood. I just comb it through, flicking the lock on the right so that it curves round, following her jaw line, and bringing the lock on the left slanting down so that you just see half an eye. As she sits there leaning back on her chair I think she looks much more revolutionary than Delphine.

The music's blaring out all the time, playing big band Glen Miller stuff. I've finished long before any one else so I can watch what the others are doing. The small dark-haired woman is on the floor on all fours, and I can hear her wails over the noise of the music, and now her model's on the floor too. She's lost a contact lens. That happened in the salon the other day, this woman's lens fell out but, just as I was thinking I'd have to get down on my hands and knees to try and find it for her, her Pekinese licked it up so I was saved the trouble.

Michel's backcombing Delphine's whole head in separate strands so they're standing out in all directions. She's beginning to look quite strange, like she's woken up to find herself in bed with General de Gaulle or something.

There's one of the competitors over the other side, with blonde hair that's cut in a way that makes it flop around as he works. His model's sitting there looking like a china doll as he darts around in his bright red shirt and kerchief with his comb and scissors. The hair's ballooning up on top as if there's a little goblin inside blowing his guts out, and then, on either side, there are these heavy locks that come round the face like fat sheaves of corn. She looks like a prize exhibit for the harvest festival.

We've all finished now and we're whipping off the lilac gowns, all except for the woman who lost the contact lens. She and her model are leaving, they're not waiting for the judging. The woman's pushing past me. There are tears running down her face and she's hissing 'je le savais! je le savais!' I knew it!

The models are taking up poses that they have to keep while the judges go round with their pens and notebooks. They're mostly middle aged men, the judges, and they're all in carefully pressed grey or blue crimplene suits. They stand there staring and noting things down. You can tell, from the amount of time they spend on each model, who's got a chance of winning. They all take one glance at me and Mathilde and pass on, except for one guy a bit younger than the others in a black suit. Mathilde's looking at him with a *Come on* look in her eyes. She's an actress so she's good at that sort of thing. He stands there for quite a while as the others just pass by with barely a glance. After he moves away, Mathilde catches my eye and smiles, which she's not supposed to do, you're supposed to keep exactly the same expression on your face, all the time they're going round.

Michel has told Delphine that she should look as if she's shouting out *Victory to the People, Down with Capitalism,* which accounts for the weird expression she's assumed, which she has to keep for at least five minutes while the judges go round. He's also told her to hold both arms up in the air with her fists clenched. I think this is a lot to ask of a girl who usually spends her days with her elbows propped on the counter and a glittery smile on her face.

The harvest festival girl is attracting a lot of attention from all of them. She's wearing a junket pink dress with a Peter Pan collar and a narrow black satin bow. She's looking up with a shy little smile on her face and she's got her hands resting demurely in her lap. They're circling round her, peering and writing things down, probably admiring the lovely curve on top of her head. I now realise that what she's reminding me of is the giant penny bun mushroom I found once on one of our boring Sunday walks.

Of course, she's the one who wins. The second prize goes to someone over the other side who's done an elaborate bouffant style on this very sexy looking red head in a plunging scarlet dress. And Michel comes third for being innovative. I'm way down the list but I get a special mention from the man making the awards - along with the tall woman with the orange hair and horn rimmed glasses - because it's so unusual to have women entering these competitions and we deserve a round of applause for our courage. 'You men will have to watch out. One day …' he says, which raises a laugh.

I suppose deep down I hadn't expected to get anywhere, I feel like the woman who lost the contact lens. *I knew it! I knew it*! I think I've cut Mathilde's hair so that she looks sensational, she looks like a woman who knows where she's going. And I know where I'm going too, I've created a style for the sixties. But these boring stick-in-the-mud judges in their crimplene suits can't recognise this. I feel sick at heart.

I go over to join Michel who's surrounded by Marie Claire, Françoise, Berthe, Jean François and Bertrand They're all congratulating him, saying they think Delphine looks wonderful. But I know he's angry, he thinks he should have come first, his style was much more original and needed more skill to do than the style that won.

'Ah, Lucy!' Jean François has suddenly noticed me. 'You did very well, too, Lucy.' Marie Claire and Bertrand say they think so too, they think Mathilde looks quite chic. But I know she looks much too odd for their taste, and I'm sure they're also thinking that the cut was good but I should have gone to more trouble, using more rollers and lacquer instead of just letting the hair hang loose like that. I couldn't expect to get anywhere. I'm feeling really depressed, I just want to get away, when suddenly there's Mathilde giving me a long hug. I'd like to go off and have a drink with her but she has to rush because she's on at the theatre this evening.

At least we don't end up in a café with them all. Michel manages that quite well - he says he has to spend the evening with his brother and his wife who live near the *Gare St Lazare*. I say I'm going home because I have a headache, which is actually true. We meet in the café across the road where we had breakfast that time in May when I found him on the doorstep. We decide we'll just have something to eat in the restaurant bit of the café. We have to get up early for him to catch the train back down to Nice.

Neither of us feels very hungry. Michel keeps saying how stupid the judges were to award first prize to that fool - that *con* - for that stupid hairdo which was so conventional and unimaginative, the sort of style that any *con*, any fool, could have managed. I agree with him, but at least he came third. He doesn't seem to realise how humiliating it is for me to have done so badly. We've decided to risk staying downstairs in the flat. As we come through the front door, he asks if it would be all right if he used the phone to ring Jeanne. She'll want to know how he got on.

'Sure, that's okay,' I say and go into my room and put *Oh yes, I'm the great Pretender* on - loud.

And then we go to bed and I'm wishing I could feel like Rapunzel letting her hair down, like the first time we were together, but I'm all knotted up inside. Michel's started on again - he's really devastated that he didn't come first. How would he feel if he'd come nineteenth like me? In the end I can't help it, I burst out

'What about me? My style was much more original than anyone else's and you really needed to know how to cut to get it to swing like that.' And then it occurs to me to add, and I really mean it, 'I think it's me should have come first.'

He laughs, thinking I'm joking. He puts his arms around me.

'Oh, Lucy, you're right, it was unfair coming nineteenth, you were much better than most of the others,' he says.

But I can tell that he thinks winning's not so important for me. Maybe Michel's no different from Juan in spite of his revolutionary politics, maybe, like Juan, he thinks that being a wife and mother is occupation enough for a woman. I'm opening my mouth to tell him that surely he knows that I'm just as ambitious as he is when he says

'George and I have been talking about setting up a salon together.'

'George and you? But don't you remember, *we* talked about setting up a salon together - *Lucy et Michel*?' I'm trying not to make it sound as if I'm whining. The magazines are always warning you against that. 'I'd thought we were going to be partners.'

He remembers but it's as if I'm reminding him of a game we'd been playing. Also he seems surprised by the name.

'I thought we were going to call it *Goldilock* or something.' He's joking but I don't feel like laughing. Is he really thinking that, if we were married, my main job would be supporting him, cheering him on, being like Ronaldo's wife back in Manchester? She was a really good hairdresser, much better than her husband, but he got all the credit. 'I don't know where I'd be without Vera' he was always saying. But it was his name above the door - *Maison Renaldo*. (His real name was Ronald). I know where you'd be, I used to think, you'd be the tea boy making the tea or not much more.

But I'm too choked to explain how I'm feeling, especially in French. What's upsetting me most is that I need to explain to him at all.

'It's not fair – C'est pas juste' is all I can manage. I sound like a child. It's what we were always saying in the playground, what I hear Catherine and Daniel saying when they're complaining to Monique. It's not fair – c'est pas juste.

'Let's get some sleep,' he says. His train for Nice is at seven o'clock.

He turns on his side, away from me, and I lie there listening to his breathing. I think of moving nearer to him, closing the gap between us, matching the curve of his body, laying my cheek against the nape of his neck but something is stopping me. I turn the other way and stare out through the grimy window at the dark sky.

Chapter 27

The guard's going along shutting the doors. I run along beside the train as it starts to move away. We're still holding hands.

'See you very soon,' he calls, leaning out as far as he can.

'Yes,' I say in a whisper he probably doesn't hear. The thought of not seeing him again very soon is almost unbearable. I stand there watching and waving until he couldn't possibly see me any more. But as I walk back down the platform my feeling of resentment towards him is returning, like a stone in my shoe. He should have cared more about the unfairness of me doing so badly in the competition. He must have known it was because I was a woman. It's beginning to strike me that, although he's a great champion of the Algerians fighting for their independence, when it comes to women he doesn't seem any different from other men.

I don't know what to do now. It's Monday so I have the day off. I could go and see Vinny but I'm not sure I want to see anyone. In any case, it's too early. I'm sure they never get up before eleven. I sit down at the buffet in the station and order a *grand crème* and a croissant. We didn't have time to have anything before we left the flat.

I keep thinking of the competition. I keep seeing the dark-haired woman rushing past me, hissing *Je le savais!* What did she know? That she was bound to lose a contact lens, or that she was bound to lose full stop? Like me, like the tall older woman with the orange hair. 'You men will have to watch out!' I keep hearing that silly twerp's voice and all those men laughing as if it was a big joke, the thought of any woman hairdresser being better than them.

'Can I sit here, mademoiselle?' A man is standing there with his cup of coffee. He looks Algerian. I tell him I'm expecting someone. There's a stocky man with red cheeks and thick wet lips at the next table who's been watching me since I sat down, looking as if he's going to say something. He opens his mouth to shout something at the Algerian as he moves away, something not very nice. It wasn't because he was Algerian, I feel like saying, I'd much prefer to talk to him than to you but I just want to be alone at the moment. I move my chair so my back is to the stocky man and get out my writing pad and pen and start scribbling, just so that he doesn't start talking. He does anyway.

'Mademoiselle,' he says, but I pretend I haven't heard him.

'Mademoiselle,' he says again. I can't stay here. I put the last of the croissant into my mouth and get up.

I wander around the streets for a bit and then I take the bus to the Latin Quarter - it takes longer than the Metro and I've got all day. I get off just before the *Boulevard St Michel* and walk down towards the Seine and *Notre Dame*. I can see its two towers through the trees. I'll say a prayer for Juan. I keep hearing his voice: 'So long as there's someone in the world somewhere who loves you....' He would have said he was now in a better place, boking down at me from heaven but I'm sure he'd never have wanted to leave this world so suddenly in that terrible way.

A group of Italians are being shown around the cathedral. They're looking up and exclaiming at the round window at the end, at the brilliant colours of the stained glass. I push past them and walk down the main aisle, with its huge pillars stretching up and up, till I'm standing in front of the Virgin and Child. You'd hardly notice the statue because it's so small by comparison.

Statues of Our Lady often have *Hail Mary* written under them in Latin - *Ave Maria*. Every time I see this I think of the silly joke about a man who couldn't decide which of two women he wanted to marry. One was called Joan and the other one was called Maria. So he went into church and bowed his head and prayed before the statue of Our Lady and when he looked up he saw the words *Ave Maria* written there. So he married Maria. 'Should I marry Michel?' I ask her now, but I don't expect an answer.

The clock's striking eleven and the heavy bells are beginning to ring out. There must be a service starting. I light a candle for Juan and leave, setting out up the *rue Saint Jacques*. I pass a fruit and veg stall. A tall woman in a bright green costume is choosing lettuces and there's a man, who's presumably her husband, standing beside her, helping her. She's holding this enormous frilly lettuce in her gloved hand and she's asking him his opinion about it, and he's pointing to others with red leaves and she's saying 'Mais non, chéri …' That's something that always amazes me, the energy the French put into food – buying, cooking, eating it, the men as well as the women. At the same stall there are all these runner beans. My Dad grows runner beans – they're green and they're all about the same size but here there are thin ones, fat ones, short ones, long ones and different coloured ones - dark green, light green, purple, maroon. If I married Michel I'd become part of this world.

I buy a bag of figs to try to cheer myself up. I love the taste and the feel of them in your mouth when you split open the tough purple skin with your teeth and inside there's this soft creamy red flesh. It'll be good sitting there eating them with Vinny and Steve, with Steve's music going on and the sun shining in. I've never been there in the daylight except for that time on the cushion with Vinny, when the rain was pouring down outside. Michel will be nearly half way to Nice by now. I don't think I'll say anything about him to Vinny and Steve. Or about the competition, unless they ask. And I don't want to tell them about Andrew either because I know they think he's dull and conventional and they'd want to make fun of him.

'How's Andrew?' Vinny would ask and I know she'd be thinking 'Don't tell me you're going to marry Andrew and turn yourself into a suburban housewife, are you?'

I don't think I want to tell them anything at all, actually. I just want to be with them, listening to Steve talking about how important it is to feel free and to be creative. I felt excited that day. It was the same feeling I had in the museum, looking at those paintings that were all colour and rhythm that made you want to shout out and dance around.

What if I stayed in Paris, and got more friendly with Vinny and Steve? It would mean going on working at Bertrand's, following fashions instead of creating them. What are the styles for this year? Are chignons still in or are they out? Have they been completely replaced by …? Wait for the next instalment of *Coiffure Beauté*. On the other hand, I could go to London. Jack said that's where it's all starting to happen. The sixties are going to be different from the fifties, he said. Things are changing, London's not the old-fashioned, conservative sort of place it was. But I want to be with Michel, a voice inside me keeps protesting.

I bang on Vinny's door but it doesn't open. Are they still in bed? I bang again and eventually the door opens and Marc is standing there in floppy black trousers and yellow espadrilles and nothing on top. He hasn't got a hair on his chest. He's scratching his armpit and yawning and telling me to come in.

It's like walking into a completely strange place. The floor's bare - Steve's tape recorder has gone, and all the books and records and dirty glasses and ashtrays spilling over with cigarette butts that were scattered about.

'I thought you were the man who's coming to buy that,' he says, pointing to a large painting leaning against the wall - great splashes of reds and oranges.

'Where's Vinny?' I ask.

'She's gone, they left yesterday, they've gone down to Avignon, somebody's lent them a flat down there.' And they wouldn't be coming back, not to his flat, anyway.

'Oh,' I say. I didn't know it was *his* flat. I'm wondering if he's going to offer me a cup of coffee but the French never do. I take out my packet of cigarettes and offer him one but he says he always rolls his own special ones. Is there any point in getting their address? Already they're beginning to feel like people I met in a dream.

'And Meriche?' He shrugs his shoulders. He tells me Meriche lives somewhere over near the

Panthéon, at the corner of *rue de la Montagne St Genviève*, in a building just next to a café. He looks at me as if he's curious to know why I should be interested in Meriche.

I can see the *Panthéon* in the distance. I start to walk towards it, back down the way I came and then a zigzag through narrow streets full of little restaurants - Greek, Russian, North African, Vietnamese. I wonder if Han and Tan's restaurant is among them. The sound of people's voices drifts down from open windows and the smell of the midday meal being prepared. An old man is shuffling along ahead of me with a mangy looking dog at his heels. They disappear inside a doorway, and then a voice behind me: 'Vous êtes seule, Mademoiselle?'

I reach the little café in the *rue de la Montagne St Geneviève* just as the voice at my shoulder is asking me for the third time if I'm English. I close the door quickly behind me, catch a glimpse, through the glass, of a worn donkey jacket and a thin grey face and greasy hair and a mouth sucking on the end of a cigarette.

The woman behind the counter is large with her hair swept up and dyed jet black and she's wearing flashy dangling pearl and gold earrings. She greets me with a big smile and I ask her for a glass of *Perrier*. Apart from two men in one corner playing dominos I'm the only person in the café. The woman looks the chatty sort but she's almost certainly noticed my English accent so she probably thinks it would be too much effort talking to me. I don't feel like talking anyway.

The place where Marc said Meriche lives is a very old building. I push the door open and I'm in a dark passage and there's a strong smell of urine coming from behind one of the doors. The door's a little bit open, and my stomach nearly turns over when I glance in - it's one of those Turkish lavatories and it looks as if it hasn't been cleaned for months. All the other doors are closed but I can hear Arab music coming from one of the rooms and I wonder if it's Meriche's. Another door opens and a man comes out who looks a bit like Meriche but much older. I ask him about Meriche and he points to the door on the left and I'm just about to knock on it when he tells me Meriche isn't in – he hasn't been seen for several days. He looks at me and I know he's thinking the same as me, about all the bodies they've been fishing out of the Seine.

I cross the *Boulevard St Michel* and wander into the Luxembourg Gardens, still thinking about Meriche. Mothers are rounding up their children. It's time to go home. Do I envy them? No. I sit on a bench and watch two little children playing in the sand pit. They keep burying this little blue teddy bear and then rescuing it.

'Sophie, Nicholas … it's time to go home.' The two children are running towards a harassed looking woman holding onto a pram with a baby bawling inside. But where's the blue teddy bear? The two children are running back, turning up the sand. 'It was there,' I call across to them, pointing to the corner of the sand pit where I'd last seen them burying it. They dig and dig but the blue teddy bear has disappeared. They don't want to leave till they find it but their mother's calling them, they have to go, it's their fault if it's lost, they should have looked after it. The little girl's sobbing as their mother hurries them down the dusty gravel walk. She'll remember the lost blue teddy bear all her life. Michel will be more than half way to

Nice by now. Maybe he'll phone me from the *tabac* before going back to the flat.

I buy some bread and cheese and a bottle of wine on my way back home. All day I've been going round feeling half my inside has been taken out of me. There's a note from Nounou for me on the hall table. Madame has phoned to say that she won't be back until tomorrow. So I have the flat to myself this evening. I think about going into the study and putting on the record I used to listen to with Juan. I could sit in one of the leather armchairs and follow the sad tune of the clarinet and maybe it would help me to think. Only I'd probably keep hearing Juan's voice in the background: 'Lucy, in two years' time you will be twenty five.' In less than two years now, actually.

Instead, I go into my own room. The letter from Andrew is still unopened on the table. I know he'll be asking me if I've made up my mind yet. Well, by now he'll have got my letter. Will the letter I get back from him – if he writes at all – be one full of hurt and reproach? It's only what I deserve.

I open the bottle of wine and put on the record he brought me of Connie Francis singing *Lipstick on your Collar*. It's my favourite record at the moment. I turn the volume down and keep the door open so I'll hear the phone if Michel rings. He probably won't - it's a lot of trouble from a *tabac* and he'll be tired after the journey. But then the phone does ring and it's him.

'Lucy, when are you coming down?' he asks me, almost immediately.

I could come down this week end. I could take Saturday off. I could get the night train down on Friday and we'd have the whole of Saturday and Sunday together. That's what I want to say but I know that what he means is 'When are you coming down for good?'

'I'm not sure. It's a big decision. I need time to think.' I say.

'I love you,' he says.

'I love you,' I say.

Back in my room I put *Lipstick on your Collar* on again. I couldn't marry Andrew because I didn't want to turn into somebody whose main purpose in life was being somebody's wife. Marrying Michel would be completely different, I'd thought. I'd even faced the ordeal of telling my parents that I wanted to marry a divorced man.

But maybe being married to Michel wouldn't be all that different. Maybe what Michel wants also is a supportive wife who will be there loyally helping him to get to the top. I'm twenty three, I know it's high time I was married, but not at this price. I love him and he loves me but that should mean that we're looking out for each other. He's not being fair. He's just thinking of himself.

Well, I can think of myself too. I get my writing pad out and pour myself a large glass of wine. *Cher Michel* ... I stare for a long time at the blank page.

Chapter 28

I post the letter to Michel on my way to work. In the salon Marie Claire says she's sorry I didn't do better in the competition.

'Actually, I liked your hairstyle much better than Michel's. Delphine would have frightened the life out of me if I'd met her in the street with hair sticking up all over the place like that.'

A bit later she says

'Lucy, do you think it would suit me, having my hair cut like Mathilde's?'

I tell her I could easily do a version for her sort of hair, which is much finer. She thinks Bertrand will like it. She seems to be getting used to him spending so much of his time with Antonia.

'He's like a child,' she says. 'He comes in looking so sad and just wants to put his arms around me.'

'He even said he'd like me to come up to the nursing home one evening with him, just to see her. 'I'd like you to meet her before …,' he said. We're in the cloakroom and Marie Claire's voice has fallen to a whisper and she's got an *I don't know what to do* expression on her face, when Bertrand comes in.

Later I have lunch with Marie Claire in the place we usually only go to on a Saturday. It's crowded and we only just manage to find a tiny table inside the door. There are people coming in and out all the time kicking my handbag which is on the floor, so I end up putting it on my lap. I tell Marie Claire I'm leaving at the end of the month.

'So you're going down to Nice,' she says in a *you've never said anything but I've known all along about you and Mich*el tone of voice.

'No, I'm not going down to Nice,' I tell her and her face brightens.

'Ah,' she smiles 'so you're going to Leeds. You're getting married to Andrew. I'm so pleased, Lucy. I'm sure you're doing the right thing.'

'No, I'm not going to Leeds either, I'm going to London,' I say. I can tell she's about to say - 'Ah, because of that boy that we met in the *PamPam* who looks like James Dean – what's his name again?' So I tell her quickly that I'm going to London because I think that's the place to be at the moment, things are beginning to happen there and I'll easily get a job in one of the salons and then one day soon I'll branch out on my own.

I'm trying my best to sound cheerful as inside I'm seeing myself installed in a dingy bedsit, not knowing anyone, trying to find a decent salon that will take me on. I open my handbag and get out the page of advertisements I've cut out from *The Hairdressers' Journal*.

'This one looks promising,' I say, pointing to *Maison Gérard* of Bond St.

'Lucy,' she says. There's such an expression of concern for me on her face, I wonder if she isn't going to burst into tears.

'I'll cut your hair this evening, if you like,' I say, 'and we can try out one of those new colours - I think the pale amber would suit you.'

'Ah non, Lucy, not the amber, with my colouring. I think the pink champagne.'

But then she remembers Antonia. Maybe she'll wait till after she's seen her. It would be awful turning up to visit a dying woman looking like someone on the brink of a new life.

'So Patrice has persuaded you to leave Paris,' Jean François exclaims later in the day when I tell him I'm going to London. I ask him who Patrice is.

'You remember, he is the French who 'as a salon in London. He was the judge in the black suit who 'as fallen in love with Mathilde.'

'But he didn't fall in love with me too,' I say.

'Oh no, but he has fallen in love with the way you did Mathilde's hairs, Lucy. Did you not realise? He has liked verri verri mush your style. And he has a salon in London very sophisticate.'

'Oh Lucy!' Marie Claire exclaims. I decide I'll write to him as soon as I get back to the flat, as well as to *Maison Gérard* of Bond St.

Back in the flat I at last get round to opening Andrew's letter. I feel terrible. Poor Andrew. But I'm sure I've done the right thing, I should have done it much sooner. He'll be heartbroken for a time because I know he loves me, in a way more completely than Michel, but in time he's sure to find somebody else. I open his letter.

'Dear Lucy,' he begins *'this is a very difficult letter to write and I don't know where to begin. Carmel offered to write instead of me but I felt it was me who ought to tell you. She and I have fallen in love and we want to get married. I'm very sorry …… temptation ....lonely ....waited so long …'.*

Sometimes you have to laugh.

It's two weeks later and we're all in *Chez Gilbert*. I'm leaving tomorrow. It's Friday so it's fish on the menu - *moules marinières, sole meunière, salade saison, tarte maison* - but I'm feeling too upset to eat anything. It's not just because I'm saying goodbye to everyone, I'm feeling Michel everywhere, like a ghost hovering. The same three men are at the next table having the same argument, the fat one still has *L'Humanité* sticking out of his pocket. For a moment I forget myself and I want to shout at them - 'But have you not seen the headline in today's paper? Why aren't you talking about what's happening now, instead of having arguments about what happened in 1936?'

Instead I turn to Jean François and Bertrand and say it to them, how it's terrible all the torture and the killing that's going on not just in Algeria but here in Paris. I start telling them about Meriche. They look uncomfortable as if they feel it's none of my business.

'You sound like Michel,' says Bertrand, so I say 'Eh alors?' That's the expression Michel's always coming out with and I've always wanted to use it. It means 'So what?' I tell them that I'm proud to sound like Michel. He isn't just interested in himself and his own little life, he cares about the world, he wants to change it so that it's a better place for people to live in. I don't say how I wished he wanted to make the world a better place for women to live in.

Claude is there as well as Monique and the children when I get back to the flat. Claude's making his pasta dish and Daniel and Catherine are helping him.

'Why don't we leave them to it and go out for a meal somewhere?' I say to Monique. In all the time

I've been there I've never been out with Monique, I've never ever seen her except in the flat.

We walk to the *Drug Store* on the *Champs Elysées* and order plates of bifteck frites and a bottle of *Côte du Rhone*. Monique was getting worried all we'd have to drink there would be *Coca Cola*. She's pouring wine into our two glasses when who should pass but Alberto, accompanied by a very tall, willowy brunette who looks American.

'Lucy!' he cries holding his arms out as if he would like to enfold me.

'Alberto.' I give him a little wave that's at once a hello and a goodbye. He moves on but not before he's had time to take a good look at Monique. He's probably wondering if she's a lesbian.

I ask Monique if she's planning on getting a job once the kids go to school but she doesn't think it would be possible because of the demands of Claude's work. He needs her to be there, he never knows when he hasn't to go off on a business trip and he wouldn't know how to pack a suitcase for himself, he'd be sure to forget his socks and his handkerchiefs. And then when he's in Paris, as Lucy knows, he often comes back to the flat for lunch, brings back colleagues, and she has to be there to organise things with Nounou. I'm looking at her neat head as she talks and remembering those portraits at Vinny's. I'm trying to imagine what the real Monique's like inside herself but all I'm getting is the neat head. I can't imagine her with any other hairstyle.

'How about you, Lucy?' I know what she means is 'Won't you be lonely setting out all by yourself like that?'

'I'll be fine,' I say. 'In a few years I may even have my own salon. It'll have LUCY in large plain letters over the door.'

'Or even LUCY AND MICHEL,' I say to myself as I wipe my plate with a piece of bread. Who knows?